The
BROTHERS OF
BAKER STREET

ALSO BY MICHAEL ROBERTSON

The Baker Street Letters

The
BROTHERS OF
BAKER STREET

MICHAEL ROBERTSON

MINOTAUR BOOKS
A Thomas Dunne Book
New York

A THOMAS DUNNE BOOK FOR MINOTAUR BOOKS.
An imprint of St. Martin's Publishing Group.

www.thomasdunnebooks.com
www.minotaurbooks.com

ISBN 978-0-312-53813-2

10   9   8   7   6   5   4   3   2

For my three brothers,
and for our parents

ACKNOWLEDGMENTS

My thanks to my editor, Marcia Markland; to my agent, Rebecca Oliver; to Laura Bonner, for representing international rights; and to Kat Brzozowski, Elizabeth Curione, Phil Mazzone, Helen Chin, and David Baldeosingh Rotstein, at Thomas Dunne Books/St. Martin's Press.

The
BROTHERS OF
BAKER STREET

LONDON, AUTUMN 1997

In Mayfair, the owner of an elegant Edwardian white-stone sat down at the garden table with unusually high expectations for breakfast.

It was a bright September morning, quite lovely indeed; the roses in the garden were much more fragrant than in many days or weeks past—more so than anyone could possibly understand—and there was every reason to believe that breakfast would be equally remarkable.

The servant girl would bring tea and scones for a start. The tea would be hot and dark and would swirl together with the milk like vanilla and caramel taffy; the scones would be fresh and warm and appropriately crumbly when broken in two, and the butter would melt into each half like rain into loose garden soil.

The breakfast would be wonderful—especially so because it was no longer necessary to take the medications that accompanied it.

No medications, no nausea. No medications, no mental dull-ness. No medications, no loss of pleasure in the ordinary, every-day elements of life.

Not taking the bloody little pills was certainly the way to go.

The wonder was why the servant girl still bothered bringing them at all.

Several steps away in the parlor, the servant girl—a young woman, who had emigrated from Russia only a few years ear-lier and shortened her name to Ilsa (because there was a tennis star of that name and people could pronounce it)—arranged a china setting on a silver serving tray, with all the breakfast com-ponents her employer was expecting.

She placed the medications on the tray as well—a yellow pill for the schizophrenia, a round blue one to alleviate the de-pression caused by the yellow one; and a square white one to deal with the nausea caused by the blue one, but apparently not to great effect. And there was a small pink one, which was re-lated to the effects of the other three in some complicated way that no one had adequately explained.

The pills had been part of the daily regimen ever since Ilsa was first hired. That was almost a year ago now. Ilsa's employer, just a few years older than Ilsa herself, had lost both parents to an automobile accident at that time, and needed some assis-tance with the daily routine. Ilsa had been brought in to pre-pare the meals, to put the medicines on the tray, and to do the housekeeping and other chores. She wanted to do all of her tasks well.

Keeping the place tidy was more trouble than it should have been. Like a cat bringing presents from the garden, her employer kept discovering and bringing in small pieces of fur-niture and such from the parents' estate. Ilsa had counted five lamps, three vases, an ancient portable typewriter, and innu-merable scrapbooks and folders and yellowed paper items, some of which her employer had begun to take upstairs alone to study in private.

But as difficult as the housekeeping was, what worried Ilsa most was the medications. A new doctor had come by—a man Ilsa did not particularly like—and said not to worry about them. So Ilsa tried not to worry. But she continued to put the pills on the tray anyway, as she had been originally told to do. It seemed to her that she still should do so. And she was uncertain of all the regulations in her adopted country; she did not want to get in trouble.

Now she brought the breakfast setting out to the garden. And she also brought a copy of the *Daily Sun*.

Ilsa placed the silver tray on the table. Her employer smiled slightly and nodded. Then Ilsa stood at the table and began to read the headlines aloud from the tabloid.

This had been become a ritual in recent weeks, and she took some pride in getting good at it.

"'Prime Minister Calls for Moratorium on Queue Cutting,'" read Ilsa.

"No," said her employer.

"'Prince Harry Fathers Love Child with Underage Martian Girl.'"

"No."

"'Liverpool Louts Stab Man in Front of Pregnant Wife.'"

"No. Page two?"

"Just adverts."

"And on page three?"

"A woman in her underwear—and nothing on top. Shall I read the caption?" Ilsa giggled just slightly, because she was beginning to understand the British fondness for bad puns, and she was looking forward to demonstrating that knowledge.

"No, Ilsa. I don't need to know about the page-three girl. Go to page four."

"Two headlines on page four," said Ilsa. "The first is: 'Taxi Drivers a Terror to Tourists?'"

It was an article about a spate of robberies and nonlethal assaults against patrons of Black Cabs. Ilsa read the headline with the proper inflexion, making it sound as alarming as the headline writer clearly intended it to be.

"Hmm." Ilsa's employer seemed disappointed and began to butter a scone.

"And the second is a lawyer on Baker Street who denies that he's Sherlock Holmes," continued Ilsa. "There's a photo. I think one might call him good-looking, in a stuffy sort of way."

Her employer abruptly stopped buttering. There was silence for a moment. Then—

"Let me see it."

It was just three short paragraphs, not even breaking news; just a follow-up piece, about one Reggie Health—a thirty-five-year-old London barrister—and the unusual circumstances of a trip he had taken to Los Angeles a short time earlier.

Ilsa watched as her employer stared at the passage for a very long time, eyes searching intently, as though there were something more on the page than just the words.

"Is something wrong?" said Ilsa.

"It's like trying to find a gray cat in the fog," said Ilsa's employer finally, getting up from the table, with the *Daily News* in hand, and without finishing breakfast. "But I think I am beginning to remember."

Ilsa did not ask what was being remembered. She took the tray away, saw that the medications were again untouched, and wished it were not so.

2

THREE DAYS LATER

Nothing is so faithful as a male goose," Laura Rankin had once said. "If he loses his mate, if she dies or becomes directionally challenged flying home from Ibiza after a holiday, the male doesn't take a new one—he remains solitary for the balance of his life, spending what's left of his sad existence at ale and darts and whatever else ganders do with their spare time."

It had not been so long ago that she said it. It had been a warning; Reggie Heath just hadn't known it at the time.

He was remembering it now, as he turned his Jaguar XJS south from Regent's Park onto Baker Street in a heavy rain. It was not a gentle London drizzle, but an angry drencher, and it suited his frame of mind perfectly.

As a result of his recent and unintentional adventure in Los Angeles, Reggie had lost most of his personal fortune, all of his law chambers' clients, and (at least he liked to tell himself the

Los Angeles events were the reason) the affections of the one woman he knew he loved.

He wanted all of it back again. Especially that last thing. When it came right down to it, he was thinking of everything else as just a means to that end.

But driving across the bridge this morning, he had heard a rumor. His new secretary, apparently unafraid to be the bearer of bad tidings, called him on his mobile to warn him, and the call had come as a shock—in part because he wasn't aware she knew that much about his personal life.

But these days, apparently, the whole world did.

He didn't want to look, and see what everyone else had already seen. But he knew he must.

He pulled into the car park in the two hundred block of Baker Street. He was at Dorset House—a building that occupied that entire block, and that was home not only to the headquarters of the Dorset National Building Society, but also to Reggie Heath's Baker Street Chambers.

Reggie parked the Jag, and with his umbrella beginning to break at the seams against the windblown rain, he crossed the street to Audrey's Coffee and Newsagent.

"The *Financial Times*?" said the attendant. He offered Reggie's usual purchase. The *Financial Times* had headlines about the PM at an economic conference in Brussels, and the inflation rate, and a proposal to bring the technological advances of satellite navigation systems to the taxis of London. None of that was on Reggie's mind.

"No," said Reggie. "The *Daily Sun*."

"Second time in a week, Heath. Developing an interest in trash?"

"No. Trash has developed an interest in me."

Reggie entered Dorset House and crossed through the lobby

in quick strides, trying not to broadcast that he was carrying the lowest form of journalism folded under his arm, but trying not to be seen as hiding it either.

The lift was empty. That was lucky. Reggie got in and pressed the button for his floor.

He paid little attention to the front-page headline—"American Couple Killed: Cabbie Caught," something about unfortunate tourists in the West End two nights earlier—and he jerked the paper open to the inside pages. He saw the teaser line his secretary had warned him of.

"Fun with Freckles in Phuket?" was the title.

"Bloody hell," said Reggie, aloud, so transfixed that he didn't even realize that the lift hadn't moved and the doors had opened again.

A tall, attractive brunette in her thirties, a loan officer for Dorset probably, got in and stood next to Reggie.

"Stuck on page three, are we?"

Reggie roused himself. Just opposite the page-two blurb he was reading was the bare-tits photo that always occupied all of page three.

"Sorry," he said. He closed the paper. Trying to explain would have been worse. Much worse.

"Oh, don't mind me," she said, as the lift reached Reggie's floor. "Hope she's pert."

Normally Reggie would have come up with a response to that, but today there was no time. He exited the lift.

"Touchy," she said, still within earshot as Reggie walked away down the corridor.

He was headed for his secretary's desk. Also his chambers' clerk's desk: it was the same desk; he had hired just one person, a fiftyish woman named Lois, to fulfill both roles. That was mainly a financial decision, but also, combining both roles in one made it less likely that the secretary would want to bash in the clerk's head. Once had been enough for that. He wanted no more murders in chambers.

Lois rolled—almost literally—out of her desk station as she saw him approach. She had the general shape of a bowling ball, and the enthusiasm of one crashing at high speed into pins. With any luck, Reggie hoped, solicitors would bring new briefs to the chambers just for the entertainment of watching her react to them.

But at the moment, he didn't want to talk. And the papers she held in her hand didn't look like something he wanted to see.

"A new brief?" he said, doubtfully, without breaking stride.

"No," she chirped. "Letters to—"

"Put them where I said earlier," said Reggie.

Reggie entered the sanctuary of his chambers office. He closed the door behind him and spread the *Daily Sun* out on his desk. He followed the page-two headline teaser deeper, past a large Tesco advert and a smaller, cleverly self-deprecating one for Marmite, until he got to the back pages. And there it was:

"'On with it or off with it?'" read the caption. And there was Laura Rankin, caught on a beach in Phuket with some man's hands—"an unnamed but well-known media mogul" said the text—either fastening or unfastening her bikini top, and doing so with more points of contact than should have been mechanically necessary.

The gall was astonishing. Lord Buxton had actually published a pic in Lord Buxton's own paper of Lord Buxton's hand trying to fondle Laura's lightly freckled left—

Bloody hell. This would not do.

Reggie read to the end of the short piece, and saw that the unnamed but well-known media mogul was said to be flying in his well-known private jet right back to his well-known media headquarters in London later on that same day the photo was

taken—his apparent mission of adjusting Laura's bikini top
having been accomplished. The *Daily Sun* wondered in print,
"Will the lady soon follow?"

The lady will return to London, thought Reggie, but not
following after the bloody well-known media mogul.

Reggie grabbed his raincoat and headed for the door. If the
Daily Sun had the itinerary right, Buxton should be back at
work in the Docklands at that very moment. Reggie could be
there in twenty minutes and help jolt him out of his jet lag.

Then the phone rang, from the secretary's internal line, and
Reggie felt obliged to pick up.

"What the hell is it?" he said, into the phone.

There was an anxious pause at the other end, as the new
secretary regrouped.

"Sorry," said Reggie. "What is it, Lois?"

"A Mr. Rafferty wants to see you," said Lois. "From Dorset
House Leasing Division."

This could not be good.

"I'm very sorry," continued Lois. "He called earlier, but you
seemed so preoccupied when you came in—"

"Quite all right," said Reggie. "My mistake."

And now he had to choose.

Deal with the emissary from the leasing committee . . .

Or go to the Docklands to confront Buxton.

Discuss annoying details with a man in wire-rim glasses . . .

Or thrash the man who was stealing Laura, and with justi-
fication that every court in the land would understand.

Easy decision.

Reggie exited his office and went to the lift. Rafferty and the
lease could wait. Lord Buxton's unsolicited and unnecessarily
public contact with Laura's breasts could not.

The lift arrived from the ground floor, and the door opened.

"Heath! There you are!"

It was Alan Rafferty—a smallish man with a tendency toward very expensive gray suits and what Reggie suspected was a bit of a Napoleonic complex, deriving in part, no doubt, from his position of power on the leasing board. He had some documents in one hand and a prepackaged sandwich in the other.

"I thought you might have forgotten," said Rafferty, cheerily. "You all right, Heath? You look a little pink."

"Perhaps this can wait until the afternoon?" said Reggie.

"Oh, no," said Rafferty. He said it calmly, with a confident smile. "I have your lease right here. Started to look at it, then thought I should pop down for a bite first. Egg and cucumber salad. Quite good, I think they've changed the recipe. But now that I've got the lease out, you may as well ride back up with me, don't you think?"

That was ominous. Rafferty did indeed have the lease right there in his hand, and his thumb was pressing so hard against one particular section that it was probably going to leave a permanent mark.

"I trust it won't take long," said Reggie, remaining in the lift. They rode up to the top floor.

There really wasn't much to the top level. It was mostly just shining hardwood floor and windows. But Dorset House wasn't the first financial institution to occupy the premises; perhaps they just hadn't gotten around to making full use of it yet.

Rafferty's office was at the far end, tucked away, with just a small desk and two chairs.

"Interesting story in there," said Rafferty as Reggie sat down. Rafferty seemed to be indicating the copy of the *Daily Sun* that Reggie still had under his arm.

"Hardly relevant to my lease, is it?" said Reggie. He assumed Rafferty was referring to the thing about Laura in Phuket, and he made no effort to disguise his annoyance. He folded the paper again to half its current size and stuffed it into his coat pocket.

"Not today's paper," replied Rafferty. "Three days ago. But perhaps you hadn't seen it? Have a look."

Rafferty took a three-day-old copy of the *Daily Sun* out of his desk drawer, opened to the intended section, and handed it to Reggie.

Reggie looked.

The headline was "Balmy Barrister of Baker Street."

He had seen it before. The story was a sensationalized account, mostly inaccurate but not quite libelous, of Reggie's unfortunate trip to Los Angeles three weeks earlier, and the letters to Sherlock Holmes—which continued to arrive at Reggie's Baker Street Chambers—that had initiated it.

"This is old news," said Reggie. "I'm not happy about it; but there you are." The *Daily Sun* had in fact run more than one of these stories. He had considered calling the reporter to complain, but his better sense told him that complaining to a tabloid writer would be like teasing a chimpanzee.

"You'll have to forgive me for not being caught up on my reading," said Rafferty. "I only just saw the story yesterday."

Rafferty looked expectantly across at Reggie.

Reggie looked expectantly back.

"And?"

"Well, of course," said Rafferty, "it does have some small relevance to your lease, wouldn't you agree?"

"I think you'll have to spell it out for me."

"Certainly," said Rafferty. "I have it right here, let me see . . . yes, right here. Article 3d, paragraph 2a, of addendum G. Would you like to read it?"

Reggie already knew what paragraph 2a said. He was painfully aware of it, and he had been avoiding this conversation with Rafferty ever since returning to London.

The best he could do now was to feign ignorance. He picked up the document.

"'Additional Duties of the Lessee,'" Reggie read aloud.

"That would be you," said Rafferty, helpfully.

Reggie gave Rafferty the look that handy tip deserved, and Rafferty settled back in his seat a bit. Reggie read the clause, though he did not give Rafferty the satisfaction of hearing it aloud:

> The undersigned lessee is aware and acknowledges that Dorset House occupies the portion of the 200 block of Baker Street that has historically been regarded as containing the residence of the Fictional Character known as Sherlock Holmes, that correspondence addressed to said Fictional Character is known to be delivered to the second above-ground floor at Dorset House, and that as the primary occupant of that floor, lessee shall have the duty of replying daily to said correspondence with the form letter attached to this codicil as Exhibit A. Under no circumstances shall lessee reply to said correspondence in any other manner other than sending said form letter.
>
> Should the undersigned lessee violate the above provisions, or fail to execute the duties described therein in any way, the leasehold shall be terminated, payment for the entire amount of the unfulfilled tenancy shall become immediately due and payable, and the lessee shall vacate the premises forthwith.

"The remedy seems a little extreme," said Reggie, after he had finished reading.

"Which?" said Rafferty, innocently. "The termination of the leasehold, or the immediate payment of—"

"Bloody all of it," said Reggie.

"Well, but then of course you did sign it, did you not?" said

Rafferty. "But there's another matter. And that is the current letters."

"I promise you I am not about to jet off to America or anywhere else again in response to any of these damned letters. In fact—"

"In fact, you have not responded to any of them at all since your return. Is that what you were going to say, Mr. Heath?"

"Well . . . yes."

"We find that unacceptable."

"We?"

Rafferty cleared his throat, and hesitated for the first time since the conversation had begun. "The committee," he said.

"I thought it was just you in charge of internal leasing. There's an entire leasing committee?"

"Well, yes, there is a committee," said Rafferty, quickly. "But the point is, I'm sure this single violation of the rules for handling the letters can be overlooked, assuming that no others occur, mind you, if only—"

"If only—what?"

"If only you will resume responding to the letters again. I mean, in the manner that you are supposed to. In the manner that it states in the codicil."

"You're saying that your big complaint is not my trip to America that was instigated by one of these bloody things, but that I have allowed a few of them to go unanswered since my return?"

Reggie said that with some heat. It was difficult to remain calm about the letters. If it had not been for the earlier ones, his younger brother, Nigel, would not have run off to Los Angeles, Reggie would not have followed, none of the Los Angeles events would have transpired, and Reggie would never have felt obliged on principle to blow the whistle on a company that he himself had invested in through Lloyd's of London. His own finances would not now be teetering as a result, and solicitors would not be avoiding his chambers out of fear it could not survive.

Granted, no good deed goes unpunished. But he had not been intending a good deed. Only what had to be done. So the outcome should have been better.

But that was history, and Rafferty was continuing. "Not just a few letters, Mr. Heath. By the cleaning lady's estimate, there must be fifty or more unanswered letters accumulated now. And our complaint is both—that you responded to one in person, and that you have not been responding to the others at all since your return."

"And you're saying you can overlook the former, if I resume the latter."

"We can overlook that one occurrence, yes. But it must not happen again. And you must resume responding to the current incoming letters—in the appropriate manner—immediately."

"Well, it may take me a bit. My brother is still in the States, and there's no one else to—"

"Immediately, Mr. Heath. Even if it means licking the envelopes yourself."

Reggie looked Rafferty in his watery eyes. Rafferty blanched—but did not back down.

"Immediately," he said again. "You are at least two weeks behind already."

Reggie smiled patiently. Sometimes one could get around the specifics of a lease, and sometimes one could not.

"Very well," said Reggie, standing. He towered over Rafferty. "I'll see to it."

Reggie exited the leasing office. On his way down in the lift, he took out his mobile phone to ring Nigel in Los Angeles.

There was a time zone difference, of course. But Reggie didn't much give a damn at the moment.

The phone rang just twice before someone picked up.

"What time is it?" said Nigel. He sounded groggy.

"Almost noon," said Reggie.

"For you, maybe," said Nigel, speaking in a low voice. "Here it's . . . it's . . . I don't know what bloody time it is, but it's pitch-black out. Even Mara is still asleep."

"I need a favor. I'm going to overnight you a package. I need you to respond to the bloody things."

"What bloody things?"

"Letters."

There was a silence at Nigel's end. Then—

"You mean *the* letters?"

"Yes."

"You told me to never touch the things again."

"Better you than me."

Reggie heard Nigel first laugh and then pause briefly, apparently considering it.

"Will do," said Nigel. "You pay the postage."

"Gladly," said Reggie.

Reggie shut off the phone, got out of the lift, and went to Nigel's former office to get the letters.

The in-basket that Nigel had used for them was still there. That was intentional. Reggie didn't want the letters to Sherlock Holmes cluttering up his own office. And he didn't want them getting in the way of new briefs, the instructions from solicitors with new cases, that Lois would be placing in his office—if they ever began to roll in again.

And neither did he want anyone else messing with the letters and creating new troubles for his law chambers.

Lois was under instructions to deposit the letters in the basket and then to flee from them as quickly as possible, which she faithfully did—although, unfortunately and with the best of intentions, she had opened all the envelopes to spare Reggie the trouble, and so the opened letters were there, faceup, staring back at Reggie now from the in-basket.

He looked at the one on top.

It was a marriage proposal. From a ninety-year-old woman in Bolivia. But it was a tentative proposal: she wanted Mr. Sherlock Holmes to first confirm for her whether he was still alive, and if so, which century he was born in.

Reggie briefly considered replying that she should not get her hopes up, because Mr. Holmes was born in the previous century and did not date younger women.

But might as well let her have the hope. And besides, he really didn't want to deal with the things at all.

And there were simply too many of them. They had overflowed out of the basket onto the floor, no doubt annoying the cleaning lady and causing her to snitch to Rafferty.

Reggie began to gather up all the letters, doing his best not to read another word of them in the process. Better not to know.

He got the largest mailer he could find and proceeded to stuff the letters into it.

It was a tight fit, and in the process a letter fell out and drifted down to the floor, settling so far under the desk that Reggie knew he would have to move the chair and get down on the floor to get at it.

There was hardly time for that. And now Lois appeared in the doorway.

"You have a call." She said this with visible trepidation.

"Yes?" said Reggie.

"A reporter. Emma Swoop from the *Daily Sun*. She wants to know if you have any comment on the story about Laura in Phuket with the unnamed gentleman who—I mean, the one with the pic of a man's fingers on Laura's left—I mean the one where her bikini top is—"

"Emma Swoop," said Reggie tightly, before Lois could dig herself in any deeper. "Why do I know that name?"

"She was the one who wrote those bits about you in Los Angeles."

"You'd think I'd done something bad to her in a past life," said Reggie. He hammered three staples into the mailer in rapid succession and with much more force than necessary.

He picked up the mailer and plopped it into Lois's outstretched arms.

"Overnight this," said Reggie. Then he said, with all the self-control he could muster, "And tell Emma Swoop that I will deliver my comments to her boss in person."

Reggie went downstairs and got in the Jag. The tires squealed as he accelerated out of the car park, heading toward the Docklands.

Lord Robert Buxton's current empire included a film studio in Los Angeles, a music distribution company, a promotional racing yacht in Melbourne, and book publishers in New York—but the flagship for it all was the *Daily Sun*. And as Reggie turned onto Wapping High Street, he could see the sign for that tabloid's headquarters a mile away in the Docklands.

Buxton's newly constructed compound was far larger than it needed to be for any practical purpose; larger, even, than that of an even more successful publishing magnate who had relocated there prior to Buxton. Reggie was pretty sure that Buxton had built his own there just for the bragging rights.

The compound was enclosed all around with a ten-foot wall; at the entrance gate was a full security station, complete with weapons screening.

Reggie gave the guard his name, the guard relayed that information, and after a few moments someone in Buxton's office—perhaps even Buxton himself—sent word that Reggie could enter.

Which Reggie did, after two aborted attempts in which his watch and car keys set off the weapons alarm.

He walked rapidly across the compound, entered the main building, and took the lift to the top floor.

Buxton's private office was three or four times the size of Reggie's law chambers. It had wide windows that looked across the Thames, a skylight, an electronic, dynamically lit map of the world and its time zones, and more large indoor shrubberies than the Royal Botanic Gardens.

Buxton—about the same age and height as Reggie, but somewhat heavier—turned from the window as Reggie entered.

"Heath! Great to see you! How have you been?"

"Hold out your hand."

"Excuse me?

"Hold out your right hand, please."

"This hand?"

Buxton held out his right hand. Reggie opened his copy of the *Daily Sun* to the photo of the hand on Laura's breast. In that photo, on the fourth finger of the suspect's right hand, was the same garish, gold signet ring that Buxton was wearing.

Reggie looked at the photo, and then at Buxton's hand, and then at Buxton.

"Thank you," said Reggie. "I just needed to be sure."

Buxton looked at Reggie, at the photo, back at Reggie again, and then made the mistake of grinning.

"The sun really brings her freckles out, don't you think?" said Buxton.

Reggie hit Buxton with a right cross. It had been his best punch in school, and he connected cleanly.

But in the same instant, there was a flash of light. As Buxton fell backward onto a potted rubber-tree plant, Reggie turned and looked behind—and saw a *Daily Sun* photographer standing there in the open doorway.

The photographer continued to snap and flash away as Reggie pushed past.

Security did not stop Reggie on his way out of the building. He did not think they would. Not if Buxton had any sense of self-respect.

But as Reggie got in his car, with the flash spots still fading from his eyes and his adrenaline throttling down, he began to realize what a huge mistake he had just made.

Buxton had obviously positioned the photographer at the ready for whatever might take place. And Reggie had fallen into the trap neatly. Tomorrow he would once again be in the *Daily Sun* doing unbarrister-like things.

Reggie drove back to Baker Street, with the stupidity of his mistake sinking in, and with the second, third, and fourth knuckles on his right hand turning blue with bruises. He bumped them twice getting out of the Jag, and again on the heavy glass door at the entrance to Dorset House.

He walked quickly across the lobby, hoping to encounter no one.

The lanky brunette from earlier in the morning got in the lift with Reggie again.

He saw her give just one quick sidelong glance at the bruises on his knuckles, and then look away with what amounted to a shrug. Of course. Today's sophisticated London woman was not impressed by the cave-man thing. In the real world, pugilistic skills did not compensate for not owning a yacht.

And Reggie saw no hope of winning Laura back while his law career—the essence of his existence for the past fifteen years, his very identity—was failing.

How would she respect a man who not only has next to nothing, but is no good at what he does? He was well past the age of getting by just on his potential.

The lift opened now, and Reggie tried to shake himself out

of that train of thought. He walked quickly down the corridor, toward his secretary's desk.

As Reggie approached, he saw that Lois was quite excited about something; she nearly leapt out of her chair in enthusiasm.

"You have a client!" She said this as if it were a rare and wondrous occurrence.

And of late, Reggie had to admit, it was.

"Where?" said Reggie, looking at the empty guest chairs outside his office.

"I mean, you are about to have, I presume. The solicitor is inside," she said, indicating Reggie's closed chambers door. "Hope that's all right. Her name is Darla Rennie. Didn't want to . . . you know . . . let one get away."

"Good job," said Reggie, with a slight smile. "Mustn't take chances. Lock them in if you must."

Lois sat back down, pleased with herself, and Reggie opened the chambers door.

The light was dim inside; Lois had apparently been bold enough to let someone into Reggie's chambers in his absence, but not to turn the lamps on for them. The two main client chairs in Reggie's office—burgundy leather in a deep, wing-back design intended to convey a sense of power and security—faced away from the door, toward Reggie's desk. From the entrance, one couldn't even tell if they were occupied, and for a moment Reggie thought his new clerk must have been mistaken in some uniquely incompetent way.

Then there was a voice from the client chair to Reggie's right. A woman's voice.

"Your clerk let me in. But don't blame her; I insisted. I hope you don't mind."

The woman had not gotten up from the chair; at the moment, all Reggie could see was the lower portion of two shapely legs in nude-toned stockings—smooth and subtly shining, like the voice.

Reggie walked around behind the desk to get to his chair, and to see her face. He still had the copy of the *Daily Sun* under his arm, and as he crossed behind the desk, he dropped the beat-up tabloid as surreptitiously as he could into the waste basket.

"I'm Reggie Heath," he said. His inflexion involuntarily changed when he saw her face. "Tell me what I can do for you."

Her hair was dark as jet, and its curls set off skin that was white to the point of translucence. She had green eyes—not warm olive green, like Laura's, but crystalline green—framed in round gold-rimmed spectacles that were so unembellished and out of fashion that Reggie guessed they had to have been deliberately chosen to add severity to the face.

She was small-boned, almost pixielike, in a forest-green wool business dress. Except for that glimpse of leg, the deep leather chair had nearly swallowed her up. She leaned forward now to speak.

"Lunch," she said, and then she smiled. "I'm Darla. I'll tell you all about my client; but first things first, and it feels like ages since I had a decent meal."

Her skin said she was in her early twenties; the sophistication in her voice suggested possibly a few years more.

"And what does decent mean?" said Reggie. From the look of her, he made it even odds that decent meant a Portobello mushroom salad with fresh spinach, or kelp-wrapped sushi and rice, or a very small and selective portion of a free-range hen.

"Anything deeply fried," said the young woman.

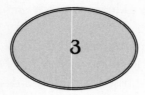

3

Reggie and the new solicitor sat down on plastic chairs at Marylebone Fish Fryer, which if not absolutely the best fish-and-chips in London, was certainly the closest. And Darla seemed unconcerned about it either way. The air was filled with the scent of vinegar and deep-fat fried food, and she seemed to almost bask in it.

"My client," she said, liberally dousing the crisp batter, "is a driver of a Black Cab. I wish to engage you to represent him in a criminal proceeding."

"What is the accusation?"

"Robbery homicide," she said. Then she paused to bite eagerly into the fish; she sat back with a contented sigh, and wiped her mouth. She looked back at Reggie watching her, and she gave a little smile.

Then she continued: "A tourist couple from America, robbed and killed after going to the theater in the West End, and their bodies found several miles away."

"I believe I saw something in the news about that," said Reggie.

"Really? I haven't seen it, so little time. I can imagine it would make the papers. But publicity is not always a bad thing for a chambers, is it?"

"Not always," said Reggie. And then he paused. It wasn't the high-profile nature of the case that caused him to hesitate. It was another reason, and the solicitor seemed to sense it.

"I am absolutely convinced my client is innocent," said Darla. "And I won't hold you to the cab rank rule if you are not equally convinced after speaking with him."

This was not a huge concession on her part. The rule, that a barrister must accept the client presented to him in the same way that the next cab in line must accept the next passenger, could almost always be got around if need be.

"Fair enough," said Reggie. "But why me?"

"For starters, I know you have not had much lately, Mr. Heath."

"Excuse me?"

"In the way of new work. My client is of limited means and he cannot afford, if you'll forgive my saying so, the rates of the current top-ranked criminal advocates."

"I see your point," said Reggie, "although I would have put it differently. But you should know that I haven't done much criminal in recent years."

"In recent years, none at all, I know," said Darla. "But what you did in years past was quite successful."

"I won the cases I tried, if that's what you mean."

"It is exactly what I mean. It's all right, Mr. Heath, really. I know what your concern is. You never lost a case you defended. Even though your last defendant was, in fact, guilty."

Reggie sat back in his chair at that. He gave Darla a hard look, but she continued.

"Please do not take offense. It is still common knowledge among the legal community. A veteran police officer with a sterling reputation was accused of killing his wife over a divorce. He swore his innocence. But the prosecution allowed themselves to be driven by media, and they brought the case without the facts to support it; their witnesses were unreliable, and you destroyed them, quite rightly, in court. The case was dismissed. And then the police officer accused of murdering his wife promptly went home and murdered his mother-in-law to boot."

Now she stopped and just looked across at Reggie. He looked directly back.

"There was little I could do at that point," he said.

"What you did was stop practicing criminal."

This was completely true; she had it right. He had indeed turned to corporate, where the consequences of successfully representing a client who turns out to be deceptive and in the wrong are—usually—less severe. But it was bad business to explicitly acknowledge such qualms to the legal community, and he did not want to do so now. He just nodded very slightly to her in response.

"Wherever would the legal system be if all lawyers shared your compunction, Mr. Heath?"

"Everyone is entitled to the best defense available," said Reggie. "That doesn't mean everyone is entitled to me."

Darla smiled slightly and said, "In my opinion, it does mean exactly that. But you've clearly paid a price for your scruples."

"How do you mean?"

"All one has to do is look about you, Mr. Heath. You have one person as both clerk and secretary. You have no junior to do the scut work for you, and no pupil seeking to train with you. I did not see another brief on your clerk's desk, or on yours, and your shelf is empty. But there is no shortage of accused clients in London. What could account for the sad state of your chambers if not your resistance to taking on any case where you're afraid your client might have done it?"

Reggie was about to answer that, then stopped. It was actually refreshing—apparently she was the one person in London who did not read the tabloids or know what that coverage had done to his chambers reputation.

He shrugged in response to her question.

"Well," she said. "You needn't worry. My client meets your strict criteria. He is innocent. And because he is, I will be able to get him the best defense available, in my opinion—I will get you—and, I hope, at a bit of a cut rate?"

Reggie had no other case work pending, and this solicitor clearly knew it.

"I'll check with my clerk," said Reggie, bluffing anyway. He paused, then said, "I'll need to see the discovery file first and meet your client. No promises beyond that."

"Of course," said Darla. "His name is Neil Walters. He's at Shoreditch police station. Can you see him this afternoon?"

"Yes, I think that will work."

"Brilliant. I have another engagement myself. But my client, of course, will be available."

She stood. She offered her hand. Reggie took it, and she left it in his possession for just a moment longer than courtesy required.

"You are just as I expected," she said. Then she let go of his hand, smiled again, and exited the little café before Reggie had a chance to ask what that expectation had been.

As she walked away down Marylebone High Street, Reggie was aware that his blood was pumping fast. This was partly because he desperately needed a new brief.

And partly because this young female solicitor was quite . . . well, no point in going there. He did not need that sort of complication.

Reggie returned to Baker Street Chambers and got the bundle of information that Darla had left with his clerk. He sat down behind his desk and opened the packet. It included both her case summary and the police report, annotated with her own elegantly formed handwritten comments.

Reduced to its essentials, it said this:

A young couple from Houston were visiting London for the first time. They took in an early show at Covent Garden and then spent a couple of hours trying to understand the English fondness for warm Guinness at a pub nearby. They exited the pub shortly after eleven, by which time both of them, according to several accounts, had fully grasped the concept and were more than a little inebriated.

The barman at the pub went to the trouble of flagging down a Black Cab for them and he made sure the couple got into it, confident that he had deposited them into the safest means of getting home in all of London.

That was the last seen of them alive. Their bodies were found the next morning in a muddy Thames tidewater channel at an abandoned power-generating station at Lots Road, on the outer edges of Chelsea. Her purse and jewelry and his wallet and Rolex were gone, but a hotel key was still in his pocket, and from that, routine work by Scotland Yard traced the two victims back to their hotel, the bar they had visited, and the single most damning piece of evidence against Reggie's potential client: the license number of the cab, which the barman claimed to remember, and which two witnesses in Chelsea claimed to have seen just moments before the time of the crime.

The proposed theory was that the perpetrator drove the American couple behind the abandoned power station to rob them, and something went wrong—the husband decided at the last moment, perhaps, to resist. The perpetrator killed the man first, bashing his head on the concrete edge of the sea wall, and then asphyxiated his wife, and then dumped both bodies into the muddy channel.

Or so the police believed from their examination at the scene.

Police had already searched the home of the cab driver, and found nothing there to link him to the victims.

They also searched the interior and exterior of the cab itself, and found nothing there either—none of the victim's personal belongings, no traces of blood or a struggle, or anything at all to indicate that the cab had been at the scene of the crime.

That fact would have been more exculpatory if only the cab had not been thoroughly and professionally cleaned earlier in the morning before it was seized by police. That cleaning itself, Reggie knew, would make them suspicious. But Reggie's potential client did have a receipt for the work, and the report said he claimed to have it done routinely every week.

That was all of it. Reggie stood and walked to the window, looking out on Baker Street as he mulled it over.

The prosecution's case really boiled down to just the eyewitness sightings. There were two independent testimonies about that, with mutually corroborating details, and despite how much he needed the work, Reggie's first thought on reading their accounts was that the defendant might indeed be guilty.

But, of course, that impression was based just on the prosecutor's report. It therefore meant nothing. At least not until he talked to the possible client.

Reggie got his coat and exited his chambers office, just in time to encounter Lois, who was approaching from her secretary's station. She had a letter in hand.

"I found this under Nigel's desk," she said. "I think you really should look at it."

Reggie accepted the letter, feeling guilty now for just having left it there earlier under the desk, for Lois or the cleaning lady to deal with. He took a look.

It was typewritten, on a very old manual from all appearances, and that by itself made it stand out. There was no return
address. Reggie read it now, as follows:

Dear Mr. Holmes:

I am not fooled.
That you survived Reichenbach Falls was never a surprise to me.
That the interests of Dr. Watson's literary agent in the af-
terlife should have led him finally to the exploration of cryo-
genics (though he must have gone to great pains to keep it so
well from the public), and that he should have passed this information on to you, and that you should have used your own
intense, though narrow, scientific focus to bring the investigation to a successful conclusion while pretending retirement in
Sussex does not surprise me either.
That you should then use that knowledge to make yourself available to what you hoped would be a more civilized
and yet still intellectually challenging time, follows naturally.
I don't know precisely when you revived, but I am sure
you find today's London eminently satisfying on the second
count, but disappointing on the first.
And I know that your current guise as a self-centered
lawyer is just that, a disguise.
I am not fooled, and I shall have my forefather's revenge.
I shall take from you what you value most.

Your Humble Servant,

Moriarty

"Self-centered lawyer." That was annoying. And the fact
that the letter writer seemed to think he was communicating

with both Reggie Heath and Sherlock Holmes at the same time was odd; all of the other letters had been intended simply for Sherlock Holmes, period.

But the letters not written by either schoolchildren or people from other cultures were almost always just jokes. Taking such things seriously was his brother's quirk, not his own, and Reggie had already wasted too much time on this one.

"It's just a prank," said Reggie. He gave the letter back to Lois. "Send it on to Nigel with the others."

Reggie took the lift down to the lobby. He left his own vehicle at Baker Street—the undercarriage of the XJS had begun to make noises on even small bumps—and he caught a Black Cab to take him to Shoreditch Police Station.

4

The police station and the adjacent magistrate's court were in a mostly unrestored area of the East End. Reggie had not spent much time in this part of London since his parents died, but it was familiar territory. He had grown up here. When the cab took the last turn onto Old Street toward the police station, he was less than half a mile from his childhood home.

They passed a parked scaffolding truck, and Reggie remembered that he and his father and Nigel had all painted a block of flats nearby, on Shoreditch High Street, many years ago. Reggie had been seventeen then, and it was his last summer working regularly with his father.

By the end of that summer, before he went off to Cambridge on scholarship, he had been able to climb to the top of a sixteen-foot, two-piece rickety extension ladder, hold a full gallon of paint in the palm of one hand, and paint the top fascia board of the house with the other. At that age he had been a bit proud of the strength and balance it took to do it. In fact, he was still, though he had not tested that skill since . . . well, since that summer. And, at least in his memory of it, he had never spilled a drop—except for once, when Nigel had been holding the ladder, standing directly below, and pointing out a flaw in Reggie's technique, on which occasion Reggie had somehow managed to let go of the entire gallon of oil-based paint.

That had been a splendid summer, and not solely because Nigel had still been trying to get the paint out of his hair two months later. But it was the last of the summers like that. Their father had died the following December, under circumstances that still rankled when Reggie was reminded of them.

But the cab came to a stop now. Reggie got out and entered the Shoreditch police station.

The exterior of the place was old and on the verge of becoming an historical landmark, but the interior conference room was quite up to standards, with the presumably calming pale green walls and plastic chairs. Reggie took a seat in one and waited, as the guard went to fetch the defendant.

Moments later the guard returned, escorting Neil Walters—a white male, something under thirty years of age, strongly built. Reggie motioned for him to sit down.

"I'm Reggie Heath. Did your solicitor tell you about me?"

"Yes. She said you are tops. She said you would save me, and not take my house to do it."

"We'll see."

"Which is good, because I haven't got one."

"No house, you mean."

"Yes. I rent in Stepney."

Walters spoke with an East End accent. Reggie had lost his own at university. But he had always assumed he could pick it up again at will, and he never minded hearing it. It reminded him of an earlier time. Of his father, and of growing up.

Walters was slightly over six feet, almost as tall as Reggie. His demeanor was both confused and defiant—which didn't tell Reggie much, because both attitudes were typical for a young working-class male caught up in the system for the first time, whether guilty or innocent.

"Tell me about the night of the crime," said Reggie.

"I didn't do it, Mr. Heath," said Walters.

"Understood. But tell me about that evening. Were you driving?"

"Yes."

"From what time?"

"I started at ten in the morning and I got home just before midnight that evening."

"Sounds like a rough shift," said Reggie.

"It's my usual. The cream fares are the morning and evening commuter crowds—but everyone wants those, and I'm new. So I work the hours I must and take the spots in the cab rank that I can get."

"It was a normal day for you?"

"Yes, and it was a good one. I ran twenty fares, and without taking a single wrong turn."

He said that with evident pride.

"Drivers keep score about that?" said Reggie.

Walters shrugged. "I do."

"Anyone see you after you got home? Did you go out, buy groceries, have friends over?"

"No. I mean, on some other Saturday I might have had a bird there. I do all right, if you know what I mean."

Reggie made a mental note that Walters should avoid that sort of bragging if this went to trial. Jurors might start inferring things all on their own about what caused the robbery to go fatally violent.

But that was assuming Reggie decided to take the case at all.

"You're single and you live alone then, and you had no company that evening?"

"Right," said Walters. Then he seemed to feel obliged to add something more, and he leaned forward earnestly.

"I have no alibi Mr. Heath . . . but I did not do it."

"Do you know why the police think you did?"

"Because I drive a Black Cab."

"Because you drive a Black Cab, and because witnesses say it was your license plate number."

"But I was on the other side of town driving home, wasn't I? I couldn't have done it when they said it happened. I was in the East End, driving home."

"Can anyone vouch for that? Did you have a passenger?"

Walters looked surprised by the question.

"To Stepney at that time of night? No one in my neighborhood takes a cab home, Mr. Heath. We're not lawyers."

Reggie nodded slightly.

"No offense meant," said Walters, scrambling quickly to correct himself. "People there just can't afford it, is all."

"Yes," said Reggie. "I know." Now Reggie was silent for just a moment, and Walters seemed to take that as a sign that he still needed to bolster his case.

"Mr. Heath, ever since I was a child, I've never wanted to do anything else but be the driver of a Black Cab. And it's no easy thing, I can tell you."

"Why is that?" said Reggie.

"Well, for one thing, there's getting the Knowledge, and then there's the chats with the examiners, which you have to do every three months and they just get harder each time, and you have to go to the Black Cab school, and you learn all the routes and at which times of day, and the location of every pub and theater and courthouse in the city, and by description, or what your fares think are descriptions, not just by addresses."

"Doesn't sound easy," said Reggie.

"Because it isn't."

"Did it make you wonder if it was really worth the trouble?" said Reggie.

"Oh no. It's worth the trouble, all right. Not everyone is capable of becoming a Black Cab driver, Mr. Heath, and even capable ones don't always get to do it. At least not until they've jumped through all the hoops to join the club."

He paused with that, and then for some reason seemed emboldened.

"Sort of like becoming a barrister, you might say."

"No, it's not at all like—" Reggie stopped himself. "Well, I suppose if all apprentice drivers must eat a prescribed number of bad meals in the same halls, just to force a sense of camaraderie and exclusivity on novices who might otherwise prefer to be seeking out more pleasant company than each other, then yes, it would be exactly like becoming a barrister."

The cab driver gave Reggie an appalled look.

"They make you eat together?"

"At the beginning, yes. And not just eat, but converse, as well."

"Doesn't sound easy," said Walters.

"It isn't," said Reggie.

"But then, you get paid very well."

"Sometimes," said Reggie.

Now Walters looked worried. "I have limited . . ."

"Your solicitor told me," said Reggie.

"I'll be paying for my cab for the next ten years," added Walters. "And there was the tuition at the Taxi Knowledge School. And then the moped."

"The moped?"

"You can never hope to learn all the routes on foot; it would take a lifetime. And doing it by car would cost too much just for the petrol."

"So you bought a moped."

"Yes. Everyone does."

"You owe significant money on the cab and the moped?"

"Yes. And some on the Knowledge School, too."

"I see."

"Is that a problem?"

"The prosecution thinks it's motive."

"Well, that would be a lousy reason to kill someone, for a few dollars, wouldn't it?"

"Agreed."

"Anyway, I've paid some of it already. My dad gave me my start. He had some savings. I got it when he died. It wasn't much, but he always made sure he gave me everything he had. He worked even harder than I do for it."

"He was a cab driver, too?"

"No. He was a housepainter."

"Really?" Reggie sat back in his chair.

"Yes. All his life. He had strength in his forearms you would not have guessed. He could hold a full gallon of paint steady in one hand, from the bottom of the can, as if it were nothing, while he used a brush with the other."

For a moment, Reggie said nothing and just studied the client. He liked it that Walters's father was a housepainter. But he didn't like coincidences.

Still, it was not an uncommon occupation for East Enders—so perhaps not so surprising that Walters's father had the same line of work as Reggie's.

The silence seemed to make Walters think that Reggie was unimpressed.

"Do you know how much a full gallon of paint weighs when

you have to hold it like this for hours?" said Walters, extending his left arm out from the elbow, palm up.

"Yes," said Reggie. "I know exactly."

"My dad told me it was no kind of life. He said the fumes would kill me if the ladders didn't. He told me to make a better life for myself."

Reggie nodded, intending nothing more than acknowledgment. But Walters seemed to take it as something more.

"Did yours tell you that, too?" he asked.

"Yes," said Reggie, too surprised at the question not to answer.

"And so you did, didn't you?"

Now Reggie did not answer, and it wasn't just because he wasn't the one who was supposed to be revealing his background. It was because he wasn't sure of the answer.

It was absolutely true, his father had done everything in his power to be sure that Reggie and Nigel would have better livelihoods than his own. And Reggie had, in fact, grown up with that expectation. The next generation would always do better.

But there is more to life than livelihood, and in recent weeks Reggie had found himself comparing his own life to his father's. At this same age, Reggie's father had a wife whom he loved, two sons full of potential if not common sense, and a hope that everything could only get better in the future. These days, Reggie only hoped he would be able to equal that, and of late, he felt some of that hope slipping away.

Now the potential client, getting no answer from Reggie, continued speaking, and Reggie refocused.

"I know I'm not educated like you, Mr. Heath, but I'm smart in some ways. I know how to get from this place to that one, and if I don't already know, I only have to do it once and then I remember forever. I knew I could be a Black Cab driver, if I applied myself. And my dad told me I could, too. It's all I ever wanted to do, and I wouldn't give it up for the world."

The guard rapped on the conference-room window now, and pointed at his watch.

Reggie nodded back at the guard. "It's all right. I've heard enough."

Walters looked up, at once both hopeful and alarmed.

"I'll call your solicitor tomorrow with my decision," said Reggie.

"My life is in your hands, Mr. Heath."

"We'll hope it's not as dire as all that," said Reggie.

Reggie left the jail and took a Black Cab back toward Baker Street.

He had not yet made his decision. He knew this case could not be the financial salvation of his chambers. Payment would come from the public-defense program and would be minimal.

But that wasn't the real issue. The real issue was whether he believed Walters.

Reggie's instinct from the interview was that Walters had not done it. But he wanted his decision to be based on more than just that instinct—even though this was a form of intro-spection that he knew a practicing criminal lawyer should not engage in.

Everyone understood how the system worked: the barrister is not the judge and jury, and it is not necessary or expected that he believe in his heart that the client is innocent. It is only neces-sary that he not know for a fact otherwise. Any lawyer who could not accept that as the operating premise should not be practicing criminal law.

But that was exactly why Reggie had stopped practicing it years ago.

He needed this client to be innocent. In some ways, the idea of defending Walters felt like the idea of defending Reggie's own family honor. The only real question was whether he believed the man.

The cab was headed up the Embankment now. It would be a few minutes before he reached chambers. He could make his decision at that time.

At the moment he still had other issues.

He took out his mobile and rang Laura.

She picked up. Her voice sounded vaguely sleepy. But it was not her woken-out-of-a-deep-sleep voice. It was relaxed and lazy, like an afternoon nap in the shade.

"Reggie," she said. "What a nice surprise."

In almost every memory he had of this voice, she was wearing either nothing or something very near to it.

"Where are you?" he said.

"In Phuket, of course. You know that."

Reggie knew that. And he knew he shouldn't be wondering about where she was or what she had just been doing more precisely than that.

"Yes," he said. "How are things going? Are you enjoying the satay? Is the peanut sauce all that it is supposed to be? Everything on schedule?

"A bit salty, but I like it. We shoot all day until four, and then I put on fifty-weight sun block, my widest hat, sunglasses the size of grapefruits, and I sit under an umbrella and pretend I'm getting sun. It's great fun, and I'm paler than ever. You know how I hate sunburn."

"You certainly don't want to get overexposed."

"No, of course I don't . . ." Then she paused. "Ohhh," she said, and then she laughed. "*That's* what this is about."

"What is?"

"You saw the *Daily Sun*."

"Never read it. Something of interest this week?"

"You saw it, Reggie. Don't lie. I know that miffed tone."

"I could hardly avoid it," said Reggie, unable to stop himself from taking on just exactly that tone. "Everyone in London is going out of their way to tell me about it."

"Really?" she said lightly. "I never knew we were that much of an item."

Reggie hoped the "we" she referred to was herself and Reggie—even though she had used past tense—but he wasn't certain.

"For him to publish that photo in his own paper—"

"It's harmless, Reggie, really. I don't mind it."

"Laura, it's his hand and your breast in his own bloody tabloid!"

Reggie had not intended to say that out loud, and the silence now from Laura confirmed the mistake. In the three long seconds that followed, he took the precaution of checking that the lever that activated the intercom between the cab driver and passenger was off.

"Reggie . . ." began Laura.

Then she paused. Gathering herself, probably. He knew he was in trouble.

And now she said: "Yes, it is his newspaper, and it is my breast, and you don't own either of them, so why is it a problem for you if one does some lighthearted coverage on the other?"

"Quite right," said Reggie, retreating. He wanted to say it was the lack of coverage that was the problem, but he managed to hold that remark in check.

Reggie noticed now that the cab driver, for some reason, was shaking his head.

"Reggie," said Laura now. "Please don't go defending my honor or doing anything similarly rash."

"Certainly not."

"Promise."

It took Reggie a moment. "I promise," he said finally.

There was another long pause. Reggie was trying desperately to think of a way to start the conversation over, but nothing came to mind.

They said their mobile-phone good-byes, awkwardly.

And now the cab driver, who before had contented himself with just an occasional glance in the mirror, actually turned his head.

"Mind a bit of advice, mate?"

"What?" Reggie looked over at the small red lever just above the right passenger door. "Is the intercom off, or not?"

"Broken," said the driver, matter-of-factly. "In the on position." Then he held up a copy of the *Daily Sun*. "This the one, is she?"

There was no way for Reggie to reach through and grab it from him; the glass partition had only a small aperture at the bottom.

"Don't miss the turn," said Reggie irritably. "Dorset House on Baker Street."

"I've never missed a turn," said the driver. "I know these streets better than any of the fancy GPS stuff that the lot are talking about now."

"Sorry to have doubted you," said Reggie, not interested in what lot the driver was referring to. He just wanted to get out of the cab without any further conversation related to Laura's breasts.

"You don't need all that futuristic crap if you've got a head on your shoulders."

"I'm sure you're right," said Reggie.

"Now about your lady friend. Know what I look for in a woman?"

Reggie looked out the window and saw that they were still

one turn away from Baker Street, the light was red, the traffic was heavy, and he would probably have to endure another two minutes of conversation.

"No," he said.

"A woman who will let me take my shoes off. My last missus got upset over that. We went on holiday to the summerhouse in Spain, and she wouldn't let me take my shoes off in the front room. So that's a trade-off right there. There is value in being able to take off your shoes."

"You have a summerhouse in Spain?" said Reggie.

"Of course. Don't you?"

"I used to," said Reggie. He thought about that for a moment, and then asked, "How long have you been a Black Cab driver?"

"Fifteen years."

"Ever want to do something else?"

"Sport fishing in Bermuda, when I retire."

"I mean, some other work for a living?"

"Not a chance. Took me too long to get where I am. Five years just learning the street Knowledge, supporting myself at my day job with the Royal Mail, then putting my skinny arse around the City at night on a moped. Could never do that now, there's no scooter big enough. Anyway, why would I want to do something else after all that?"

"And you gave up a perfectly stable government job for this?"

"Of course I did. Easy choice, mate."

They were slowing now.

"Here's your Dorset House," said the driver.

Reggie paused before opening the door.

"Wouldn't give it up then, driving a cab?" said Reggie.

"Not for anything," said the driver.

Reggie got out of the cab and gave the driver a better tip than he had originally intended. He had made up his mind. He went directly to chambers and rang the solicitor from that morning.

It was late in the workday, but she picked up almost at once. Her voice was bright.

"I will represent your client," said Reggie.

"Brilliant," said Darla. "I couldn't be more pleased."

"Who is prosecuting?" said Reggie.

"Geoffrey Langdon, over at Stiles Court. Is he any good?"

"Deceptively so," said Reggie. "He wants you to underestimate both him and his case. Bludgeons you with self-effacement. He'll stand up before the judge, hesitating like a schoolboy, and next thing you know, you're flat on the floor. When is the preliminary hearing?"

"Two days."

Bloody hell, that was soon. Reggie said nothing for a moment.

"Is that a problem?" said Darla.

"It's not much time to poke holes in the prosecution's case."

"But it is just the committal hearing. There will be sufficient time before trial to create a defense, surely."

"If it comes to that," said Reggie. "But better to get it tossed at the outset, wouldn't you say?"

"Why, of course," she said. "I'm such a dunce, I don't know what I was thinking—except that I thought that they surely had a prima facie case in any event. Do you see major flaws?"

"We at least need to test the prosecution facts a bit. They might have got it wrong, you know."

"Oh," she said, as if it had just occurred to her. "Of course. Tell me what we can do," she continued, sounding eager to make amends.

"Did you get anything at all from your private investigator?"

"I had him interview the witnesses who said they saw the cab. He's sending his report, but he said he didn't turn up a useful thing. Used up all his paid legal-aid hours on it, too. Sorry, did I botch that as well? It seems we're on our own for the rest of it."

"No," said Reggie, feeling a bit more friendly toward her now. "No, it was worth a shot. But we need a look at the crime scene. Will you set that up?"

"Surely," she said.

An hour later the phone rang. Reggie picked up.

At the other end of the line was Geoffrey Langdon.

"Heath—hear you're taking the Black Cab case."

"Yes."

"Didn't realize you were doing criminal again. But I do always have the devil of a time keeping up."

"It's an exception," said Reggie.

"Well, it would be a wonderful opportunity, I think, for me to learn from you, Heath. No doubt about it. I mean, if it were to go to trial. But you're going to plead it out though, aren't you?"

"Thank you for bringing that up," said Reggie. "I was just about to ring and see if you want to drop the charges now or wait until I contest the committal hearing."

"Drop them? Oh, dear. No, I'm afraid I can't do that. No. Considerate of you to suggest it, I suppose. But no, we can't do that. The case is quite . . . well, rock solid, really. You're sure you won't plead?"

"I can't ask an innocent man to plead to homicide."

"Well, of course, if he were innocent, but—"

"And if I didn't believe him, I wouldn't have taken the case."

"Yes, understood. Quite scrupulous of you, of course. Well, see you in two days, then. Say, have you seen the *Daily Sun* this morning?"

"No," said Reggie, and then he hung up the phone. He didn't need to hear another question about Laura in Phuket.

In any case, it struck him that Langdon had been just a little too anxious to get a plea.

Reggie picked up the phone and rang Detective Inspector Wembley.

"I'd like to buy you a pint," said Reggie.

"Why, Heath? You're not doing criminal again, are you?"

"A one-time thing, I expect."

"What's the case?"

"The Black Cab driver accused of homicide."

"You can buy me the pint," said the inspector. "But, of course, I'll tell you nothing you shouldn't already know."

Reggie regarded that as a fair bargain. Wembley sometimes overestimated what everyone else should know.

Reggie exited Baker Street Chambers and took a cab to the Stick and Whistle pub on Tothill Street, just one block over from New Scotland Yard.

A small crowd of police officers boisterously watched a match between Chelsea and Arsenal on the big-screen telly. Reggie went to the bar and bought two pints, paying no attention to the match. He had been a great fan of football as a child, but not in the years since.

Inspector Wembley was already seated at the bar. The inspector was middle-aged, with white hair and the stubbornly declining build of a man who had once wanted to be a prize-fighter. He was leaning intently toward the wide screen as Reggie approached, his shoulders moving in a subconscious punching motion, as if he were about to jump into the match himself and flatten a defenseman who was giving Arsenal trouble.

Reggie sat down and put a beer in front of Wembley.

"Damn, that was blatant! Red card him!" shouted Wembley.

"Been a while since I've taken a criminal brief," said Reggie, as Wembley turned his attention from the screen just long enough to seize the pint. "Anything I should know about this one?"

"Don't really have much choice, do you?" said Wembley. "From what I hear, your calendar is pretty much open."

"True," said Reggie.

"The prosecution's case is solid, Heath. If you want my advice, plead your client and be done with it."

Reggie nodded. "You always think that. And so does Langdon when he's working for the Crown. But is there anything I should know?"

"I'm sure Langdon will send you his file," said Wembley, casually turning his attention back to the sports screen.

"He did," said Reggie, "but prosecuting barristers always manage to leave something out. What should I know that isn't in the file?"

"If it isn't in the file, I've no idea," said Wembley. "But what is in the file is that we have identified the suspect by his cab number, and he has no verifiable alibi. We don't withhold facts, Heath, you know that."

"Yes," said Reggie. "But if all this happened according to the prosecution's theory, wouldn't you expect there to be substantial evidence in the Black Cab itself?"

"You might," said Wembley. "Unless the perpetrator had it properly cleaned after. Which appears to be the case."

"Still seems to me the prosecution is rushing this one a bit," said Reggie.

"No comment," replied Wembley. But then he actually turned his attention from the sports screen and looked over at Reggie.

"All I can suggest is that you think about the victims for a moment."

"Bloody rot; you don't need to remind me to have empathy for victims, Wembley."

"That's not what I meant, Heath. I only meant, think about who the victims were. Their profile."

Reggie did so.

"American tourists," said Reggie after a moment. "And it's still high season."

"Spot on," said Wembley. "And this isn't the first of the crimes. So before you get yourself too deep in this, consider it from the City's point of view."

"Spell it out for me."

"The Black Cabs are known throughout the touristy world as the most reliable and crime-free mode of transportation devised by man."

"Perhaps a slight exaggeration," said Reggie.

"No, it's a fact. They're safer than your mother's baby carriage. Nothing is more risk-free. There has not been a single crime or allegation of a crime associated with anyone's ride in a Black Cab in more than twenty years. I can tell you that for a fact. No rape, no robbery, no murder, no nothing."

"A credit to all of London," said Reggie, nodding.

"But in the past two months," said Wembley, "there have been seven."

Reggie waited for a moment, then asked.

"Seven what?"

"Assault, robbery, and now murder."

Reggie said nothing. He was astounded.

"Seven of *each?*"

"No, no—I mean seven total incidents."

"I see. A sort of variety pack, then."

"A cab driver bopping about London and harassing American tourists is like having that shark roaming around offshore in—where was it, Nantucket?—in *Jaws.* Bad for business. You don't really want anyone to know about it. But once it hits the papers and everyone knows about it, you want it over with, right quick. Especially when someone dies. Really, Heath, you need to learn to appreciate the politics of things. Read the daily rags once in a while."

There was a chorus of outraged shouts at the wide screen now, and Wembley looked back over his shoulder to join in.

"Bloody hell, will they ever red card that wanker?"

Then he turned back to Reggie.

"I mean," said Wembley, "if you can get past all the ink they're devoting to yourself. And to Miss Rankin."

"That's a red card, Wembley," said Reggie, and then he put down his beer and left the pub.

5

Despite Wembley's endorsement of tabloid reading, Reggie had had enough of the daily rags. He hoped that the private investigator's report would prove to be more useful. It arrived at chambers the following afternoon, and Reggie had just enough time to review it before setting out to meet Darla Rennie at the crime scene.

But the report had little that was helpful.

The investigator had interviewed both the barman at the pub in Covent Garden and two Chelsea residents who said they saw the cab some twenty minutes later. All of the witnesses acknowledged that they had not been in a position to get a look at the driver's face. If it went to trial, Reggie would hammer on that.

But the identifications of the license plate were another matter. The barman distinctly remembered the letters in the middle of the license number—WHAMU1—because they happened to form an acronym for West Ham United, a popular football club. A jury would believe his reason for remembering those letters.

The second sighting was on King's Road, near Chelsea Harbor, where the cab had apparently rounded the corner in a hurry, narrowly missing two middle-aged women who had just stepped into the street, splashing both of them from the recent rain—and to such an extent that they wrote the number down and actually called in a complaint to the police.

Reggie knew he could argue that the second witnesses might have written the number down incorrectly, but their call to the police established a solid time line—and the number they wrote down included the same acronym that the barman recalled so clearly.

On top of that, the private investigator had taken the time to check all the current Black Cab license numbers in London—a check that the prosecution would surely do as well—and there was only one cab in the city with that acronym in its license number, and that was the one owned by Reggie's client. That could not be a good thing.

Reggie took the turn now from King's Road in Chelsea. He drove down a narrow street, lined with trendy out-of-the-way furniture shops, to the abandoned power station at Lots Road, on the north bank of the Thames.

He passed two large, sooty redbrick buildings, one with a thirty-foot smokestack on top; between those buildings, a dozen feet below the little bridge where Reggie crossed, was Chelsea Creek—some twenty feet wide and lined with concrete to contain the changes in water level from the Thames.

There was razor wire all around the perimeter of the structures, but in some places it was not in good repair, and

Reggie guessed there would be spots where it could easily be traversed. If you wanted to do something away from the public eye in Chelsea in the middle of the night, this would be the spot.

A police officer opened a rusty metal gate (which now had a shiny new lock), and Reggie drove inside. He parked at the far end of the main building, near the river.

It had rained overnight. The afternoon sky now was gray, and a cold wind off the river greeted Reggie the moment he opened his car door.

He saw that Darla was already there, chatting with an officer who looked quite eager to cooperate with her.

When Reggie approached, she handed Reggie a copy of that morning's *Daily Sun*.

"I see that you agree with me," she said. "About a little publicity, I mean."

Reggie accepted the paper from her. She had it open to page two, with this headline: "Balmy Barrister to Defend Death Cab Driver."

"I thought you didn't read this trash," said Reggie.

"A friend alerted me to it," she said. "But no harm done, that I can see."

Reggie glanced at it. It was a short, one-sided account of his excursion the day before to Buxton's compound, followed by a note that he was now representing the notorious suspect in the "Black Cab Killings." It was no worse than he had expected. He folded the paper and tucked it away.

"Let's take a look at something real now," he said.

"They say there won't be much to see," Darla volunteered as the officer escorted them to the crime scene. "What with the rain last night."

"It wasn't covered up?" said Reggie to the officer.

"No need," said the officer. "Forensics completed their work before it started. Photographed every square inch. We'll send the pics over, if you like."

"Yes, I should like," said Reggie. "But you'd expect Scotland Yard could afford a tarp. It rained the night of the crime as well, didn't it?"

"Yes," said the officer. "I believe it did."

"So, no footprints were distinguishable?"

"Don't know that, sir; you'll have to ask the forensics team."

"I will do, but I expect that's why forensics didn't bother protecting it—whatever footprints there were, if there were, and tire tracks as well, if there were, had already been obliterated by the time the police arrived."

"Was that a question?" said the officer.

"No," said Reggie. "Where were the bodies found?"

"This way," said the officer.

The building ended at about ten yards from a concrete sea wall, about three feet high, with an opening where the old power station had received deliveries by boat at some time in the distant past.

They walked on for the width of the building, until they reached a flimsy metal fence. The fence was in serious disrepair and had been flattened down at several points; whether from sheer neglect, or deliberate activities of the demolition crew, or some other force, it was hard to tell.

The office stepped over one of the flattened sections.

"They were found down here," he said. "But it was low tide then."

Reggie and Darla joined the officer and looked down at Chelsea Creek. The Thames flowed into this channel at high tide, and ebbed from it at low. At present it was filled with dark river water.

"How low was it when the bodies were found?" said Reggie.

"It was just mud in the creek, if that's what you mean."

"Were they weighted down with anything?"

"No. But they didn't float out into the Thames, because they were caught up on that jutting rebar you see down there."

"Caught up on which side of it?"

"Not sure, I expect forensics will have photos."

There was nothing more to see. Darla walked up close to Reggie as they headed back toward the gate.

"This is good, isn't it?" she said in a low voice. "They have no footprints. Nothing to indicate he was at the scene really, do they?"

"So far. But I would like things better if it had not rained, so that the prosecution could offer no logical explanation for why our client's footprints are *not* present."

She thought about that for a moment, then said, "You said on the phone that the motive seems weak. Why? What's weak about it?"

"It takes years of effort to become a Black Cab driver. It's almost as tough as becoming a barrister," said Reggie, and then in a quick afterthought, "Or a solicitor. You wouldn't expect anyone to jeopardize all that for a simple robbery. Or even a string of them."

"I see," she said. "I hadn't thought of it that way. Then we're in decent shape, with low motive and little or no forensic proof?"

"No," said Reggie. "They still have the ID on the cab. Without a verifiable alibi, that will be enough for the indictment to stand. Our client says he was driving home at the time in the East End, but we have only his word for it. The prosecution, on the other hand, has two witnesses who reported seeing his cab, and its license number, thirty or so minutes away in the West End. If we can't overcome that—and right now I don't see how we do—this will go to trial, and if it goes to trial, anything can happen."

"We'll think of something. I have full confidence in you."

"Noted and appreciated, but we have just two days to think of it."

"Perhaps a pint would help?"

Reggie turned and looked at her. What he heard was a purely casual invitation between two lawyers working the same case, and not at all inappropriate, even though they had already hashed out all the lawyerly issues they could for the moment. But her emerald eyes were glimmering and she was standing quite close, as if she wanted to tuck herself inside his raincoat, making him at first highly inclined to accept the invitation, and at second thought, concerned about the consequences of doing so.

He was not prepared at the moment for a determination on this subject. He decided to ask for a continuance.

"Save the pint till after?" he said.

"Done," she said.

Reggie drove back to chambers. He rang Laura on his mobile along the way, but he got no answer. The message service picked up—but he wasn't quite certain what he wanted to say. That he thought the young female solicitor was hitting on him? No, probably not a good subject for conversation. That he had finally acquired a new case, the first since he had returned from Los Angeles, but that it wasn't going particularly well? No, probably not that either. In fact, it was probably a bad idea to leave any message at all. He shut off the phone.

Half a moment later, it rang. It was Laura.

"Did you call?"

"Yes," said Reggie.

"Why didn't you leave a message?"

"I . . . didn't have all that much to say, really."

"You are allowed to call without an agenda."

"Noted. Just thought I'd mention that I got a new brief, actually."

"That's wonderful," said Laura brightly. "What sort is it?"

"Robbery homicide."

There was a pause.

"Well, double homicide, actually," added Reggie, in a tone that was halfway between bragging and apology.

"I thought you didn't do criminal," said Laura, with just a slight note of concern.

"Circumstances are . . . exceptional."

"I see. Well, I am glad you rang . . . or that you sort of did at any rate, because I was just about to ring you."

"You did just ring me."

"Oh, of course," she said with a laugh, and as awkward as Reggie was sure he sounded a moment ago, now it was Laura who seemed just a bit flustered.

"I just wanted to let you know I'll be back in town tomorrow.

"I thought you had another two weeks on the shoot."

"There's a short break. A good time for us to talk, I think."

Now she did not sound flustered; now she just sounded tense and formal. Chills went down Reggie's spine.

"Of course," he said. "Just give a ring."

"I will," she said. "Have to go. Must pack."

That was all.

When Reggie returned to the Baker Street building after that call, he once again went straight to his chambers as a refuge.

There was something wrong in Laura's sudden need to visit. He did not want to think about what it was, but in any case, he had a great excuse not to do so. He had a hearing to prepare for.

He pulled the police files and the private investigator's report out of his desk and pored over them once again. All of it confirmed his initial impression: it just didn't make sense that a dedicated Black Cab driver would jeopardize his career by committing a string of low-yield robberies—much less a murder.

But Reggie's gut feeling carried no weight in court, and he knew he did not have enough to get the charges tossed at the preliminary hearing. As overeager as the Crown Prosecution Service appeared to be, it only needed a prima facie case to get an indictment. And if Reggie contested that indictment at tomorrow's hearing and failed, he would not only annoy the court, he would be prematurely revealing and seriously undermining the defense that he would need to present at trial.

Reggie got up from his desk. He would sleep on it. In the morning, if no other strategy came to mind, he would have to call Langdon and initiate a retreat, and accept a trial date.

Reggie exited chambers, but he had to pause at Lois's desk; the fax machine was screeching and blinking.

Reggie picked up the fax as it creaked out. Perhaps Darla had come up with something.

But it wasn't from her. It was from Nigel, and it said:

READ THE BLOODY THING!

Reggie picked up the next page that came through, and when he saw it, he had to laugh.

It was a fax of the same typewritten letter that had fallen from the top of the stack the day before. The letter from Moriarty. Apparently, Nigel was taking it seriously.

Which Reggie found amusing—because any halfway decent evil genius wouldn't use a manual typewriter, which might well be traceable and reveal your location. He would go to the library and use a common laser or ink-jet. Even ink analysis could reveal no more than which brand.

Reggie crumpled the fax and tossed it into the wastebasket. He had no time to deal with a letter from a fictional villain to a fictional detective, threatening or otherwise.

6

Reggie returned to chambers the next morning and saw Rafferty, just ahead of him, heading for the lift.

Reggie slowed his pace, but it was too late—Rafferty had seen him. Rafferty held the doors open, and Reggie could not turn away without seeming to flee.

"Hear you have a new brief," said Rafferty.

"Word travels fast," said Reggie, not adding that it was also traveling farther than he preferred.

Rafferty just smiled and nodded—and he said nothing more, until the doors opened on Reggie's floor.

"Letters under control, I presume," said Rafferty then.

"Of course," said Reggie.

Rafferty nodded, as if to indicate that perhaps he would take Reggie's word for it. Reggie quickly exited the lift with no further discussion.

As he approached his secretary's desk, Reggie looked back

over his shoulder. At least Rafferty wasn't actually following him. That was something.

"Any new posts this morning?" he asked Lois.

"Um . . . by new posts , do you mean, well . . . addressed to whom, exactly?"

"To me, of course."

"No. Sorry."

Reggie nodded and proceeded toward his office.

"But there was this," Lois called out.

Reggie paused and came back to her desk, puzzled and hopeful.

"Yes?"

With some trepidation, she handed Reggie the one letter from the in-basket. From the look on her face, he realized now to whom the letter must be addressed.

Mercifully, there was only just the one. There was no need to send another package off to Nigel and then have to deal with more faxes. Given it was just one letter, Reggie could send the form response for this one himself, and keep Rafferty at bay.

He opened the laser-printed letter, gave it a perfunctory glance—and then paused. The first sentence caught his eye:

Dear Mr. Holmes:

I read much in the papers about that Black Cab driver and how he murdered that American couple. A most horrible thing.

But I don't see how he could have done it, Mr. Holmes. I read in the *Daily Sun* that the cab was in the West End near midnight. But I saw that cab myself at that very time in the East End at Lower Clapton Road. I saw the license plate WHAMU1 while waiting for a bus.

I cannot come forward, Mr. Holmes. I am a married

man, and I do not wish to divulge the nature of my business
at that hour on that corner. I am writing to you because I
know you can be discreet, as you were in "Scandal in Bohe-
mia" and I expect in many scandals in other places that we
never heard about.

I am not so sure of that poor man's barrister. But there
are many television cameras in the East End now, as I'm
sure you know. Please go to the corner of Lower Clapton
Road and Newick Road. Look up. And then help an innocent man.

A Concerned Citizen

There was no return address. The postmark was from the
previous day.

Reggie, still standing, read the letter again. He read it once
more again after that, and then he went into his chambers office, sat down with the letter on the desk in front of him, and
read it yet again.

An alibi. An alibi witness.

But the preliminary hearing was scheduled for that afternoon. There was no possibility of tracking this anonymous
letter writer down within the next five hours, if it could be done
at all. And in any case, how much credence could be given to
a witness who provided a tip by writing a letter to Sherlock
Holmes?

Still, none of that would matter if the tip in the letter was
correct. With all the new CCTV cameras being put up of late,
there might be some hope.

Reggie picked up the phone and rang the Traffic Authority.
He gave them his credentials and purpose, and after a few moments, he was connected with a traffic engineer.

"You are asking for a CCTV location?" said the engineer.

"Yes," said Reggie. "Do you have a camera at Lower Clapton Road in Hackney?"

The engineer took a moment to check, and then said that indeed yes, there was a camera at that location.

"Is it operational?"

"Yes."

"How far back does it go before recording over again?"

"Seven days."

"Have you had a request in the last week from the police to pull the tape?"

The engineer took another moment to check, and then said no.

"Thank you," said Reggie. "You will receive such a request shortly."

Now Reggie rang the prosecuting barrister.

"Heath," said Langdon, answering. "You've reconsidered? Not really going to contest the hearing, are you?"

"Your disclosures said the police reviewed the relevant CCTV tapes."

"Of course."

"And found nothing."

"Nothing conclusive. CCTVs don't capture everything, you know that. Lorries get in the way, buses, any number of things can obscure a vehicle that was actually there."

"Which routes did they check?"

"Why, they checked the pick-up site at the pub, the location where the cab was sighted in Chelsea, and the entire route between those two points."

"Did they check the cameras along my client's route home?"

Langdon was silent for a moment. Then, in a small voice, "No. Seemed a waste of time, given that we already had witnesses that placed the cab across town—"

"I'm asserting an alibi defense," said Reggie, "and I want

all the traffic tapes pulled on the route my client says he traveled to get to his home in the East End at the time in question." This was a demand; Reggie knew the police were obliged to do this, and so did Langdon.

"You mean simply in time for trial, correct?" offered Langdon, hopefully. "I don't know all that much about such things, but I trust you don't want to use the court's time today to—"

"Now, for the preliminary hearing," said Reggie. "And if you think the court will be annoyed by the time it takes today, consider how unhappy the Crown Prosecution Service will be if I get the whole thing tossed out at trial because you didn't check all the relevant CCTVs."

"Very well," said Langdon. He was annoyed now, and the tone of false humility was beginning to fade. "You'll have your tapes. Hope you know what you're doing, Heath, for your sake."

Reggie hung up the phone, hoping the same thing.

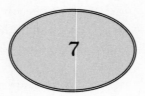

7

A cold rain had begun to fall when Reggie left Baker Street Chambers that afternoon, and he decided to take the precaution of a cab rather than drive his own car. The case had become high profile, and there would be parking issues. And the noise from the undercarriage of the Jag was getting more noticeable.

The preliminary hearing had been moved to Horseferry Road Magistrates Court, a venue for high-profile cases, which this case now was. The earlier Black Cab crimes had been relegated in most newspapers to a few lines on the back pages. But those little blurbs had been building momentum, and the murder of American tourists was such a spectacular event that Reggie knew it would generate a media circus at the courthouse. If the case got to actual trial, it would be moved to the Old Bailey, and it would then become the largest of all circuses.

But not if he could prevent it. If he did his job properly, this hearing would be the end of it, and his client could go home to Stepney and back to work.

As Reggie's cab approached the courthouse now, he saw that all the legal and most of the illegal parking spaces along Horseferry Road were already occupied—in almost all cases by Black Cabs.

Quite an unusual number of Black Cabs, Reggie thought as his own cab double-parked to let him out, even for central London.

Reggie approached the security entrance. He knew what his plan was. But something about the physical act of going through the courthouse security station made the extreme risk in his strategy begin to sink in. Was he making a mistake?

He did not know who the letter writer was. He did not know for certain what the tapes would show. Perhaps they would show nothing. For all he knew, the letter was a red herring and Langdon himself had written it. It would be a brilliant and unethical ploy, if he had done. Reggie's defense would be destroyed.

Reggie showed his security credentials to the guard now, and he saw that Langdon had already arrived—just a few steps ahead of him.

Langdon was pulling a small trolley that was stacked high with thick legal case books, several bundles of documentation, and—Reggie was pleased to see—perhaps a dozen black plastic videocassettes, of the size and type used in closed-circuit television, attached to the trolley, a bit haphazardly, by a bungee strap.

Langdon hadn't seen Reggie yet, and was just about to roll his trolley on past the security desk, when suddenly the bungee strap shifted for some reason, and the entire stack of videocassettes spilled out with an abrupt clatter onto the gray-tiled floor.

"Oh, dear. I suppose I'll never learn, will I?" announced Langdon, to no one in particular and to anyone who happened to be listening.

The security clerk dutifully nodded, and Langdon got down to the floor and began to gather the cassettes together. Within a couple of moments he had all of them—or almost all of them— assembled on the trolley again. He struggled back to his feet— apparently not noticing that in the process he had inadvertently kicked one of the cassettes just out of sight under the security desk.

Langdon said, "There. That should do it. My wife always tells me I'm never any good at packing."

"And quite right about it, too," said Reggie.

Langdon turned. "Oh. Heath. There you are. Well, you've caught me making a fool of myself again, I'm afraid."

"No harm done," said Reggie. "But I believe you missed one."

Without getting down on the ground, Reggie pointed one finger in the general direction of the cassette that Langdon's foot had propelled under the desk.

"Oh?"

Reggie nodded, and pointed again. "Must have skidded a bit."

"Quite right," said Langdon. He got down on the ground to retrieve the cassette. "You have sharper eyes than mine, Heath."

"Lucky thing," said Reggie. As Langdon put the cassette back in the stack, Reggie noted its position and the date written on the label.

And now Reggie breathed a sigh of relief. Langdon might be clever enough to try to sucker Reggie with a letter providing a false tip to unhelpful evidence. And he might be clever enough to try to temporarily lose a piece of helpful evidence on his way into the courtroom. But surely he was not clever enough to be doing both. Langdon was trying to hide the tape, so it certainly had to be both real and exculpatory.

Or at least, probably so.

"Did you say something, Heath?"

"No," said Reggie. "After you. Lead on."

Moments later Reggie took his seat in the courtroom, at a long oak-veneer table that gave him more room than he really needed. There was a chair available at his table for an assistant, but Reggie had none, and a chair for the solicitor as well—but she had yet to arrive.

To Reggie's left was a similar but separate table for the prosecution. This was just the preliminary hearing, not the trial, and so Langdon, like Reggie, was working without an assistant. He was making full use of the table space though. At the far end he placed a large, open binder containing photographs and diagrams of the crime scene. But that was almost certainly just for show, given how little the crime scene investigation had yielded. The prosecution's only real case was the witness statements. Langdon had the transcripts of those directly in front of him.

The CCTV cassettes, however, remained on the trolley next to Langdon, behind the table.

Reggie glanced over his shoulder at the spectator's gallery. The magistrate had opened it to the public, but there were no cameras allowed. No doubt there would be a media frenzy outside to make up for that. There were reporters present, most of them in the front row with their note- or sketchbooks in hand, but after studying the gallery for a moment, Reggie concluded that most of the spectators—the back three gallery rows—were neither reporters nor members of the general public. They were cab drivers.

Now all the faces in the gallery turned, and Reggie turned to look as well. The defendant had been brought in. He was escorted into the dock and stood there, looking about apprehensively. It was the correct look. Given a choice, you really didn't want a client in the dock who looked like he was accustomed to being there.

Walters now looked in Reggie's general direction, and at the same moment there was a soft hand on Reggie's arm. He turned. Darla had arrived.

"Sorry I'm late," she said. "The security guard got very chatty." Walters had caught her eye, and she nodded very slightly back in his direction before she sat down.

Reggie leaned over and whispered to her. "If it goes to trial, you won't want to be seen doing that. It will look like coaching."

"Of course," she said.

Now the bailiff, the court recorder, and the magistrate entered; Reggie, Langdon, and Darla all stood and remained standing until the magistrate had assumed his place.

The magistrate read the case number, and then Langdon stood and matter-of-factly read a statement charging Reggie's client with murder in the first degree.

"Very well," said the magistrate, not looking up. "I see that the Crown has properly delivered initial discovery documents to the defense. No need to waste time. Do I hear any objection to a trial date two weeks hence at Central Criminal Court?"

"You do, my lord," said Reggie, standing.

Now the magistrate looked up.

"I do?"

"Yes, my lord. The defense contests the committal to trial and requests that the prosecution's prima facie evidence be read now into the record."

The magistrate frowned.

"Heath, is it?"

"Yes."

The magistrate looked at the case schedule in front of him. "Reggie Heath?"

"Yes."

The magistrate lowered his spectacles and peered over them at Reggie.

"I don't think I've seen you in my court before, but your name rings a bell for some reason. Something to do with a shrubbery."

"My lord?" said Langdon helpfully. "If I may. My learned friend Mr. Heath has been out of the country recently. You may have seen his name in connection with some minor matters that gained public attention overseas, or perhaps locally regarding an indoor planter at a certain publisher's compound near Tobacco Dock. I'm really not quite sure; I'll admit, I have difficulty keeping abreast of such things . . . as it were . . . but none of that, I'm sure we all agree, has any bearing whatsoever on this case."

Langdon looked over at Reggie as if to accept thanks for having done him a great favor. Before Reggie could formulate a properly cutting response, Langdon continued.

"And because of that short absence, and . . . well, if I . . . if I may say so, because he has been out of criminal practice for some time, I believe, my learned friend may perhaps be unaware of our recent attempts to streamline the committal process?"

"Well, indeed we are trying to do that, aren't we?" said the magistrate, nodding.

"My lord, yes," said Reggie now, "But recent changes to the Criminal Procedure Act notwithstanding, it is still within your discretion to hear the case read, and I think you will find it will take only a moment of your time."

"Well, a moment is rather a subjective measure, though, isn't it? How long a moment do you mean, Mr. Heath?"

"Two minutes, my lord. I will be astonished if my learned friend can drag it out any longer than that, no matter how many well-placed hesitations he includes, because the prosecution's case is quite that short."

"Really?" said the magistrate. "Two minutes?"

"At most," said Reggie. "That's how little substance there is to the charge."

The magistrate pushed back the edges of his left sleeve and looked at his watch.

"I have two minutes," he said. "Mr. Langdon, do you?"

Langdon cleared his throat. "My lord, yes, of course. I will . . . do my best to condense it, if I may."

"No condensing necessary, Mr. Langdon. Spill it all, and if Mr. Heath's estimate proves to be wrong, that will be something for me to remind him of when he next appears in my court."

"Very well," said Langdon. "I shall start then with the forensic examination of the scene, although it may not be within my skills to cover it in so short a time—"

"My lord?"

"Yes, Mr. Heath?"

"The defense will stipulate to the facts shown in the forensics reports as currently provided by the prosecution, for none of those facts implicate the defendant in any way. Nothing was found at his home, nothing in his cab, and nothing that directly tied him to the scene."

The magistrate looked over at the prosecutor.

"Mr. Langdon?"

"Well . . . my lord, yes, it would be correct to say that the prosecution does not base its case on the forensics of any of those locations. Other than, of course, the forensics that establish that two unwitting tourists from the States were horribly killed, and the time at which their deaths occurred."

"That much is known. But on what does the prosecution base its case that it was the defendant that did it?"

"On eyewitness statements, my lord. Two of them. Highly credible and mutually corroborating."

"Then let's spend our two minutes on those, shall we?"

"Of course, my lord."

Langdon now recounted both of the witness statements that Reggie had already seen, investing them with as much high drama as could be done in reciting the numbers of a license plate. He included the significance of the barman's WHAMU1 mnemonic with much emphasis. He carefully delivered the very damning evidence that the second witnesses had called in the sighting the moment after it occurred, and that call was captured on a police recording that indisputably established the time of it. And then Langdon delivered the coup de grace:

"My lord, in the entire registry of Black Cabs in London, there is only one license that contains the characters WHAMU1, and that is the license of the Black Cab that belongs to the defendant."

Langdon stopped on that. Reggie said nothing. The magistrate checked his watch.

"One minute and forty-five seconds," he said. "Well done, Mr. Langdon. Brief and to the point. To just one single point, admittedly, but with no contradiction, it is sufficient to go to trial. Mr. Heath, do you have anything to say?"

"Yes, my lord. My learned friend has forgotten to mention the CCTVs, which the police went to some pains to collect."

"Mr. Langdon?"

"My lord, yes, CCTVs were collected, but as they revealed nothing conclusive, I did not think to mention them."

"How many of these tapes are there?" said the magistrate.

"Eleven in all, from various locations, covering more than a hundred hours," said Langdon.

"More than a hundred hours," said the magistrate, drumming his fingers. "Mr. Heath, if you attach some importance to the CCTV tapes, I believe it will have to wait until trial at Central Criminal Court. The Old Bailey has much better AV equipment anyway."

"My lord," said Reggie, "I attach significance to only one of them. The tape for Lower Clapton Road. I would guess it is the third one down in the stack of cassettes that Mr. Langdon still has on his trolley. All the others simply demonstrate that despite their best efforts, the police found no CCTV tape to show that my client's cab was anywhere near the scene of the crime when the crime occurred. But the Clapton Road tape shows where my client actually was at the time the crime was occurring. In other words, it irrefutably establishes his alibi. We need not review the whole thing; simply fast forward to—oh, say—11:45 P.M. on the night of the alleged crime, and go from there?"

The magistrate stared for a moment at the witness transcripts before him. "That's just five minutes after the sighting in Chelsea."

"Exactly," said Reggie. "And several minutes prior to the earliest possible time of death as established by forensics. If my client's Black Cab appears on the tape at Lower Clapton Road at that time, then it is completely impossible for it to also be the one that drove the unfortunate Americans to their demise on Lots Road."

"And does it appear there, Mr. Heath? Are you certain what the CCTV will show?"

"I'm asking that the court take five minutes to find out."

Langdon started to say something now, but the magistrate motioned for silence. He thought about it for a moment longer, and then turned to the bailiff.

"Queue it up. Let's hope it is worth the fuss, Mr. Heath."

Langdon sighed.

The bailiff now spent several minutes getting the tape into the player, and getting the portable television configured to display it at such an angle that the magistrate could see it clearly.

Finally it was ready. The bailiff started the tape, then fast-forwarded, showing quite some proficiency, to the time in question.

The magistrate leaned in earnestly to look, and after perhaps thirty seconds, his eyes grew wide and he leaned in closer.

"Stop there. Back up a bit, please. There. There, you have it."

The magistrate sat back in his chair, and on his gesture the bailiff turned the display for the lawyers to see.

Reggie breathed a sigh of relief, and he felt a little tingle of victory go down his spine.

Darla looked as though she were about to dance in her chair.

Langdon stared at the screen for a moment longer, said nothing, and then began to pretend that he was looking for something important among his documents.

"Mr. Langdon," said the magistrate, "I believe what we see is a Black Cab with the WHAMU1 license number your witnesses reported, at the time they reported it in Chelsea, but it is obviously not in Chelsea—it is on Lower Clapton Road in Hackney, some forty minutes away. Would you agree?"

"I . . . it would appear so, my lord."

"Have you any explanation how that can be?"

"Not . . . quite yet, my lord, but I'm sure something will turn up."

Now the magistrate's tone showed some annoyance: "And have you any explanation why this tape was not specifically called out in the prosecution's bundle of discovery documents, so that both the court and defense would know of its significance?"

"I can only say that there were many hours of tapes, and little time to prepare, and the police are only human, my lord."

The magistrate nodded, but with a frown. For several seconds he stared at the video display, rubbing his forehead with his fingers. Then he looked up.

"Be sure everyone takes a little more time if you try again, Mr. Langdon. I am dismissing without prejudice; you may refile when and if you think you've got it right. In the meantime, the defendant will be released forthwith."

There was an audible murmur now from the gallery behind Reggie, but just what it meant he could not tell.

The judge stood, and in spectacularly anticlimactic fashion exited the courtroom.

"I knew there was a reason I chose you," said Darla, smiling up at Reggie. "No matter what anyone said. I'll collect our client and meet you at the side exit?"

Reggie nodded.

Darla looked back over her shoulder, her face glowing from the victory, and smiled at Reggie again as she exited.

Reggie left the courtroom now himself and he went to the barrister's cloakroom to pack up his wig and gown. Then, as he exited the cloakroom, he encountered the prosecuting barrister in the corridor. Langdon's usual put-on self-effacing manner was gone.

"Congratulations, Heath," he said. "You have not lost your touch, it seems."

"Thank you."

They were about to continue in opposite directions down the corridor, but Langdon turned.

"It was a bit of luck, though, wasn't it?" he said.

"In what way?" said Reggie.

"CCTVs are quite imperfect. So many things can prevent a

CCTV camera capturing the license of a vehicle as it passes by. Lampposts. Double-deckers. Pedestrians with large umbrellas. You had no time to review the tapes. How did you know what you needed would be there?"

"I knew it when I saw you kick the cassette under the desk," said Reggie.

Langdon thought about that for a moment, then shook his head in the negative and laughed. "But that really was just an accident, Heath. There was no time for me to review them either. I had no idea what the tape would show."

"A bit of luck on my part then," said Reggie.

Langdon nodded very slightly in the affirmative at that and then, looking at something past Reggie's shoulder, he said, "Good evening, Heath."

"Good evening."

Langdon walked away in the opposite direction down the corridor.

Reggie turned now and saw that Darla and Walters had come up behind.

"I wondered how you knew that, too," said Darla.

Walters said, "I'm just bleeding glad you knew to do it. Thank you, Mr. Heath, thank you."

Reggie just nodded and shook the man's hand. It still seemed unwise to acknowledge to anyone that he had been relying on a tip letter written to Sherlock Holmes.

They reached the end of the corridor now, and an usher opened the door at the side exit of the courthouse. Reggie stepped out first, into a heavy rain, and he took a quick look about.

At least two news vans from the BBC, along with perhaps a dozen reporters and photographers from the paper media, were assembled at the far end of the street, waiting at the main exit on Holborn.

At the near end of the street were five parked Black Cabs—oddly parked, facing the wrong way. But in any case, all of them had their out-of-service lights on. That was not good.

Reggie opened an umbrella, attempting to shield Darla and Walters from both the rain and the news hounds on Holborn, and hoping to find an active cab and be gone before anyone knew. But the media were vigilant—a scout at the intersection was watching, saw the side door open, and shouted out. Cameras and reporters began to hurry toward them, in a flock of black umbrellas; the news vans began to turn around. It was not looking good.

But now the five out-of-service Black Cabs—all purely black, with no adverts to distinguish any of them—started their engines and turned on their lights. Then each pulled into the narrow street.

One cab stopped in the middle of the street, blocking a news van approaching from Holborn.

The other four cabs all pulled up curbside in front of Reggie, Walters, and Darla.

"I'll take this one," said Walters, jumping into one. "He's a mate. You take another, and we'll lose them."

Passenger doors opened in all four cabs. Reggie began to hustle Darla into one, just as the reporter in the lead position of the running flock—a young woman, with short blond hair and fresher legs than all of the other reporters apparently, and flashing a *Daily Sun* badge—shouted out to Reggie, loud enough for all on the street and the BBC cameras to hear, "What technicality did you use to get your client out, Mr. Heath?"

She was accompanied by a photographer, close on her heels. She had not identified herself, but Reggie had an idea who she was. And although he knew better than to respond, he could not resist. He paused just for a moment before following Darla into the cab. "The technicality that he was twelve miles away when the crime was committed," he shouted back. Then, with cameras flashing, Reggie jumped into the cab, and shut the door.

All five cabs now took off down Ellis Street. The running reporters—even the young blonde woman—gave up the chase, and now there were only two BBC news vans to deal with.

At the intersection, the lead cab stopped and remained in place, and the other four split off in pairs in opposite directions. At the next intersection, the pair split off as well.

Reggie looked through the back window of the cab and saw that they had shaken their pursuit.

"Nice trick," said Reggie to Darla. "How did you arrange it?"

"I had no idea of it," she said. "I only called for the one cab."

"Nicely done," said Reggie to the driver now. "But they all know where Walters lives. They'll just go directly there."

"I'm sure they will," said the driver. "And they'll have a nice long wait for him, too. We'll just drive him about for a time, have a pint and a chat, and bring him back when all the news mongers are too tired and hungry to care anymore."

There was silence for a moment, as their cab mingled anonymously now among the traffic on the Embankment.

And then the driver said, as if they were just any fares that had gotten into his cab, "So where to, then?"

"We can drop you first, if you like," said Reggie to Darla, "And then I'll go back to chambers for my car. Where is your office?"

"Why on earth should I want to go back to my office? You can drop me at home, or we can go to the Seven Stars to celebrate. Those are the options."

"How far is home?"

"Not far, if it's one way."

Reggie looked at her and pondered her expression for a moment, but he wasn't quite certain she had meant what he thought she might have meant.

In any case, he decided that he wasn't taking chances.

"A rain check?"

She laughed a little at that. "If it makes you feel safer," she said. She smiled as she said it. Reggie looked away from her for an instant, looked back, and she was still directing that smile at him.

"The Seven Stars," she said to the driver. And then, to Reggie, "Alone if I must."

The Seven Stars was only blocks away. They were there within minutes, mercifully.

"A rain check, then," she said to Reggie as she got out, still with the smile.

The driver turned to look back at Reggie.

"Blimey, mate, if I were you—"

"Bloody hell, just drive," said Reggie quickly. "Dorset House on Baker Street."

The driver complied, and several minutes later they pulled up.

Reggie started to get out of the cab without having paid.

"Forgetting something, mate?"

Reggie stopped, halfway out of the cab.

"Sorry." He paid the driver.

"I suppose you were expecting a free ride, for what you did in the courtroom today?"

"What? No, not at all."

"That's good. 'Cause you're not likely to get one. Not from me, not from any Black Cab driver."

Reggie paused outside the cab and turned back toward the driver.

"What's your point?"

"The last thing in the world we want is one of our own out whacking people. Bloody hell, people trust us with their frail old grand mums. What's going to happen if they think they can't anymore?"

"Point taken," said Reggie. "But have you considered that he didn't do it?"

"Better not have," said the driver. "And if the police don't soon put away who did . . . well, I know blokes who aren't above taking care of it themselves."

On that disturbing bit of bluster, Reggie shut the cab door and went to his car.

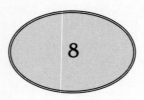

8

The next morning, in the garden of the Edwardian town home in Mayfair, Ilsa brought a full breakfast—deliciously greasy singed bacon, with stewed tomatoes and baked beans, and all the juices intermingling. Her employer was quite hungry, having worked hard the day before.

With the meal, Ilsa she again brought the *Daily Sun*.

"Page one," said Ilsa: "'Balmy Barrister Bails Black Cab Killer.'"

"Really?" said her employer. "Page one?"

"Yes."

"I like that. I presume we have a photo or two?"

"Yes."

"Let me see."

Ilsa unfolded the paper so that they both could look.

The grainy *Daily Sun* photos showed the defendant getting into one cab—and the lovely leg of the solicitor as she got into the other cab—and the villainous visage of Reggie Heath as he got in as well.

"Is that him?" asked Ilsa. "The barrister?"

"Yes," said her employer. "An evil man, thwarting Londoners in their legitimate desire to be free of the Black Cab menace."

"Is that in the editorial page? What you just said?" The phrasing sounded quite journalistic to Ilsa.

"Not yet. But it should be, shouldn't it?"

"He does look mean," agreed Ilsa.

"Indeed, he does."

Ilsa's employer sat back with a satisfied sigh, then said, "Ilsa, do you know what the binomial theorem is?"

"No," said Ilsa.

"Neither did I, until just recently," said her employer. "I paid so little attention to mathematics in school. But I'm rather catching on now. These things run in the family, you know. Perhaps some day I'll write something about it myself."

Ilsa nodded. "Yes," she began, agreeably, and then her employer quickly interrupted her.

"You may now address me as Professor."

Ilsa hesitated, puzzled over that request. "I didn't know that you are a professor," she said, quite respectfully.

"Well, technically perhaps not yet. But soon, I expect."

"I'm sure you can be one if you want," said Ilsa. "Your doctor said that you are the brightest woman he has ever known."

"My doctor is rather a fool," said Ilsa's employer, seizing a piece of bacon. "But he is right about that much."

"Yes"—said Ilsa, and then, quite carefully—"Professor."

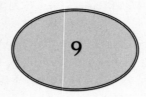

9

Reggie stopped at Audrey's Coffee and Newsagent across from Dorset House, to pick up a cold sandwich on his way to chambers.

Audrey's had installed a small cappuccino machine more than a year ago, and the output from that was part of Reggie's usual purchase at breakfast. But not so much recently.

He wasn't on a budget. Not exactly. It was just that after the loss of his entire Lloyd's of London investment, it made no sense to pay two quid for milk foam.

But all told, things were looking up. He had won his case. That was good in and of itself, but more importantly, it meant that if Laura called today, he need not necessarily feel like a complete loser when he spoke to her. That was a start. A step closer to being himself again.

"The camera makes you look old," said the clerk at Audrey's.

"Excuse me?"

The clerk nodded at the news rack—the one close at hand by the register, with the cheap daily rags like Buxton's.

Reggie saw the *Daily Sun* story. It was page one; it could not be missed. And it was another Emma Swoop byline.

Reggie was in the foreground of the largest photo, scowling villainously back at the press, and at an angle that made it look like he was developing a bit of a paunch.

The solicitor Darla Rennie was visible only in the flash of a shapely bare leg.

It seemed unlucky, and possibly bad form, to buy the paper and take it with him. But a queue was building in the little shop, and the woman behind him kept peering around Reggie's shoulder at that front page and then glancing up at Reggie's face.

Reggie bought both the paper and the sandwich and hurried out.

Once again he was entering the Baker Street lobby with the lowest form of journalism tucked conspicuously under his arm.

He got in the lift, pressed the button, and as the doors began to close, he opened the paper and followed the story onto page two.

But the lift doors hadn't closed yet; a slender hand caught them before they did, and the same tall brunette from a few days before stepped inside. Reggie acknowledged her presence with a quick nod, but stayed focused on the story.

As the lift went up, the woman's eyes shifted to the outward-facing front page—with Reggie's photo—and then she craned her neck ever so slightly to see the interior pages Reggie had opened to: page two and, once again, page three with that day's bare-breasted lass.

"You're making progress," said the woman, as the doors opened on Reggie's floor. "One more page, and you'll be right up against her."

Reggie couldn't take the time to even think about a response. He got out and headed quickly down the corridor toward chambers.

Once safely inside, he opened the *Daily Sun* again and read the article about how he had used insidious legal trickery to get an obviously guilty killer released.

It was complete rubbish. But Buxton owned the paper. He would have the last word, and there was nothing Reggie could do about it. Or almost nothing.

Now the phone rang, and Reggie dismissed, for the moment, the fantasy of going to Wapping to punch out Buxton again.

He picked up. It was Laura.

"I should like to speak, please, to a cynical champion of the dark dregs of society. Is there one available?"

So she had seen the tabloids.

"A dreg or a cynical champion?"

"Can I get both in one?"

"Any time you like."

"I would like an early dinner and a chat, then," she said. And then she added, "She has fine legs, Reggie. But shouldn't proper solicitors wear opaque tights or the like to court?"

"I . . . I told her exactly that myself," said Reggie.

Laura laughed again. "It doesn't matter, Reggie, really."

"What time shall I pick you up?"

There was a short pause. "Why don't we just meet?" said Laura, too brightly. "I know you're quite busy."

"Fair enough," he said. "The Olde Bank pub at four?"

"Do they still serve shepherd's pie?"

"So I'm told," said Reggie.

"Brilliant," she said.

Then she was off the phone.

Reggie was worried the moment she had hung up.

What was all this about a chat? Why did she not want Reggie

to pick her up? And why did the flash of the lady lawyer's legs not matter?

Reggie pondered these things until the late afternoon and then took a cab to the pub to meet Laura.

The Olde Bank on Fleet Street was as large and ornate as a pub could be and still be a pub and not a cathedral doubling as a boozing convention center. Pints were drawn from a bar in the center, and in concentric circles around that were three levels of standing areas and tables and booths for the public, and at the top level, a closed room for private functions.

The place had a smattering of tourists in the booths, but was mostly populated by dark-suited barristers standing at the counter of the center bar.

Many of them turned to look as Reggie and Laura walked by. Some just shifted their eyes, or tried to subtly twist their necks, but those on their third pints took no such precautions and overtly turned to look.

Reggie knew almost all of them from court.

"I think your peers are surprised to see you here," said Laura.

"Peers is a good description for them at the moment. But it's not me they're staring at."

"Well, I don't think it's me; the movie hasn't even come out yet."

"It's you. I'd tell them to borrow cameras from the tourists and take a picture, but some would probably do it."

At least Reggie hoped they were just tourists. One of the patrons near the front of the bar—conspicuously not staring, but in Reggie's opinion, stretching his peripheral vision to the limits—had a camera bag that looked pretty high end.

"Let's keep on to the back," said Reggie.

They went up the steps to the next level and found an isolated back corner booth, just across from the closed private function room.

"I thought you never came in here," said Laura as they sat down. "Although I'm not sure you've ever told me why."

"Tonight is an exception," said Reggie.

"Why?"

"Why an exception, or why I rarely come in here?"

"Let's do the whole bag of them: why it's an exception, why I've never known you to come in here even once, and why you've never told me why."

Reggie knew he should have been communicating more. Perhaps it was time to rectify that.

"They wouldn't let me in once."

"Really? When did that happen?"

"When I was twelve."

"You couldn't get a pint when you were twelve, and you're still annoyed?"

"I didn't want a pint. I wanted a word with one of the barristers."

Laura laughed.

"What's so funny?"

"Any other twelve-year-old boy is annoyed that he can't have a pint with the grown-ups. But not the twelve-year-old Reggie Heath. He's annoyed that he can't go and argue with them. But go on, tell me why."

"For my twelfth birthday my father took me to a professional football match. It was in the finals, between Chelsea and Manchester United, and the tickets cost a small fortune. It was just me and my dad, who was a huge fan; my mother didn't care for the sport, and Nigel was still too young to bring along, though it was a job telling him that.

"I had a Man U cap that I had saved for weeks to buy. Because our seats were, unfortunately, in the Chelsea section, my father gently suggested as we left the house that I leave the cap at home. But I refused. I was full of pride for our team, afraid of nothing, and I insisted on wearing the cap.

"It was the first professional game I had ever seen live and the most wonderful game ever played, even though our team lost finally on a penalty kick. The winning fans were boisterous, and as we exited, a hooligan ran by and snatched the Man U hat off my head. My father just reflexively reached right out and took it back. And then the Chelsea yob turned back toward us, along with two of his drunken friends. But a bunch of Manchester fans had seen the exchange, weren't putting up with it, and a brawl ensued.

"The bobbies arrived eventually and arrested anyone who was too injured, drunk, or slow to flee. And with me in tow, my father was not quick enough."

"I'm sure you were moving as quickly as possible."

"I'm afraid I kept trying to get back into it with the Chelsea louts. I took my football very seriously then. But the end result was me sitting in a room with a police matron while they booked my father. Then my mother arrived, Nigel with her, posted a bond, and we all went home.

"There really should have been nothing more to it than that. But there had been a stadium trampling just a few weeks earlier; people had been killed, and now the London tabloids were all on a tear about footballer hooligans. The Crown Prosecution Service gave in to the public frenzy and brought felony charges—even though it should have been just a misdemeanor even if my father had started it. Which he hadn't.

"The sensible thing from that point would have been just to try to plea to a lesser charge. But not my dad. 'Our livelihood depends on my good name,' he said, and so it went to court.

"He went to Lincoln's Inn to meet our barrister, and I went along."

"That sounds like trouble," said Laura. She was leaning

forward on the table, toward Reggie, paying quite close attention.

Reggie felt encouraged. He continued.

"The barrister sat behind this huge mahogany desk, green felt writing pad in the center of it, a wooden case with shining gold pens, and a brass lamp. I was impressed. I was sure we couldn't lose when I saw all that."

"Your desk is like that," said Laura.

"My desk is larger."

"Of course it is. Go on, then."

"Well, then came the day of the trial. One of the Chelsea fans had sustained a broken arm—probably from repeatedly bashing it on my dad's hard head. This wanker got on the stand, showed off the locations of various contusions, and said how it was my father who had done it.

"It was nonsense, every bit of it; my father had been too busy herding me out of the way to take a swing at anyone. The man was lying, and no better at it than a schoolboy.

"I kept waiting for the judge to turn his head to the jury and roll his eyes. And at any moment I knew our barrister would leap to his feet, point to the man in the witness box, and demand: "'Sir, are you or are you not a sniveling liar who has concocted this gigantic fiction of an injury for no other purpose than to support a concurrent civil suit and enrich yourself and the mistresses you seek to entertain?'"

"Or words to that effect," Laura volunteered.

"Yes. But the judge never did. And the barrister never did. In a case that should have been shown the door at the preliminary hearing for a contemptible lack of evidence, my father was found guilty and sentenced to thirty days, and required to pay a five-thousand-pound penalty that captured every bit of savings our family had.

"After the proceedings, my mother and Nigel and I walked

by this very pub on our way to the tube. The two barristers—
the one who represented my father so ineffectually, and the one
who prosecuted him without cause—were standing right down
there, under the first chandelier, buying each other pints. I
found it annoying, and I wanted to go inside and set things
straight. But they wouldn't let me in."

"Self-preservation on their part, I suspect," said Laura.

"My father never recovered from this," continued Reggie.
"I knew he wouldn't, even then; I could feel what it would do to
him. He lost his business. He lost his health. He died just before
I got to Cambridge on my scholarship."

There was a pause now. Laura was looking at Reggie as
though she hadn't seen him in years.

Reggie himself seemed a bit embarrassed, and he focused
instead on his Guinness.

"For quite a long time after, I wished that I had not worn
the cap," he added, in a sort of mumble, looking down into the
warm beer, and Laura almost didn't catch it.

"Why have you never told me that story before?" she said.

Reggie shrugged. "You never asked?"

"It's not a woman's job to ask everything, Reggie; how can
she possibly know just what question to pose? You're supposed
to volunteer something now and again and leave some bread
crumbs."

"I'll try to remember."

"So. You stayed away from the traditional barrister haunts
all these years while you became the best barrister any barrister could hope to be, and then you stayed away some more, just
to rub it in, and to really prove the point, you established your
chambers all the way over on Baker Street. And now, just when
it's looking like you can't make that work, you've proven all
those naysayers wrong, in spades. And so now you come in, for
your victory lap."

Reggie shrugged.

"But it's more than that," said Laura, studying his face. "This is the victory lap for your father."

Reggie gave that some thought, then nodded very slightly. He looked across at Laura, who had now begun to seem perturbed.

She looked back at him and said, "I can't believe this. You pick tonight to start telling me things? You are completely impossible."

"I'm communicating. On the right track now, aren't I?"

She shook her head. She seemed to not want to make eye contact, clearly still annoyed.

"So then . . . what is it you wanted to tell me?" said Reggie.

Laura leaned back in the booth now and began looking about the room—anywhere but at Reggie.

"Have you ever noticed how many clocks they have here?" she said.

He hadn't.

"And none of them with the right time. What time is it, do you think?"

"Quarter past."

"Had no idea we've been here so long. Time to push on, don't you think?"

"It's only been thirty minutes."

"Well, yes, but even so—"

"They haven't even brought your shepherd's pie yet."

"They'd better bring it in the next five minutes then. And when they do, less talking, and more eating."

Now she folded her arms and sat back, in a sort of mock-pleasant way, that said very clearly that she was not involved, and not intending to be, in any intimate conversation of any sort of significance.

"The lights are so lovely here, don't you think?"

Clocks. Lights. She would be commenting on the furniture next, and just hours before she had said they needed to chat, and here he was perfectly willing to do just that, and just generally communicating like bloody hell, and now she was clamming up like a corporate officer in the dock for fraud.

It was aggravating, and though something was telling him not to, he pressed the issue.

"You said we should have a chat. And I am here, ready to chat."

She stopped looking about. She looked directly at Reggie. She sighed. She looked away again, then back at Reggie once more, and then she put her hands on the table and blurted:

"Robert Buxton has asked me to marry him!"

The acoustics in the pub were remarkable. Or perhaps some words were heard less often than others and attracted more attention. Whatever the reason, several lawyers standing at the near side of the bar on the lower level looked up.

And then the comfortably dark shadow of the corner booth was broken by a bright white flash.

Laura raised her hand to shield her eyes; Reggie turned and looked behind to see the source of it, and then the white flash happened again.

Reggie stood, blinking, and thrust his arm out, but wasn't able to grab the photographer, who retreated quickly back onto the stairs toward the lower level.

"How will we ever get out?" said Laura.

"This way."

Reggie saw the red neon lights of an emergency exit at the near end of the corridor; he grabbed Laura's hand, pushed the door open, and they made their way down the stairs to the street.

They stepped out into a light rain. The alarm bell was ringing from the emergency exit, but there did not seem to be any paparazzi still in pursuit.

The rain was beginning to increase. Reggie waved for a Black Cab.

But there was no need. Before the cab could pull up, a white limo drove in front of it and stopped at the curb.

The limo driver jumped out and opened the door for Laura.

She hesitated. She seemed almost about to keep walking toward the cab instead, but the limo was right there in front of her, the driver expectantly holding the door.

And then, from somewhere deep inside the limo, Robert Buxton's voice called out, "Heath! Good to see you!"

Laura turned to Reggie and said, "Why must you insist on communicating so damn bloody much?"

"I thought . . . communicating . . ."

"It's quite the cat's pajamas, but I didn't want to tell you this. I mean, not now . . . with all that you told me, and with me still—"

"You still what?"

"Nothing," she said, and she got in the limo. "I didn't want to talk about this. You made me."

"But I didn't think that—" Reggie began, but he didn't get to finish. Without even waiting for the driver to help, Laura got in next to Buxton and yanked the limo door shut.

The limo pulled away. Reggie remained standing flat-footed at the curb.

In the limo, Laura settled in—sort of—next to Buxton.

Buxton had his briefcase open, and he was on his mobile. But now he looked up at Laura.

"Sorry," he said. "Tomorrow's edition." He shut off the phone.

"Of course," said Laura. "One must always be looking ahead."

"Did you tell him?"

"You mean Reggie? Tell him what?"

"That we're getting married?"

Laura hesitated. She had not given Buxton his answer yet. She was acutely aware of that fact, even if he was not.

"Actually, we were talking about that," said Laura, in just a bit of a lie, pointing at a copy of the *Daily Sun* that Buxton had in his open briefcase.

Buxton picked up the paper to see what she was referring to, then said, "If he's still bothered that anyone else in the world should catch a glimpse of the world's most perfect breasts, then I'd say he'd better get used to it."

Laura nodded very slightly but said nothing. She assumed Buxton meant Reggie getting used to Buxton seeing her breasts, not the rest of the *Daily Sun*–reading world seeing them, but his meaning wasn't entirely clear. She decided to let that go— for now.

She had an impulse to look back through the window at Reggie as they drove off, but it would have been rude with Buxton next to her there, especially under the circumstances, and she resisted it.

Whether Reggie stood there watching, or simply shrugged and walked away, or ran down the street after the limo, waving his arms like a lunatic, she would not get to know.

Pity. She did want to know.

And in fact, Reggie did stand there watching. But as Laura rode off in the limo, lawyerly onlookers had accumulated at the entrance to the pub, just a few yards away, and there was a danger of a return of paparazzi.

So now Reggie turned on his heels and walked quickly away in the opposite direction on Fleet Street.

Reggie walked rapidly, covering several blocks in a very

short period of time, though clearly it would make no sense to walk all the way back to Baker Street. He wasn't paying much heed to anything, but the rain was coming down heavily now, getting under the collar of his macintosh, and he realized that in the rush he had left his umbrella in the pub booth. He continued walking. But in another block, getting drenched, he began to wish that he had not let the cab go.

And then, just as he was thinking about trying to flag down another, a Black Cab, already occupied, pulled up to him at the curb.

The door opened, and the passenger called out to him:

"Is this a good time for the rain check?"

It was Darla.

"Couldn't be better," said Reggie. He got into the cab beside her.

"Then let's make it a proper one," she said. "I'm buying you a pint. Where shall we go?"

"Wherever you like."

"The Olde Bank pub on Fleet Street," she said to the driver.

Bloody hell, thought Reggie, that's an unlucky and almost certainly unwise choice, and he considered countermanding the instruction, even though he had invited her to choose, and even though his umbrella was still there at that pub.

And then he replayed through his mind the sight of Buxton's white limo driving off with Laura inside, and he asked himself whether it actually mattered what he chose at this point. With that in mind, he said nothing, and in a few moments he was once again walking into the Olde Bank pub with a woman that any of the male barristers, and possibly some of the female ones, would gladly give up their wigs for.

"Why is everyone staring?" asked Darla, as they sat down in a booth.

"Not sure," said Reggie. "I don't come here that often."

"I thought all lawyers did," she said. "Why don't you?"

"I'd rather not talk about it," said Reggie.

"Oh. All right then." She took a very small sip of her drink, and then set it down.

"You don't like what you ordered?" said Reggie, looking for an excuse to change the subject.

"I ordered it out of habit," she said. "I used to think I liked crème de menthe. Recently I discovered that I don't."

"Do you often discover that you don't like things that you thought you liked?"

"Yes, and the reverse. I'm a very changeable person. Or so I've been told."

Reggie noticed that her green eyes were changeable as well—going from emerald to beryl in an instant—depending on the light, apparently.

Those eyes were flirting with him. And so was the rest of her. He knew that. And the knowledge alone was beginning to produce a reaction.

Reggie decided that he needed another pint. He excused himself and went to the bar.

As the pint was being drawn, Reggie looked back toward the booth and saw a couple of lawyers stopping to chat briefly with Darla. Then, as Reggie headed toward the booth with his fresh Guinness, they moved on.

Reggie sat down, and Darla said, "They thought you might want this." She held out the umbrella Reggie had left behind earlier.

"Good of them," said Reggie, accepting it. Then Darla said, "Is it socially deficient of me not to know who this Laura Rankin is that they are so on about?"

"No," said Reggie, "but you may have seen her in Covent Garden once or twice in the past six years or so."

"An actress, then, is she?"

"Of course."

"I didn't get to the theater much six years ago. I was too occupied with my A-levels."

That meant she was no more than nineteen at the time, and she seemed to want Reggie to know it.

Reggie almost said something defensive about how young Laura was when she first debuted at Covent Garden. But he didn't quite. The Guinness he had just finished was pleasantly warm, so was the voice of the woman who had been concerned about her A-levels just six years ago, and there was no need to be confrontational.

"I'm sure you aced them," he said instead.

"I did indeed," she said. She smiled as she said it, leaning forward, and somehow wiggling her whole body in the same motion, as though the A-levels were just yesterday.

Reggie put down his empty pint glass, and reached into his pocket.

"Are you getting another Guinness?" she said.

"I'm calling a cab," said Reggie. "One or two of us have had enough."

"I think it's you. But you'll give a lady a ride home, I hope?"

Moments later they were in a radio-dispatched Black Cab. The passenger seat, as in all Black Cabs, was wide and smooth, with plenty of leg room, and nothing in the middle to impede easy access between one passenger and another. It made the trip excruciating. Her knees bumped into his with just the slightest imperfections in the road, and she allowed her hips to slide across to his with every curve. When the cab took a left turn and came to a stop on a street in Mayfair, she ended up pretty much in Reggie's lap.

"Well," she said, as the vehicle came to a stop. "And here we are."

"Yes," said Reggie. "We very much are."

She paused before she got out of the cab.

"You know, you really shouldn't be driving all the way from Baker Street to Butlers Wharf in your condition."

"What condition?"

"Your obvious condition. I can propose an alternative, if you like."

Reggie concluded that she wasn't merely suggesting that he go back to Baker Street and sleep on a chair at chambers. And once again, as he considered her invitation, the image of Laura getting into the limo and riding off recycled through his mind.

But perhaps the jury was still out on that. Or perhaps the jury was back, but there was still opportunity for an appeal.

And perhaps it was best to act as though there were still hope, even if it seemed there was not.

"I'll just take the cab home," said Reggie.

"If you insist," said the solicitor.

Reggie saw two expressions cross her face now: First, a smile to suggest to Reggie all that he would be missing, and then, for an instant, a flash of annoyance just as she shut the cab door.

Reggie returned to chambers. There were two calls from the reporter Emma Swoop. There was another fax from Nigel about the Moriarty letter. But there was no message from Laura.

Reggie briefly considered returning Emma Swoop's calls to let her know what he thought of the coverage she'd been giving him. But he thought better of it. He ignored everything and went home.

10

Well on toward three in the morning, a smallish figure in a hooded mac stood at the far end of an isolated dock in the Limehouse district. The wooden base of the dock was dark brown-gray, the Thames beneath and beyond it was slate gray, the hooded mac that cloaked the figure was medium gray, and the fog that had begun to steal in around the pilings was light gray, almost white gray, almost pleasant to look at as it swirled gently up, over the planking of the dock. Standing at the end of the dock and looking out, one could almost see shapes, like small animals, leaping up out of the dark gray river into the light gray fog, darting chaotically about, swirling in cat curves and then vanishing, out of focus, like lost thoughts.

Then there was a sound.

A hulking man at the land end of the dock had put one foot on the boards, but now he hesitated. The fog was bone-chillingly cold, and probably he did not want to go farther out, farther into the wet gray mist; his knee-length black leather coat would not be sufficient protection.

But he could not turn back now; he had been seen, and he had no choice but to proceed.

He walked forward, hesitantly in the first few steps, but then in long, rapid strides, as if to convey confidence.

The strides were a bluff, and he stopped several yards off.

"You exceeded your authorizations," said the cloaked figure.

"You said to raise the stakes," said the man.

"True."

"I . . . raised them."

"You murdered a woman."

The man hesitated. "If you had said specifically what you wanted me to avoid—"

"Some things should be apparent."

"I presumed you saw my history."

"Yes. That makes it my mistake, of course. But no matter."

The man began to relax just a little, and ventured, "I should like very much to remain in your employ."

"Don't worry. I still need you."

"Yes, ma'am," said the man, feeling just a bit reassured.

"You may call me 'Professor' now."

"Yes," said the man quickly. "Professor."

Professor Moriarty was smiling; the light on the wharf was shadowy and she was wearing a small hooded mac, but it was still possible to see her smile, and it was almost enough to counter the man's first impulse, which had been to run from the pier as fast as possible.

"You can go now," said Moriarty.

"Right then," said the man. He took a step back, saw that Moriarty was still smiling, and then, with something that was almost like a quick smirk in response to that smile, he turned around and began to walk away.

That smirk might have been the fatal error, or perhaps it made no difference at all.

But the man did not walk far.

11

At Butlers Wharf, something woke Reggie out of a very pleasant dream, so real that he had to turn and look to be certain that there was not in fact a woman lying there with him.

There was not. Perhaps that was just as well this morning, because although the dream had been about Laura, his memory of the night before was clearing, and if a woman were there, simple logistics said it would have been someone else.

The heaviness in his forehead said three pints of Guinness, or perhaps four, which would have been nothing in his Cambridge days, but lately was beginning to have some after-effect.

He took aspirin with water, walked out to the garage to get in the XJS, and realized that his car was still at Baker Street. He stood in the cold wind at the base of Butlers Wharf to get a cab, and then, as he rode across the bridge, he reviewed the events of the night before to make sure he indeed recalled them all accurately.

There was the dinner at the pub with Laura, followed by

her riding away in the limo with Buxton. The sight of that still ached.

Then there were the pints with the young female solicitor—bloody hell, had that been at the Olde Bank as well?—and clear signals from her, and then the cab ride home. And yes, he was certain that she had indeed gotten out at her home, somewhere in Mayfair, surprisingly—must be family money—and then he at his. Thank God for that. No damage done. If there was still a relationship left with Laura to be damaged.

By the time Reggie's cab dropped him at Baker Street, the dull ache in his temples had dispersed into all the junctions in his body, turning what had been a nicely localized pain in the head into a more generalized sense of not-well-being.

He stopped at Audrey's Coffee and Newsagent. He bought an Americano—two shots of espresso cut by a bit of boiling water. The clerk offered the *Daily Sun*.

"No," said Reggie. "I'm back to the *Financial Times*."

"You'll want the *Sun*," said the clerk. "Looks like they're the only ones who got the story."

"What story?"

The clerk just gave Reggie a look and handed him the paper.

Reggie glanced at the front page.

"Black Cab Killer Casts Body over Bridge."

Bloody hell.

A crowd was gathering behind him. Reggie tucked the paper under his arm and made a dash into the Dorset House lobby.

Once in the lift, he immediately opened the tabloid and turned page three inside out, so that the day's bare-breasted nymph would confront anyone who got in with him. With luck, the distraction would prevent gawkers from asking about the sensational Black Cab headline. And it pretty much worked; three Dorset House employees, one male and two female, rode up in the lift with him, but Reggie managed to exit without any of them saying a word. He made it all the way to his secretary's desk.

But Lois looked up as he approached, and she reacted to the paper under his arm.

"You've seen the headline?" she said, quite genuinely concerned.

"Yes," said Reggie. "No need to worry yourself over it."

"Of course."

"Any briefs this morning?"

"No."

"Well, that will soon change. Nothing gets the clients rolling in like the possibility that ours was guilty and we got him acquitted."

Then Reggie went into his chambers and closed the door behind him.

He folded the page-three girl back to her usual position and read the story on the front page.

Shortly after three that morning, according to the reporter's account, a Black Cab had pulled over on Blackfriars Bridge. The driver and another individual had gotten out, opened the passenger door, and shoved a body over the railing and into the Thames, violating any number of ordinances in the process. There were witnesses and the police had already recovered the corpse. And now, wondered the reporter in print, for just how long would cunning and unscrupulous barristers like Reggie Heath be allowed to manipulate the system and turn known murderers loose upon the unsuspecting citizens of London?

The story was short on details and long on hyperbole. It

offered no reason at all to think it was Reggie's client who had done it.

Reggie checked the byline: It was Emma Swoop once again.

But now the phone rang. It was Wembley.

"Morning, Heath. Just thought I'd see if you happen to know the whereabouts of your client."

"Which one?"

"Well, you've only got one at the moment, haven't you?"

"If you want to get technical about it, at the moment I've got none. The case was dismissed, and my work is done."

"He may have need of your services again. Quite soon. Be aware that we would like a chat with him. I've already spoken with his solicitor."

Reggie knew Wembley was waiting for him to ask.

"Why? What's happened?"

"You haven't heard?" Wembley related the same account Reggie had seen in the paper.

"This is known fact?" said Reggie.

"It is."

"There are witnesses, then?"

"Two fishermen on the near bank, and at least two passing vehicles, one in each direction. Traffic is light on the bridge at that hour, but not light enough to push a body over and go unnoticed."

"Has the body been recovered?"

"Yes."

"And?"

"We're still working on it. No wallet, no watch, no rings, no ID, and the face mangled beyond recognition; apparently some river traffic ran across him before we did. But well-dressed, or had been based on what we recovered, and from general appearances, this looks like another victim robbed—and then murdered—by our Black Cab driver."

At least Wembley said "our," not "your." That meant there was room for doubt.

"Anyone get a cab number?" said Reggie.

"Not this time."

"Anyone actually see the face of the driver? Or the accomplice?"

"Not that we know of."

"A little soon to be suggesting it's Walters then, isn't it?"

"No one's suggested anything until you did just now. But for what it's worth, I sent a car out to your client's place just as soon as we got the first report."

"And?"

"And he wasn't there. His cab was, but he wasn't."

"He might have been out with friends for the evening. It happens."

"Just thought you'd want to be aware of the situation, Heath. Given your history."

Reggie bridled at that.

"You mean the situation where London does not become crime-free in the wake of my client being released?" said Reggie, with some heat.

"You didn't like it much last time you got a murderer free and he killed someone, Heath."

"No, I didn't," said Reggie. "And it was my mistake, of course. I shouldn't have taken his word for his innocence just because he was a Scotland Yard copper."

Reggie waited for Wembley's response. The officer in question had been in Wembley's department. In fact, Wembley, who knew from personal experience how effective Reggie was in court, had asked Reggie to take the officer's case.

"Yes, it's my history too," Wembley said, finally. "But do let us know when you hear from your client." And then he was off the phone.

Within two minutes it rang again.

It was Darla. "I'm glad I caught you," she said. "I was afraid you might still be sleeping it off. Have you heard?"

Her voice was entirely that of the professional solicitor, with no hint of what Reggie had thought might have been seduction the night before.

"Heard what, exactly?" said Reggie, feeling obstinate for some reason.

"There's been another crime," she said. "By a Black Cab driver. Allegedly. Have you really not heard at all?"

"Sorry. Force of habit. I was just talking with Wembley; tends to make me evasive."

"Oh. Well, then. So you have heard. What should we do?" asked Darla.

The truth was, if this were the worst-case scenario—that the client they had released had been guilty and had now committed another crime—it was too bloody late to do a damn thing.

"What did you have in mind?" he said.

"I'm not sure, exactly. But I . . . I just thought you might know."

"I think perhaps we should get the facts before assuming our client did this."

"Oh, quite right, I know that, of course. But the tabloids will flog us both about this, especially you. Should we call them and point out that there might very well be more than one Black Cab driver doing bad things?"

"You can do if you like. But I won't be able to complain about the prosecution bowing to tabloid pressure if I start playing the media game myself."

"Good point. Should we just check on our client, then?"

"To make sure he isn't about town murdering and dumping bodies?"

"I mean, check that the police aren't still knocking on his

door, that reporters aren't camped on the pavement, that . . . that whatever." She was sounding just a bit defensive and flustered now.

"Sorry," said Reggie, and he was. He was being sharp with her, and he knew it, and he knew the reason—the possibility of having released a guilty man disturbed him more than it did her. "It's been a rough morning," he offered.

"Quite all right."

"Did you ring him?"

"I did. No answer."

"So you want to take a drive to Stepney, then?"

"Well, I think one of us should, don't you? I don't know the area myself though. I'm directionally challenged, or so people have told me. I've always had him come to my office."

"So you want me to have a look?"

"I'd be happy to ride along if you like. Unless you're afraid I'll attack you."

Now another call was coming in.

"I'll get back to you," said Reggie, and he picked up the other line.

It was Inspector Wembley. Again.

"We've found something. I'll let you see it firsthand if you can get to the generating station in forty minutes. Otherwise, you can wait for our report.

"Can you give me a hint?"

"No. Just get here if you're interested."

Reggie got off the phone with Wembley and rang Darla back. Though she had obviously been there just moments before, now he just got her answering service. He left a message that the trip to Stepney would have to wait.

Then he exited chambers, told Lois not to return any calls to the press, and drove to the generating station at the end of Lots Road.

The morning was heavily overcast, the Thames running blue-gray as steel.

It was low tide, and the river water that made up Chelsea Creek had receded, leaving mud and tidewater stink. Police cars lined the fenced perimeter of the generating station.

Reggie parked. He found Wembley just inside the gate.

"Thought you might want to see it as we dredge it up, Heath. The divers reported it about an hour ago."

"Dredge what up?"

"Just come along. Might be fun."

They walked past the tidewater channel to the platform at the far side of the site, facing the Thames. Wembley pointed in a direction about ten yards offshore.

There was something black, rounded, and metallic in the river. And just at the water line, intermittently visible in the little waves and troughs, was the glass FOR HIRE sign that sat atop the roof of the cab.

"This morning was the second lowest tide we'll see all year," said Wembley. "I'm sure whoever drove it off the ramp thought it would stay hidden. But a jogger saw it this morning and called it in. We hope to have it winched out of there before the tide covers it again."

Divers were already attaching the cable as Wembley spoke. Now the police crew started the winch. There was a high-pitched squeal from the cable, and then a deep mechanical groan from the undercarriage of the vehicle, and then a series of rhythmic clanks as the cab began to be pulled slowly toward the shore.

The black rear bumper became visible first. Then the boot, and then the white placard that showed the ID number for the taxi. And then the yellow-and-black number plate for the vehicle itself:

WHAMUl.

Reggie stared at the numbers as they surfaced ever more clearly.

He knew that Wembley, who obviously had advance knowledge from the divers, was looking at him for a reaction. He didn't want to give him one. Truth was, he was urgently trying to think of an explanation himself.

"I believe that is the same number as your client's cab, is it not?" said Wembley, sounding just a little exasperated with Reggie's silence.

"It is the same number," said Reggie, putting no inflexion on it at all.

"Any idea how that can be?"

"Of course I don't know how that can be," said Reggie. Then he added, "Unless someone used my client's number to frame him after the fact. Do we know when this vehicle was deposited in the river?"

"Not yet," said Wembley. "But we've now got two cabs with the same number, so we know something's wrong somewhere. And forensics has gotten quite good at these things, especially given the windows were still up when it went in. River water or no, I think we may soon know which of the two cabs was used in the crime, and we'll also know which one really belongs to your client."

Reggie said, "I hope we do."

"I know you've been picky about who you represent, Heath. More so than most. But this could put your client's alibi in a different light. And you could have some explaining to do about that CCTV tape. I mean, just how did you know it would show what you needed? Nine times out of ten the CCTV camera doesn't catch what you want it to, just the back of someone's arse."

"It was a guess."

"Damn lucky guess," said Wembley. "What kind of luck, we'll see."

Reggie could only nod. He watched as the cab was winched slowly from the river, dirty water pouring out from the under-carriage.

The crew was moving at a painstaking pace. Wembley had been embarrassed at how little information they had gotten from the cab found at Walters's home, and clearly he intended to make sure this one was done right. It would take hours.

Reggie thanked Wembley for the heads-up and turned to go back to his car.

In mid step, he almost fell over someone standing directly behind him. There was a blinding flash, and Reggie instinc-tively thrust his arm out, grabbing the source of the flash by the collar.

There was no struggle. Reggie realized almost immediately what the flash had been; it had just been so close to his face that there wasn't time to think.

"Probably you should let him loose," Reggie heard Wemb-ley say.

Eyes blinking, Reggie relaxed his grip and let go of a photo-grapher from the *Daily Sun*.

And standing right next to the photographer was a *Daily Sun* reporter. It was Emma Swoop—her press badge said so. And he recognized the face as well. It was her, with this photo-grapher close on her heels, who had been in the lead of the press attack outside the courthouse.

The photographer didn't want a confrontation, he just wanted photos, and he took a step back from Reggie now. But Reggie could see that Emma—early twenties and no doubt ambitiously at the beginning of her career—felt obliged to say something.

"Very nice," she said to Reggie. "Would you now like to take a free swing at me, too, like you did our boss?"

She spoke in a clipped, perfectly enunciated, rapid-fire speech pattern that gave the listener no time to think. You couldn't pretend you didn't hear all that was said, because it was said so perfectly; but it was said so quickly that you had no time to formulate a response as you were hearing it.

A useful skill, for journalists as well as lawyers. It was the sort of style that one acquired only from the best public schools. She had family money, no doubt, and certainly that family money must regard this sort of grubby journalism as beneath her station. Reggie guessed she must have a chip on her shoulder.

He knew better than to respond to her question. Anything he said would end up misquoted in the next day's paper. But he took a free swing anyway.

"Your parents don't approve, do they?" he said.

She recoiled a bit in surprise, looking almost hurt—and in that moment Reggie turned again to leave.

But first he looked back at Wembley. "Did you invite them?"

"It wasn't me," said Wembley. "But as long as they don't impede the investigation, I've no legal right to keep them out. Or so my superiors have said."

Reggie continued on to his car, with the photographer and the reporter running close behind, flashing photos and tossing questions at him along the way. And the young reporter wouldn't let up. She had the defiantly head-on attitude of a spoiled adolescent freight train.

"How do you explain a second cab with your client's license number? Do you regret getting your client released? Do you feel any sense of responsibility for this new murder?"

Emma Swoop had assessed Reggie's sore points every bit as well as he had assessed hers. So much so that he actually considered responding to her questions.

He looked back at her. Her eyes lit up with journalistic anticipation. And Reggie caught himself just in time and said nothing.

He got in his Jag, shut the door quickly, put it in reverse to avoid running the *Daily Sun* duo over, and then, fishtailing just a little in the mud, he fled the scene.

He knew the headlines in the morning would be flaming, more so than anything he had yet seen. The *Daily Sun* would not wait for the forensics; it would start whipping up the firestorm now.

Reggie rang his client's number as he drove from Lots Road. No response. He rang Darla's number as well. No answer there either, which was a little annoying—she should be making herself more available. He left another message on her machine.

Then he drove on to New Scotland Yard, to do what he knew he should have done at the outset—look at the tapes himself.

At the Yard, a cautious and watchful evidence clerk made the alibi CCTV tape available to Reggie in a small, overly air-conditioned viewing room.

Reggie reviewed the tape repeatedly, but he could find nothing to indicate that it had been tampered with in any way—no breaks, no flickers, no repeated or out-of-place content. Besides, the chain of evidence was intact from the moment the police had taken the tape from the camera to the moment they had delivered it to Langdon at the Crown Prosecution Service. And as sneaky as Langdon was, even he would not falsify evidence. It wouldn't be worth the risk to his career.

So the tape was real and valid; that was the working presumption. But there were two cabs with the same number, and no proof—at least not yet—of which one Walters had been driving. At this moment, Walters had no alibi.

And aside from the damage done to his client's defense, Reggie knew that the certainty with which he had pressed the issue at the preliminary hearing would make it look now as though he had had advance knowledge of what the tape would show—as if, in fact, he had been complicit in arranging that one cab be at that location at that time for the express purpose of establishing an alibi for the other.

He had no good answer for that. It simply would not do to say that he had received a tip in a letter addressed to Sherlock Holmes. He needed the actual source of the information. He needed to know who had sent the letter.

Reggie left New Scotland Yard and drove back to Baker Street Chambers. Lois greeted him and told him, quite apologetically, there were no messages—not from the solicitor, or from the client, or from anyone else.

Reggie went to his chambers office, unlocked the bottom drawer of his desk, and took out the letter to Sherlock Holmes that had provided the CCTV tip.

There was no return address on either the letter or the envelope it had arrived in. The postmark was from Bath. The letter was printed on what looked like very common printer paper with what looked like very common laser-jet ink.

He studied it for nearly half an hour, but could infer no clue to its origin. This was the sort of thing that Nigel liked to deal with, and Reggie wished now that he had just sent this letter on to him when it first arrived.

Or, better, that he had just ignored it entirely. Too late for that now. Reggie locked the letter back in his desk.

The only thing he could be reasonably certain of was that whoever wrote the letter must have at some point been near the location of the CCTV camera—otherwise, they could not have known about either the camera or the cab.

Reggie exited his chambers, got in the XJS, and drove to the East End.

It was early evening when he reached the intersection at Lower Clapton Road. It was a major thoroughfare, but the neighborhood itself was just a mix of garment factories and residential blocks of flats, and small take-away restaurants and launderettes to service them.

The evening commute was still in process, and heavy with bus traffic and private autos—not so many people taking taxis in this part of the city.

Reggie parked and walked to the corner, craning his neck upward, looking for the camera.

It didn't take long to find it. The deployment of CCTV cameras in London was mainly in dodgy public areas—including bus shelters on streets that seemed to need the supervision. This camera, mounted on a traffic signal, had a field of view that included the bus shelter and probably an additional fifty feet or so.

There was a convenience store within just a few yards of the bus shelter. Of the establishments within a reasonably close line of sight, it was the only one that could possibly have been open at the time Walters's cab was caught on tape.

Reggie approached the shopkeeper, paused for the loud diesel whine of an approaching double-decker to subside, then introduced himself. Two minutes later, another bus rolled up, and the conversation paused again.

"Is it always like this?" said Reggie.

"Always," said the shopkeeper. "Day and night."

Reggie thought about that.

"Excuse me just one moment," he said.

Reggie went back to the corner where the camera was positioned. He looked at the angle of it, as yet another bus rolled in, stopped, and then moved on.

The extraordinary thing—given the frequency and height of the double-deckers, obscuring a clear view of anything on the other side of them from the camera—was that the camera had been able to capture the cab number at all. What incredible luck that had been, to catch a Black Cab license number without a bus or lorry getting in the way.

Still, it could happen. Obviously, because it had happened.

Reggie walked back to the shopkeeper.

"You're open late here?"

"Till midnight, usually."

"Were you here the night of the murders in Chelsea?

The shopkeeper thought about it. "Four, five nights ago, was it?" Then he nodded. "I was here. Pretty much always am."

"Notice anything out of the ordinary?"

"What would I notice here about murders in the West End?"

"Nothing, of course. I just mean anything at all out of the ordinary."

"No. Everything was . . . ordinary."

"Thanks for your time."

"Now, the night after, that was memorable."

Reggie stopped and came back.

"In what way?"

"A real stunner came in. Lovely little chippy, never seen her before. She got out of a cab right over there. Great legs. She walked to the corner, just sort of looking up, kind of like you did just now. Then she went over to the bus shelter and studied the schedule. I think she wanted to write something down, but her pen wouldn't work. My good luck, I thought, because then she came right in to my shop to buy one of these fine implements."

The shopkeeper held up a cheap touristy ballpoint, fashioned to resemble a tiny plastic Big Ben.

"I gave it to her free. She was that much of a looker."

"Anything else?"

"I asked if there was anything else I could do for her, if you know what I mean." He laughed. "She gave me a look that would freeze hell over. I mean, I've had my share of turndowns, but to get that kind of look—and from the greenest eyes I've ever seen—that was something. Then she went back into the cab, and away she went."

"Green eyes."

"Yes."

"What kind of green?"

The shopkeeper gave Reggie a blank stare.

"Green, like I said. I'm not an optometrist."

"You would recognize her if you saw her again?"

The shopkeeper grinned. "You bet I would. I recorded every bit of that bird up here, for replays as needed."

"Think you might recognize the driver of the cab if you saw him again?"

The shopkeeper shook his head. "That's not who I was looking at."

Reggie turned to leave. The possible identity of the stunning woman was so disturbing that there seemed little point in asking anything else.

But then he remembered the most obvious question:

"One more thing. Ever happen to write a letter to Sherlock Holmes?"

"Say again?"

"Have you ever written a letter to Sherlock Holmes? Especially in the last few days or so?"

The shopkeeper gave Reggie another dumbfounded stare.

"Or do you know anyone who has?" said Reggie.

"Are you daft? Or is it just you think I am?"

"No more so than most. Thanks for your time."

Reggie went back to his car, got his mobile, and rang Darla's number again.

It seemed to ring interminably, but the answering service did not pick up. Then the phone switched over to another line and there were several more rings.

And then Darla picked up. It was her; the call was staticky, probably her mobile, but it was clearly her, there was no mistaking her voice. The tenor of it, though, was one Reggie hadn't heard from her before. She was worried.

"He called me," she said.

"Who did?"

"Our client. Didn't he ring you as well?"

"No."

"I told him to call you at chambers. You're not there?"

"No. I'm at the intersection of Lower Clapton Road and Newick. Do you know that intersection?"

"Yes. That's where he was seen on camera, isn't it?"

"Yes. And I just had a chat with a shopkeeper near the CCTV camera."

There was a pause. "A shopkeeper?"

"Yes, a shopkeeper. At the news agents. Where they sell tourist pens. Pens shaped like Big Ben, for tourists, if they ever get any, and for people who forget theirs."

Another pause. Then, "Why in God's name are you telling me about a shopkeeper and pens?" She was sounding frantic now.

"You have no idea?"

"I am trying to tell you about our client, and you are prattling about bloody pens!"

"Where are you?" said Reggie

"I'm on my way to his place now. I'm only minutes away. I'll meet you there."

"Whose place?"

"Our client's, for God's sake. Will you meet me there?"

Reggie tried to take a moment to think about that, but when he did not respond instantly, she said:

"Please meet me there," she said, sounding on the verge of tears, whether from frustration with Reggie or from something else was hard to tell. "I don't want to confront him alone."

And then there was a beep and the connection was gone.

Reggie started the XJS and drove south.

The anger he had been feeling toward Darla just moments before was gone. Certainly she had not found a way to falsify evidence for a client and make Reggie the fall guy for it. He was churlish to even have begun thinking along those lines.

Now, as Reggie sped toward Stepney, he wasn't angry at her. He was afraid for her.

Twenty minutes later he turned the corner onto Locksley Street in Stepney.

It was night, not terribly late, but there was little activity on the street, and all of the townhomes—some of them recently renovated, and others quite decrepit—were lit only weakly by lamps on some of the front porches.

Reggie pulled up to Walters's brownstone, at the more decrepit end of the street. He saw that Darla had still not arrived.

He got out of his car and looked up and down the street. There was no traffic at all approaching from either direction. There were only a few parked cars, and none of them visibly occupied.

Darla wasn't here. But Walters's Black Cab was.

There was no point in waiting for her to arrive. Reggie walked up to the unlit front of Walters's townhome, and then paused. It hadn't been obvious from the street, but the front door was ajar. And there was a sound coming from inside—an intermittent, high-pitched mechanical screech, and then, behind that, a sort of rhythmic chug.

Reggie stood on the porch and knocked, without pushing the door fully open. He knocked again, and then called out for Walters. No answer.

Now Reggie pushed on the door. The sound continued; it was coming from farther inside the home.

He called out again for Walters. He stepped just inside the doorway, waited for his eyes to adjust to the dark interior, and looked about.

Reggie could see two doorways from the living room; one was direct to the kitchen, and the other was to the hallway.

The living room was what one would expect for a single working-class male—inexpensive, but as garish as possible to impress the ladies.

Most of the furnishing money had been spent on the black leather couch, and the surround-sound stereo, and a two-person dining table with a top of blue-black glass that reflected the little bit of light from the neighbor's porch.

There was an opened bottle of wine on the dining table, though Reggie could see no wineglasses.

Also on the table top was a brown leather satchel, lying open, and just visible inside it was something that glinted slightly. It looked like a man's watch band.

Reggie called out Walters's name again. Still no response. The machinelike clunking from the rear of the house continued.

Reggie wanted to assure himself that the faint glint in that leather bag was not what he was afraid it might be. Surely it was not; surely the police search would have turned it up in their initial investigation.

Reggie was already standing in the doorway. In for a penny,

in for a pound; he took two steps into the room, and without touching anything, leaned down to get a better look into the bag.

Bloody hell.

In this light, and without touching and taking it out of the bag, he couldn't be certain—but it looked like a gold Rolex, the watch stolen from the murdered American tourist.

Touching that—or the bag, or anything else—was out of the question. A new reason to be accused of messing with something that might be evidence was not something Reggie needed. It was time to leave the premises.

But there was still that noise from the kitchen.

Reggie took three steps to the kitchen entry. He looked in.

It was a narrow kitchen. There was a pine breakfast table with two chairs, a worn-out Formica counter with some dishes in a porcelain sink, and a paper shopping bag in the corner containing crumpled food wrappers and empty beer bottles.

But the noise was not coming from the kitchen. There was another small room at the other end, with the door partly closed, and the noise was coming from there.

And Reggie recognized the sound now, or at least part of it. It was a washing machine. He had no use for one himself in recent years, sending all of his laundry out to be done. But his mother had one when he was growing up, and her small laundry room had also been adjacent to the kitchen.

It was such a normal and comforting sound that for a moment Reggie doubted all the worries that had begun to occur to him. As if the door was not ajar in the middle of night and the bag on the dining table did not contain anything that might have been related in any way to the Black Cab murders. None of that could be so, because there was a washing machine running, as there had always been in the most ordinary of days in Reggie's childhood home.

But this was not Reggie's childhood home, and now he heard that metal screech again.

Reggie moved on through the kitchen toward the laundry room. The noise was much louder here; clearly this was the source of it.

The laundry-room door was just partly open; it was too dark and the aperture too narrow to see anything inside. He pushed on the door.

It didn't open. There was resistance; something was blocking it.

Reggie put his shoulder against the door, shoved hard, and forced it open.

The door opened suddenly and banged with a thud against the adjacent wall. With the door fully open now, Reggie saw the washing machine and heard in full force the racket it was producing.

In the dim light, he saw that there were two more doorways in the little laundry room—one, open, led to the bedroom; the other, closed, led to the outside.

And then he looked down for the source of the resistance against the door—and he saw the body.

It was Walters.

He was faceup, motionless, his feet toward the door.

There wasn't much doubt, even in this light, but Reggie knelt down and checked. No life signs. Blood saturated the floor and the silk dress shirt Walters was wearing.

All this time the washing machine had continued loudly chugging. Now the chugging ceased and the machine again emitted a loud shriek. It was an unbearable sound, and Reggie instinctively stood and opened the lid to make it stop.

It did not stop. Reggie looked down into the washing compartment and saw dark sudsy water, but he didn't know why the noise was continuing.

He reached into the hot water and found something that was much too hard and sharp to be an article of clothing. He withdrew the item immediately, and as he set it on the top of the machine, he realized he had cut himself in the process.

It was a kitchen knife, but something else must have cut him, because he had withdrawn the knife by the handle.

As Reggie looked at the cut in the palm of his hand, a shrieking noise continued, but Reggie realized that the sound he was hearing now wasn't coming from the machine at all. It was coming from outside.

It was the sound of sirens, which were winding down now, directly in front of the house.

For a moment, Reggie wondered whether his fingerprints would register on the sudsy knife, and whether, in his carelessness, he might have dripped his own blood onto the body or the floor. But there was no time to think or do anything further about it. The police were already at the porch.

Since he could not possibly run, the only thing to do was go meet them. He walked quickly into the living room and managed to get his mobile phone out of his pocket, as if he were about to ring for help, just as the police came onto the porch.

"Back there, through the kitchen," said Reggie to the first officer who paused at the door. Reggie only wished that his hands hadn't still been dripping with blood and suds when he said it.

12

In Chelsea, Laura sat alone at breakfast at the Bluebird Café, just a few blocks from Sloane Square. She watched through the window, waiting for the younger Heath brother to arrive.

She was wearing faded jeans and a black top, looking much like a graduate student from King's College, and hoping to blend in among them and all the Sloane's rangers shopping in the square.

It wasn't working. She should have covered her striking red hair. But it was ingrained habit not to; she had gotten teased about it as a child, and so had taught herself early on to never cover it up, out of defiance. And then later, by adolescence, the boys had begun to notice in a different way, as they were doing now, and so she hadn't wanted to cover it up.

She was drawing stares, even though she had been deliberately loud in telling the maître d' to leave both settings. She hoped Nigel would get here soon.

It was an odd thing. She had known since age seven that she

wanted to be an actress. And now she was living that dream, and on top of it, she had one of the richest men in the world trying to lavish everything imaginable upon her.

So why did her life now seem like such chaos?

Everything would get more complicated, not less, when the movie came out, she knew that. But thankfully there were no cameras in the side breakfast room of the Bluebird Café this morning. And thank God no one had managed to get them into the bloody mobile phones.

Finally, Nigel came in sight. He was on foot, having taken the tube again, apparently. Nigel seemed to never feel that he could afford a taxi, though she had always seen him tip as frequently and overgenerously as an American. She had always liked that about him.

But she made a mental note to tell Mara soon that if Nigel ever began to make any money, he would need some training in how to spend it.

Nigel seated himself across from Laura at the little table.

"How was your flight?" said Laura.

"A bit long. Three stopovers. Have you heard of this thing called Priceline?"

"A game show?"

"Very similar; you take a guess and hope for the best."

The waiter came over.

"I'll get the continental breakfast," said Nigel.

"Brunch is on me," said Laura.

"Won't hear of it."

"Yes, you will, or I won't pay for your flight either."

"In that case, I'll get the lobster omelet."

"Better. I'm having that as well."

The waiter went away.

"Mara did not come with you?"

"She has an exhibit. I intend to be back before it closes," said Nigel. "So Reggie had better listen to reason."

"We can always hope," said Laura.

Nigel proceeded to unfold a letter from his coat pocket.

"I alerted him to this when it arrived, of course, but he just made light of it."

Laura took the letter, placed it flat on the white tablecloth, and read it.

She started to laugh halfway through, then looked up and saw Nigel's expression, and managed to read the remainder with a straight face.

"Well," she said when she was done, "I suppose it is a bit threatening."

" 'I shall have my forefather's revenge'? I'd say more than a bit threatening."

"Well, all right then, if you get past the 'forefather' part of it. But the threat is against Sherlock Holmes, not Reggie."

"No, the threat is against the barrister at 221b Baker Street whom the letter writer *thinks* is Sherlock Holmes. And that barrister is Reggie."

"Nigel, the letter is signed 'Moriarty.' It's a joke."

"It is not inconceivable that there might be a person out there with delusions of being Moriarty."

"I suppose," said Laura doubtfully.

"Such a person could be dangerous."

Laura looked at the letter again, nodded, and said, "You're right, I suppose. It just seems so . . . theoretical, compared to what has actually taken place."

"I knew it!" Nigel almost jumped out of his chair. "I knew you were holding back. You didn't pay my airfare just to see this letter. What has happened?"

"He's in jail."

Nigel settled back down and breathed a sigh of relief; clearly he had been expecting something worse.

"For murder," Laura added.

Nigel perked up a bit. "Not someone in chambers. It will give him the devil of a time hiring."

"No."

"Who then? We don't have many relatives to choose from."

"A client."

Nigel paused to take that in, then said, "He does get annoyed when bills go unpaid."

"The police said it was because Reggie's client fooled him, made him a party to falsifying evidence, and then committed a murder while out on the dismissal that Reggie so cleverly obtained."

"Hmm." Nigel stirred some sugar into his tea.

"That's an awfully weak motive, isn't it?" said Laura.

"Well, just the getting-fooled part might be enough for Reggie."

"That does seem to bother him even more than getting arrested. But honestly, Nigel, how likely is it a barrister will kill his own client just for being guilty?"

Nigel shrugged. "I wanted to kill one once. And that was just a tort case."

"Well, I thought you were the exception. And anyway, you didn't."

Nigel nodded, put some butter on his toast, and said, "Do you know why my brother stopped doing criminal a few years ago?"

"No. But he told me why he started."

"He did?" Nigel seemed surprised.

"Yes, just the other night."

"About Dad and the football match and all?"

"Yes," said Laura. "Why? It's all true, isn't it?"

"Yes, but I've never heard him talk about it. Nice work for you to pry it out."

"I didn't actually have to pry all that much," said Laura, allowing herself to take just a little satisfaction in that. But then she noticed that Nigel was continuing to butter the same piece of toast.

"What is it, Nigel?" said Laura. "Speak."

"He told you why he started with criminal. Did he tell you why he stopped?"

"Not directly."

"It was a bit before your time. I mean, before either of us met you."

"Yes, I understand what before my time means."

"There was a veteran police officer accused of killing his wife over a divorce. Reggie got it tossed out at the preliminary hearing, and then the copper promptly went home and murdered his mother-in-law to boot."

"I think I have heard rumors of that."

"Reggie never accepted a criminal case again after that. But there was more to it than just the one bad client. Reggie told me at the time that he'd had it with criminal anyway. He said, 'I thought I would be defending people being railroaded by the system, like Dad. Instead I'm defending people like the louts who roughed him up.'"

"Yes," said Laura, quietly. "I can see how that would annoy him."

"He hasn't done a criminal case since," said Nigel. "Which sort of makes me wonder why he accepted this one."

Laura considered that, then said, "I've heard him talk about this client. How hard he's had to work. How he's dedicated to his career and improving himself. I think he thought he *was* defending your father—or someone like him as a younger man. He said he wanted to make sure it turns out right this time."

Nigel thought about that, then nodded affirmatively. "Unfortunately, that just supports the prosecution theory about why Reggie would be so angry at getting fooled."

"But they can't convict just on motive, can they?" said Laura.

"No. Do they have anything else?"

"Hardly. Just Reggie's prints on a kitchen knife, and on the washing machine, and a drop or two of his blood on the floor, and Reggie himself at the crime scene with a cut on his hand just ten minutes or so after the time of death."

"Well, how in bloody hell did all that happen?"

"One foolish step led to another, I think. Like anything else. Anyway, I got the police report from Reggie's chambers," said Laura. She took that document out of her purse and gave it to Nigel. "For what it's worth, they also found a broken wineglass in the washing machine where Reggie fished out the knife."

"A wineglass and a knife were in the washing machine?"

"Yes," said Laura. "And they found a man's Rolex in a bag on the dining table."

Nigel studied the report. "The knife wound was from the front, and there were no defensive wounds. Was there a second wineglass? Not in the washing machine?"

"I don't know. Does it make a difference?"

"All the difference, probably. Trust Scotland Yard not to mention it one way or the other. Fingerprints?" said Nigel, still searching through the report.

"Not yet, apparently. But I presume they won't be able to get anything from what was chugging away in the hot suds?"

"No," said Nigel. "But it looks to me like the victim knew his attacker, and the attacker didn't wear gloves, and so had to try to clean up after, and your average murderer just isn't sufficiently neat and tidy to wipe away every possible print."

"And if the murderer isn't average?"

"Somewhere there's going to be some square inch of a print that didn't get wiped down. It's just a matter of knowing where to look."

"I hope you're right," said Laura. And then she said, "Powder or liquid?"

"Sorry?"

"Boxed, or bottled? Does the report say what sort of detergent it was?"

"No," said Nigel. "Does it matter?"

"Boxed, I hope, and as poorly constructed as most," said Laura.

"Why?"

"Nigel, haven't you ever done your own laundry?"

"Of course I . . ." began Nigel, and then he stopped and thought about it. "Well, that might be a long shot," he said. "But I'll ask Wembley to make sure they check it."

Nigel continued reading the report. "Damn. They say the Rolex has the initials of the male tourist Reggie's client allegedly killed."

"Do we have to say allegedly even when the person who probably did it is already dead himself?"

"Let's do," said Nigel. "It will make my brother feel better to think there is still some doubt about him having released a guilty man."

"Well, it has made him very mopey. I could get hardly a word out of him at the jail. He's being very dense about it. That's why you're here."

Nigel looked back at Laura as though she had paid him a compliment. The look surprised her; she thought she had stated the obvious.

"Have they indicted?" said Nigel, almost authoritatively now.

"Yes. This morning. The magistrate who heard it was the

same one who released Reggie's client two days ago, and he was not at all pleased. He immediately committed Reggie's case to the Old Bailey."

"And when is the bail hearing?" said Nigel.

"It's this afternoon."

"We'll need a barrister. The court won't like it if Reggie gets up and argues for his own bail."

"Reggie said to get Geoffrey Langdon," said Laura. "Is he any good?"

"Yes," said Nigel. "And scary as hell, if you ask me. Very sneaky fellow. But all the better for us, when he's on our side instead of the prosecution's. What about the solicitor that engaged Reggie for the client? Does he have anything that can help us?"

"She. And she seems to be either missing, or accidentally out of town, or deliberately unavailable, depending upon whether you are talking to Reggie, or to New Scotland Yard, or to me. Reggie said she sounded as though she were in some distress. He hasn't heard from her since, but she has an answering service, and the service says she left word that she will be out of town on holiday for a few days."

"Well, that's bloody convenient for her."

"That's what I thought as well."

"So because of that message she left with the answering service, the police aren't looking for her?"

"Right. At least not yet."

"All right," said Nigel. "I'll see if I can track her down while you and Langdon are at the bail hearing."

"You won't be there?" said Laura.

"Me and Reggie at the same bail hearing?" said Nigel. "I don't think so. Not unless you want to see us both locked up."

13

When Nigel entered the Dorset House lobby on Baker Street, he was surprised at how different it felt.

So far as he could tell, nothing had changed: the glass doors at the entrance, the marble flooring of the lobby, the security station with the elderly guard, the nicely business-seductive attired women moving to and from the financial floors—all seemed pretty much the same.

Perhaps the difference was that the last time he was in this lobby, he had been rushing frantically out for Heathrow and the next plane to Los Angeles, with the knowledge that there was a dead body in his office on the next level up.

Yes, that might be the difference.

Nigel got in the lift. Just before the doors could close, someone put a hand in to stop them.

A man whom Nigel had not seen before got in and pushed the button for the top floor.

The man looked over at Nigel as the lift began to move.

"You're a Heath, aren't you?" he said.

Nigel would have just nodded politely, but the flight had been very long, and although the brunch with Laura had been quite pleasant, the subject matter of their conversation—and Nigel's present task—verged on stressful. And so Nigel was in a short mood.

"Are we a species, then?" Nigel replied.

"I wouldn't know that," said the man, "but wouldn't rule it out. Just thought I saw a resemblance between you and, I presume, your brother Reggie. My name's Rafferty."

Nigel studied the man for a moment, then said, "The leasing committee."

"Ahh," said Rafferty. "I thought so. You're the brother who notices the details."

Nigel said nothing to that. He didn't know whether Rafferty was referring to the Sherlock Holmes letters themselves or to the clause in the lease that made them so important to Reggie's chambers. But either way it sounded like a problematic discussion, especially so because Rafferty gave the impression of being just a little too impressed with himself.

But fortunately, Rafferty did not seem intent on continuing the conversation, and the lift doors had opened. Nigel nodded quickly in Rafferty's direction, and then exited the lift, heading for his former office.

The walk down the corridor felt odd, and Nigel realized after a moment that it was not because he had been away for a while. It was because the floor was quieter than it should be in the middle of a workday. Reggie's practice could not be going well. Between the lift and the secretary's desk, which he was approaching now, he had encountered no one, and that was not a good sign.

But the secretary was there—the new one, whom Reggie had hired after the events in Los Angeles.

As Nigel approached, Lois got up from her desk, maneuvering as quickly as she could between the corner of it and the edge of the cubicle.

"This is Baker Street Chambers, Reggie Heath QC," she announced eagerly.

"Yes," said Nigel. "I'm Nigel Heath. I'm—"

"Oh yes," she said. "I've heard of you."

"That I'm the taller, better-looking, and more responsible one?" said Nigel. All of this was patently untrue, of course, except for the better-looking part, which Nigel regarded as subjective.

Lois was stumped for just an instant, her eyes fixing at some nonexistent point in the distance as she tried, no doubt, to think of the appropriate lie.

"Yes," she chirped, with a wide smile.

"Well put," replied Nigel. "You know Reggie's situation?"

"He's in—"

"Go ahead, you can say it."

"Indisposed," she said, bravely.

"Quite right," said Nigel. "That's exactly how you should respond to the odd solicitor that might drop by. Or close enough. But you and I know where Reggie is, though it's not good business for a barrister to be there."

"Yes," she said in a low voice.

Nigel continued. "Every day that goes by with Reggie still accused is another day that he will get no briefs and another day of being slammed in the tabloids to the point his chambers might never recover. We might have several weeks until the trial date to find evidence to keep him from going to prison. But we have only days to save his career. And—unlike me, as you may have heard—Reggie values his law career."

"Yes," she said. "I have noticed."

"Very well. The bail hearing is already in good hands. I've

got Reggie's arrest report, but there are some other things I'll need: the prosecutor's disclosures from Reggie's Black Cab case, the solicitor's instructions in that case to Reggie—and we need to hunt up the solicitor herself as well."

"I've been trying to reach her," said Lois. "Reggie told me to do so when he called from . . . that place where he is . . . but I get no answer."

"Yes, I heard that she's been hard to get hold of," said Nigel. "Which is odd, because even if she regards her case as over and done with, you'd think she'd read the papers this morning and check in."

"Perhaps she's on holiday?"

"Perhaps. Do you have her address?"

"I'm sure it must be in Reggie's office," she said. "I'll get it."

Lois was about to move off toward Reggie's office, but Nigel paused and looked toward the smaller office, the one just across from the secretary's desk, that he himself had occupied until the events in Los Angeles.

"Is that locked?" he said.

"No, you can go right in. It's your old office, isn't it?"

"Yes," said Nigel. "You go on; I'll just be a moment."

Lois bustled off to get the briefing papers.

Nigel entered his old office. He shut the door behind him and leaned back against it. He wanted to get a sense of the room once more.

He had not been in this office since discovering the body of the previous clerk, Robert Ocher, just a month earlier.

In the time since, he had gone to Los Angeles and solved Ocher's murder, rescued Mara or been rescued by her (depending upon how he looked at it), got his solicitor's license suspended without regretting it, and, finally, set Reggie back on the right course with Laura—or at least tried, to the extent one sibling could do for another without crossing the line.

So it was surprising, after all that, how the office itself still seemed familiar.

The old wooden file cabinet that had hidden the crouching secretary was still there in the corner.

And there was still an in-basket on the desk, into which the new secretary was still collecting the letters addressed to Sherlock Holmes. One thing had changed in that regard, and Nigel had to smile at it: Reggie obviously wanted Lois to have no doubts about who would be responding to the letters; on the edge of the basket he had taped a note in broad felt pen strokes: "For Nigel."

At this moment there was one new letter in the basket. Presumably everything else had been in the packages that Reggie had sent on.

Nigel picked it up.

It was a rather short letter:

Dear Mr. Holmes:

What you value most.
Your humble servant,
Professor Moriarty

That was all it said.

Nigel sat down in his old chair. Perhaps one letter from Moriarty could be ignored by more sensible minds than his own. But two such letters indicated a continuing delusion, in Nigel's view, and should not be taken lightly.

Nigel took the first letter from Moriarty out of his pocket and compared it to the new one.

In the second letter, the writer seemed to have been promoted to "Professor"—and for a moment, Nigel considered whether the letters might have been written by two different people.

Both were done on the same stationery. That didn't mean much by itself, it was a common brand.

Both letters were also done, apparently, in the same typeface. So one stationery, one typeface—probably one person, in the absence of evidence to the contrary.

But who?

Neither letter had a return address, of course. And no handwritten signatures.

Nigel looked at the backs of the sheets. Nothing. He held them up to the light—nothing. He looked at them sideways—of course, nothing.

He knew he wasn't focusing properly. He was in the office, he was sitting in the chair, the letters were on the blotter. There must be something important in them beyond the obvious message but he just wasn't getting it. Something was impeding his concentration.

But what was it? Finally, Nigel thought to open the top left drawer of the desk, the shallow drawer for pencils and paper clips and such.

Thank God, there it was. Reggie had not had the drawer cleaned out.

There was still an unopened tube of chocolate Smarties.

Forty minutes of sugar rush ought to do it. Nigel started in on the candy-shelled discs and then, careful not to smudge, again picked up the letters.

Nigel looked more closely at the typeface on each. It was blunt, uneven in impact, and irregular in alignment. A manual machine. A very old one.

Nigel picked up the letters and went to find Lois, who was just about to exit Reggie's office, papers in hand.

"I have the bundle the solicitor brought in for the Black Cab case," she said. "Her business phone just gets an answering service; we tried that earlier. But I did find her mobile phone number."

"Let's give it a try then," said Nigel.

Lois picked up Reggie's desk phone, put it on speaker phone, and rang Darla's mobile number. It rang continually, until finally it switched over, and an automated voice from the mobile phone company identified the number they had called and said to leave a message.

"I hate these things," said Nigel to Lois. Then, into the phone, he said, "This is Nigel Heath, Ms. Rennie. Kindly call Reggie Heath's chambers and assist us in getting him out of jail over your client, if it is not too much trouble."

Then he hung up.

"You'd think she'd have a secretary," said Nigel. "But I'll try her office in person. Meantime, there's something else I need, if you aren't too busy with your regular duties."

Lois looked over at the shelf where she was supposed to collect the briefs for new business incoming from solicitors. Nigel looked, too. The shelf should have been full of documents, each rolled up and tied with the traditional purple ribbon that solicitors used when delivering new case instructions to barristers.

The shelf was empty.

"I just might have time for it," said Lois.

Nigel gave her the letters from Moriarty. "These were done on a very old typewriter. Please see what you can find out about them."

She gave Nigel a blank look.

"Such as?"

"Letters done on typewriters are traceable to the machines on which they were typed. The characters tend to arrange themselves in their own particular angles and impressions."

"Yes, but how do I find—"

"Try some repair shops. Maybe there's a typewriter museum? I don't know. Someone must have something you can compare it to. If you can get the make and model, perhaps we can even find out where and who purchased the particular machine that typed this. For that you'd get a gold star."

Her look back at Nigel had not improved much. "I . . . I'll certainly try," she said, gamely.

Nigel thanked her and turned to leave the office now. But then he stopped inside the doorway.

There was a scent. At first, just a very pleasant and interesting scent, of roses and other things—but then he began to remember where he had encountered it before, and the memory aroused mixed emotions.

"What perfume are you wearing?"

Lois looked shocked at first, and then, very quickly, quite pleased.

"Nothing, really. Just what I put on in the bath." She blushed immediately after saying that.

Nigel sniffed the air, then took a step toward one of the guest chairs. Lois watched him, wondrously, as he looked first behind the chair, and then underneath it.

And then, having found nothing, he boldly put his hand into the crease of the chair.

He found something. He grasped it carefully between the tips of two fingers, and withdrew it.

It was the solicitor's business card. Darla Rennie's business card. It was slightly scented. And the scent was familiar.

"Oh," said Lois. "Yes, she sat there the other day. She must have taken it out of her purse and dropped it?"

No cause for alarm, Nigel told himself. He might be misremembering the scent. And even if it was the same scent, it could be coincidence. Two different women could wear the same scent. One of them might even put it on her business cards.

And in any case, now he had the solicitor's address.

Nigel left the chambers and hailed a Black Cab. He showed the driver Darla Rennie's business card.

"A solicitor at that address?" said the driver.

"Yes," said Nigel. "Tottenham Court Road."

"Oh, I know where it is all right," said the driver. "I know every address in London you can name. But there's no lawyer's office at 369 Tottenham Court Road."

"You're sure about that?" said Nigel, skeptically.

"Of course I'm sure. I know the street, I know what's on it, and I don't need any bloody satellite navigation system for it either," said the driver, with slightly more heat than one would expect.

"Didn't mean to offend," said Nigel.

"Pay me no heed, guv. I'm just a bit annoyed that they're trying to jam this thing down our throats."

"A navigation system, you say?"

"Don't read the papers then, do you?"

"I've been out of town," said Nigel.

"Well, there's a public hearing tomorrow, and I'll give them a piece of my mind."

"You should," said Nigel. "Clearly you have some to spare. But for now, let's just verify this lack of a solicitor's office, shall we?"

"Right you are," said the driver.

They reached the 300 block of Tottenham Court Road—featuring a newly installed American hamburger chain, a Tesco express, a launderette—and Nigel had to admit it was not where one would expect to find a high-end solicitor's office. But as he could personally attest, not all solicitors are high end.

But now the cab pulled to a stop, and Nigel looked out the window at the address.

"Bloody hell," said Nigel. "It's a mail-box rental."

The cabbie looked back at Nigel and nodded in a self-satisfied way.

"Right you are," said Nigel.

14

Shortly after one that afternoon, Laura arrived by cab to meet Geoffrey Langdon at the entrance to Central Criminal Court.

She saw a man standing anxiously at the curb in a barrister's chalk-stripe suit. He was smaller than she expected—thin-faced, with bright, darting eyes, as if always on the alert for some sort of attack from unexpected quarters.

He stepped toward her as soon as the cab door opened.

"Mr. Langdon?" she said.

"Yes, Ms. Rankin; we'll go right inside, if you don't mind. The court has allowed some media for this hearing; but let's give them as little spectacle as we can."

"I quite agree," said Laura.

Laura tagged along with Langdon to get admitted through security.

As often as she had seen the outside of it, she had never before been inside the Old Bailey. The lobby was quite spectacular, with its arches and murals—or would have been, if one weren't there for a criminal proceeding, which of course was the only reason to be there.

Langdon escorted her quickly up the stairs, and then through a short, narrow corridor into the courtroom.

"Sit one row back of me, as if you are Heath's family," said Langdon.

She did so, although the "as if" sounded odd somehow.

The prosecuting barrister entered, and sat at a table to their left.

And then a side door opened, and a sergeant entered, escorting a tall man in a regulation beige jumpsuit. It was Reggie.

Reggie stepped into the dock—a raised platform with four-foot glass sides, positioned at the end of the aisle between the defense and prosecuting benches. He managed a subtle wink at Laura as he took his position.

And now a door at the front of the courtroom opened, and the judge entered. Everyone stood. The bailiff called the court to order and announced Reggie's case.

The judge, not bothering to look up, routinely asked if there would be application for bail.

"My lord, we request that the defendant be released on his own recognizance pending trial."

Langdon said this in a low voice, matching the judge's matter-of-fact tone as well as he could. But it didn't work. The judge looked up.

"The charge is homicide, Mr. Langdon."

"Yes, my lord, but the defendant is a respected member of the legal profession."

"But we don't want one standard of bail for members of the legal profession and another for everyone else, do we?" The judge intoned this with an inflection that made it clear what the right answer should be.

"Certainly not," said Langdon, correctly. "The relevance of my client's profession is simply that he must be free in order to properly prepare his own defense."

"That's a consideration. But can you cite any instance in recent memory where a London court has released a homicide suspect—one from the general population—on his own recognizance?"

"No, my lord, but I can cite many for which bail was granted on bond to a defendant who has had no prior violent acts, is of solid reputation, and has strong ties in the community."

"Well, yes, on sufficient bond. That may be something we can consider."

"Thank you, my lord."

But now the prosecuting barrister spoke.

"My lord?"

"Yes?"

"As to prior violent acts—I believe there was an incident just a few days ago at Fleet Street in which a well-respected London publisher was violently deposited by Mr. Heath into a rubber tree plant."

"No charges were filed," said Langdon quickly.

"And yet another incident in which a photographer duly doing his job at a crime scene was violently accosted—"

"It was a rumpled collar, my lord, nothing more, and again no charges filed."

The prosecutor sighed, very slightly, in a way intended to convey that it was a shame that multiple instances of no charges being filed could not in themselves add up to something.

The judge looked at him and asked, "Is there more?"

"Only, perhaps, that of which we are not aware," offered the prosecutor, rather desperately.

"I believe that means 'no,' my lord," chirped Langdon.

"I believe so, too," said the judge. "But perhaps you will now give us your list, Mr. Langdon."

"My lord?"

"The strong ties you were referring to. What are they?"

"The defendant has been a practicing barrister in London for fourteen years."

"So I understand. Although I believe his chambers are not actually in the City of London proper, is that correct?"

"Umm, true, my lord. His chambers are in Marylebone, on Baker Street."

"Rather unusual."

"Unusual, but not prohibited," said Langdon.

"And he is at present the only barrister at Baker Street Chambers, is that also true?"

"Well, yes, he is at this moment a sole practitioner."

"Somewhat reduces the strength of his connections with the legal community, in my view," said the judge. "But go on."

"My lord?"

"Ties to the community in general? Family?"

"Both parents deceased, my lord."

"Does he have children?"

"Ahh . . . I'm not . . ."

For some reason—probably to avoid craning his neck at the upward angle to look over at Reggie—Langdon looked at Laura, who thought about it, and then shook her head rather uncertainly.

"We think not, my lord."

"A wife?" The judge was still addressing Langdon, and not Reggie.

Laura shook her head emphatically and Langdon relayed that to the court.

"Any family contacts at all?"

"A brother, my lord," offered Langdon. "Nigel Heath."

"Ahh, yes," said the judge. "I've heard the name. But not here in London, is he?"

"No," said Langdon.

The judge breathed a sigh of relief at that, but Laura noticed his reaction too late. She had already whispered a correction to Langdon.

"Correction," said Langdon to the judge. "Nigel Heath is, in fact, now in London."

"Is he?" said the judge. "Nigel Heath has returned?"

"Yes."

The judge frowned. Laura looked over at Reggie, who seemed to be holding his breath.

The judge settled back in his chair to think about it a bit, then cleared his throat.

"So, in London at this moment," said the judge, "we have one Heath brother who is accused of murdering his own client, and another who, if memory serves, had his license suspended in a row over an attempt to return a client's tort fee to the opposing litigant."

The judge still looked at Langdon, not Reggie. Langdon shrugged meekly. "My lord?"

"Perhaps you can tell me, Mr. Langdon. Are the Heath brothers genetically inclined to despise their own clients? Or is it the legal system in general they object to?"

Langdon hesitated in responding, and finally Reggie could bear it no longer.

"My lord, I'm certain that our attitude toward our clients is no different than the attitudes you will hear expressed by any of the barristers at the Wigs and Briefs after their third pint."

The judge paused and looked at Reggie in astonishment, and Laura realized that Reggie must have spoken out of turn.

"Or at the Seven Stars, on Chancery Court Lane."

The judge was clearly gathering himself for a rejoinder.

"Or at the Crown and Penance on Fleet Street."

"Enough," said the judge. "I did not address a question to you, Mr. Heath. In any case, we are all familiar with their locations, and I, for one, will not apologize for a Foster's at the end of the day. Though any lawyer who cannot hold his tongue in a pub should not be allowed a pint at all. But at the moment, sir, your ties to the community are looking a little thin. As is your capability to post bond, should I decide to grant it. Nevertheless, as Mr. Langdon points out, the court recognizes some need for you to assist—or totally destroy, as the case may be—your own defense. Bail is therefore set in the amount of one million pounds."

"Might as well just remand, if you're going to do that," said Reggie.

"Well put," said the judge. "Let's make it two million pounds. Have that on you, do you? No? Then this hearing is adjourned, and the defendant is returned into custody."

Everyone stood up, as the judge exited in one direction and Reggie was hustled away in the other by the sergeant.

Langdon turned to Laura. "Doesn't have it, does he?"

"Might as well ask if he can retire the whole bloody national debt."

"I'm sure the judge will demand just that, if Heath opens his mouth again."

They went into the corridor, heading toward the courthouse side exit. Laura thought Langdon seemed just a little uncomfortable walking with her, which she attributed to his reputed shyness.

"I thought he took it fairly well, though," Langdon said, awkwardly.

"I thought he looked like a fish just now hauled onto dry land," said Laura.

"We can appeal the bail amount at the next hearing, before a different judge," said Langdon. "That won't be for a week. But I'll do the appearance for it, no charge, and we'll hope for a better result."

They stepped out to the pavement.

"Thank you," said Laura. "I hope he keeps for that long."

Now, a long white limousine pulled to the curb in front of them. This was happening frequently, and Laura was no longer surprised by it.

"Must be yours," said Langdon, with an awkward laugh. "I'll be in touch."

Langdon walked on. The limo door opened.

Inside was Robert Buxton. He had a portable computer opened on his lap, and although he had reached over to open the door for Laura, he allowed the driver to come around and hold it.

"I'd have taken a cab," said Laura, getting in. "It doesn't all have to be a production."

"They aren't safe."

"You believe too much of what you print." She wasn't sure why she was annoyed with Buxton at the moment, but she was.

It didn't seem to register with him, though. That's good, she thought, as they drove on through the city toward Wapping. At least in some ways it is.

The limo drove past the walls of Buxton's secure publishing compound to the gate, which immediately opened. Buxton was on his mobile the whole way, but he shut it off when they pulled up in front of the main entrance to his headquarters.

It was just at the end of the business day, with most of the employees of Buxton Enterprises still exiting the building. Laura expected that she and Buxton would take a side entrance, for some minimal privacy—but they didn't. They walked through the lobby, her arm in the crook of his, Buxton setting a pace that was almost a stroll, while he grinned and nodded at the exiting journalists who had the temerity to make eye contact.

They got in the lift; that, at least, was private. As they rode up to the penthouse, Laura pondered why the walk through the lobby seemed to remind her of the prerace parade at Royal Ascot.

And by the time the lift doors opened at the top of the building, she had realized who the prize mare was.

Not entirely a good thing, she thought.

A short time later, in the early evening, lights were beginning to reflect on the Thames. Laura and Buxton sat down to dinner on the rooftop patio of the Buxton Enterprises building, with its hothouse, its authentic Spanish pavers, and its bubbling hot tub. Buxton was a man of such wealth that he was not limited even by the London climate.

It was spectacular.

Looking out across the Thames, Laura could see Reggie's much smaller rooftop flat, on the opposite bank of the river at Butlers Wharf—with no lights on, naturally, given where he was at the moment.

Buxton turned his mobile off now and put it down on the white linen tablecloth. He opened a bottle of champagne, working the cork out himself, and saying something about the year of it. A household servant brought plates of scallops on black pudding, which Laura knew Buxton knew was her favorite (except for shepherd's pie, which Laura knew Reggie knew was her favorite). The warm scent of the current meal brought her back to where she was now, as opposed to what she was thinking about across the river, and she began to pay attention to something Buxton was saying about the champagne.

Then a mobile phone rang.

Laura made a displeased face.

Buxton picked up his phone, but the ringing continued.

"Oh," said Laura. "Sorry."

She took her own mobile out of her bag and answered it. She watched Buxton watching her as she took the call.

It was Reggie.

"Oh, no, not all," she said into the phone. "You didn't catch me at a bad time, I'm having rather a good time actually."

Buxton smiled slightly, and rather smugly.

"I didn't know they allowed you to place calls from jail in the evening," she continued, and now Buxton's smile faded.

"I see," Laura continued. "Well, one is enough, I suppose, if it's the right one. What do you need me to do?"

Buxton sighed and sat back in his chair, visibly annoyed, as Laura took out a small notebook and a pen, and actually began to write herself a note.

"Yes. Yes. Do you really think so? Well, yes, it's certainly worth investigating. Right, then. But wait, wait—how are you? Are you all right? Are there rats? Are the showers really communal? Oh. Well, one hears of people who have heard awful stories."

Now there was a pause, as Laura listened to what Reggie was saying. When the moment came, she looked over at Buxton, with an expression that said he would just have to put up with what she was going to do next. And then she turned to face away from Buxton and spoke in her lowest voice into the phone.

"Reggie, I do understand. Really. But everyone makes decisions every day—not just lawyers, but everyone—that impact someone else in some way. It seems to me you usually make the right ones, certainly you always try to do, and isn't that all anyone can ask?"

There was a pause, and then she turned back toward Buxton, but still talking into the phone. "Well, that's my best speech anyway, so it will just have to do. Was there something else? Because there's a very delicious second course on its way and—oh, I see.

Yes. Yes. Do you really thinks so? Well, yes, it's certainly worth investigating. Right, then. But wait, what about bail, don't you want me to ask Robert if . . . well, I'm sure he would if . . . but it would be no trouble, he's got just tons of . . . well, that's just silly, no one's trying to cut anything off at all, and you're just being stubborn. Good-bye then."

Laura closed the phone and put it back in her bag, checked the note she had written to make sure she got it right, and then carefully put that away as well.

"Holding up well, I hope?" said Buxton, quite casually.

"You'd think he'd be worried about being in jail. But he isn't. He's worried about the possibility that he might have done the wrong thing getting his client released."

"Is he?" said Buxton, seeming genuinely interested.

"Yes," said Laura. "Does that make sense to you?"

"Not in the least."

Laura was beginning to be impressed by Buxton's evident level of concern. He was actually listening to her, and carefully so. "Well," she said, "it's just like him to—what is that?"

"What is what?"

"You were looking at something below the table."

Buxton shrugged and shook his head. "Nothing," he said.

Laura, suddenly alarmed, half stood from her chair and leaned across the table.

"What is it that you have in your right hand?"

"Nothing," said Buxton, like a child with a stolen biscuit.

"Robert, show me," demanded Laura.

Buxton, reluctantly, raised up his right hand and placed his mobile communicator on the dining table.

"You were taking notes?" she cried out.

"No," said Buxton. "Well, just that last part. "About him thinking his client might be guilty."

"You were sending this to one of your reporters?"

Buxton quickly pressed a button and closed the phone. "No," he said. "Canceled. Nothing sent, Laura, I promise."

Laura sat back down, but was still staring across at Buxton.

"Not one word," she commanded Buxton. "Not one word I have ever said to you about Reggie Heath shall ever find its way into print."

Buxton looked back directly at her, and blinked.

"Of course not," he said.

"Not one word. Ever. Not print, or any other form of media. Ever. Whether currently existing or as yet uninvented."

Buxton sighed.

"Understood," he said.

Laura allowed herself to breathe now, and she sat back.

"I don't want him to get depressed," she said to Buxton

"No worries," said Buxton. "I'm sure they take his belt away."

She showed no reaction to that remark. She took a sip of the champagne. Then she set the glass down and said:

"Reggie says under no circumstances am I to ask you to stand surety for his bail. Apparently, it's some sort of manhood thing. I think he's afraid it will de–alpha male him, or something to that effect, though he expressed it in other terms. I don't understand it. Do you?"

"Completely," said Buxton, showing interest again. "How much will it take?"

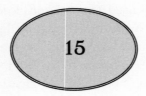

15

At quarter of nine the next morning, Nigel arrived at Baker
Street Chambers to meet Laura. He was uncharacteristically
early for their appointment—he was concerned about the solicitor's lack of an actual business address, and he had been
unable to reach Laura by phone in the evening to tell her
about it.

But as early as he was for their appointment, Laura was
there before him.

Lois pointed toward Reggie's closed chambers door. "She
said she didn't want to be disturbed."

"Yes," said Nigel, "but she didn't mean me, did she, or she
wouldn't have flown me out here?"

"Oh," said Lois, in an uncertain voice.

"I need Darla Rennie's home address," said Nigel, before
opening the door to the chambers. "If it's not in the files, try
some public documents. Or see if you can get it from her

mobile provider. Tell them you are her and you're changing your billing address. They get very anxious about that sort of thing."

"I'll try."

"Worth a shot, anyway."

"Yes," she said.

"Oh," said Nigel, "And the typewriter face? On the Moriarty letters?"

"Still working on it."

"Let me know," said Nigel.

Now he opened the door to Reggie's chambers and looked in.

Yes, there was Laura. She was sitting in Reggie's leather barrister's chair; she had scooted it over to the exterior window and swiveled it to face the street. She did not look up when Nigel came in; she seemed lost in thought.

Nigel, still standing in the doorway, decided to get directly to it.

"The solicitor who engaged Reggie to take this case," said Nigel, "may not exist."

Laura immediately swiveled the chair to face Nigel.

"What exactly do you mean by that?" she said. "And just because you caught me staring out a window doesn't mean I want us to get metaphysical."

"Her office address is a front," said Nigel, "and I checked for her name in the Law Society records."

"And?"

"She doesn't exist. At least not by the name Darla Rennie, not as a licensed solicitor in the London area. There is no official record of her."

"How could she bring a client to Reggie, then? How was she able to practice at all?"

"A magistrate's court can be quite informal when it gets

busy. If you get past security—and most of the smaller courts
don't have any—and know half of what you're supposed to do
and say, you're in, and you can come back and do it again the
next day, too."

"So you're saying she's not a solicitor at all?"

"It's possible," said Nigel. "It's also possible that she has
or did have a practice, but under another name." Nigel moved
from the doorway now and pulled one of the smaller guest
chairs up to the desk, opposite Laura. "But either way, something is wrong about her. Have you ever actually seen her in
person?"

"No. But Reggie has, of course. And anyone who was in the
court with them."

"If anyone took notice. The barrister is the one who stands
up and does all the talking. Right now, so far as the prosecution is concerned, Reggie might just as well have made her
up."

"They can hardly say that, Nigel; there was a photo of her
in the papers. And of Reggie. Very explicit—very clearly, both
of them together."

Nigel peered across at Laura, trying to get an accurate
reading on her tone.

"That's good," he offered.

"Yes," she said. "Of course it is."

"Do we have that paper?"

Laura hesitated; then she reached into her purse and pulled
out a copy of the *Daily Sun,* from the day after the Black Cab
hearing. She put it on the desk in front of Nigel.

Nigel leaned in closer for a better look.

A very long look, it seemed to Laura.

"I can't make out her face," said Nigel, still staring at the
photo.

"You're certainly giving it a good try."

"All you can see is her legs."

"Well, that is the angle the paparazzi seem to prefer." She paused. "You can stop ogling now."

"Sort of rings a bell," said Nigel, trying to push the tabloid and its photo away, but then looking back at it again.

"Oh, is that what we're calling it now?"

"I mean, I think I've seen them before. Those legs"

"Oh, Nigel, come off it."

"What?"

"You're telling me you can recognize a woman just from a photo of her legs?"

"Some legs. Varies by the woman, what you remember."

Laura sighed, and she gave Nigel a look that said she didn't believe him, but that if she did believe him, she wished she didn't.

Nigel squirmed just a bit. Then, for some reason—almost a sort of chivalry—he felt obliged to make a confession.

"Do you still have three freckles, one dark, two lighter and smaller next to it, behind your left knee?"

He tried to look her directly in the eye as he said it, but he couldn't, he broke eye contact the moment she looked back in response. And so he didn't get to see her blush.

"All right, I believe you," she said quickly. "But no more about my knees. Or my freckles. Or—"

"Done," said Nigel, even more quickly.

"So where do you think you might have seen our enigmatic solicitor's legs before?"

Nigel hesitated. Now that it had come down to it, he didn't really want to say.

"I could be quite wrong about it. As you said, what could I possibly know just from seeing legs in a photo?"

"There's more to it than that, Nigel, or you wouldn't have brought her up. So what is it?"

"I'd rather not say just yet."

Laura stared at him. Nigel shifted uncomfortably and seemed to shrink back in his chair.

"I've got the secretary tracking down her home address," he said. "When she gets it, I'll pay a visit, and we'll know more."

"No," said Laura, peering at Nigel and trying to discern the reason for his suddenly defensive posture. "I will do that visit."

"Why you?" said Nigel.

"Because I don't care about her legs, and therefore she won't be able to handle me like putty," said Laura. "Which, I'm beginning to suspect, is more than can be said for the Heath brothers."

Nigel took just a moment to analyze that remark. "You're concerned that Reggie might like her, then?"

"I didn't say that," said Laura, sounding now just a little defensive herself.

"Fair enough," said Nigel. "But if you and she get in a wrestling match, either tape it or ring me."

"Let's just focus on the matter at hand, shall we?" said Laura.

"Yes, let's," said Nigel.

"Right, then," said Laura. "Reggie said on the phone last night that we should be focusing on the tip letter and who wrote it."

"Very sensible," said Nigel. "But I've been through the bundle Reggie got from the solicitor, and the police report, and Reggie's own file. I've been through it all, and the tip letter isn't there."

"He said it's in his desk. The bottom drawer, I expect, because that's the one that's locked," said Laura. "And that's presenting a problem."

"Doesn't Lois have a key?"

"No; it's a combination lock, and she doesn't know it. I tried to call Reggie at the jail, but I couldn't get through."

"First thing they do in jail is confiscate your mobile," said Nigel. "But no need. We can do this ourselves." Nigel came around to the other side of the desk to get access to the lock. "I'm betting you know the combination."

"Nigel, Reggie doesn't give anyone the combination to his office desk."

"No, but between the two of us I'm sure we know it. When were you born?"

Laura laughed. "And that's relevant because?"

"He wouldn't use his own birth date; too obvious and on too many public documents."

Nigel looked at Laura expectantly.

"So you think he used mine?" she said.

"Of course he did."

"Well, I doubt it."

"If he didn't," said Nigel, "I'll pay my own airfare when I go back to the States."

"Done," said Laura.

Nigel leaned in toward the locked drawer, and then stopped.

"Well, go ahead, try it," said Laura.

He looked sheepishly back at her.

"Nigel . . . you never took note of my birth date?"

"I don't think I ever knew the year."

"But the rest of it?"

"Sorry."

"You'd better remember Mara's."

"I do."

Nigel willingly moved aside now, and Laura swiveled

Reggie's chair in closer to the desk drawer. She entered her birth-date numbers into the combination lock. She looked up at Nigel before pulling the drawer, daring him to be right.

"Well? Last chance to save your airfare."

"Go ahead."

She pulled on the drawer. There was an obstinate metallic clunk. It didn't open.

"See?" she said. She was more disappointed than she allowed her voice to show.

"Try it again," said Nigel. "Use four digits for the year."

Laura tried it again.

Again, the annoying mechanical clunk.

Laura sat back from the drawer, unhappy, but quickly covering. "I win. You can pay me back for your flight in installments."

Nigel regarded the desk with a perplexed look. "It should have worked," he said. "The desk combination is something Reggie uses every day. He would choose a number of something else that was important to remember, and he would use the desk combination to remember that other number."

"If you say so, but I knew he wouldn't use my birthday."

"You're wrong," said Nigel. "He would . . . unless there was another number more important."

"Well, that's comforting. When you learn who it is that has the more important birthday, do let me know. Or, better— don't."

"I guess we don't have time to figure it out. Paper clip—one of the large ones?"

Laura found a paper clip in a container on the desk and gave it to Nigel. Nigel twisted the paper clip into a more useful shape and knelt down by the drawer.

"Reggie won't like it if I scratch his mahogany desk," said Nigel.

"Scratch away," said Laura, sounding only a little cross.

Nigel inserted the paper clip and picked the latch. He pulled the drawer open, reached inside, and then stood.

"Here it is." He had pulled a single sheet of paper from the drawer. He read it quickly. "This is the anonymous tip letter. The letter to Sherlock Holmes that told Reggie about the CCTV alibi."

Laura thought Nigel sounded almost disappointed.

"What's wrong?" she said.

"I was hoping it would be typewritten, matching the letters to Sherlock Holmes from the person who believes himself to be Moriarty."

"Why?"

"It would simplify things," said Nigel.

"I think you need to forget Mr. Moriarty and concentrate on the letter at hand. Anyway, if it's not typewritten, what is it?"

"Laser-printed, or high-quality ink-jet, hard to tell."

"So are all the papers in the solicitor's bundle," said Laura, picking them up.

"So you think she sent the tip letter?"

"It's a possibility," said Laura.

Nigel put the tip letter out to compare.

"They're a different font," said Nigel.

"But you can choose different typefaces when you print on these things, can't you?"

"Yes," said Nigel, still comparing the two sheets. "But it's different paper as well. Even the ink looks different."

"Well, all right then," said Laura. "Perhaps the solicitor didn't send it. It was just a thought."

"Why are you so determined that Darla Rennie sent the tip letter?"

"It would simplify things," said Laura, repeating Nigel's words from a moment ago.

"In what way?" said Nigel.

Laura just shrugged.

"Well, in any case, I don't see anything in common in the documents," said Nigel. And we're overlooking the most obvious possibility."

"Which is?" said Laura.

"That Reggie's client, Walters, sent the tip letter. That he set the whole alibi up for himself in advance."

"Clever man if he did," said Laura. "But if he was committing the crime in Chelsea, then who drove the cab that we see on the CCTV at Clapton Road?"

"You're right," said Nigel. "Perhaps Walters did the killings in Chelsea. Perhaps he also killed the victim whose body was pushed over the bridge. Or perhaps he did neither and has been framed. But someone was driving the alibi cab in the East End when the two American tourists were getting murdered in Chelsea. Two Black Cabs in different places at the same time takes two Black Cab drivers."

"Let's hope the frame theory turns out to be the case," said Laura. "For Reggie's peace of mind, if nothing else."

"I think we need a closer look at the cabs. I'll go to New Scotland Yard and have a look at what they fished from the Thames."

"I'll go with you," said Laura.

"They won't let you. The Yard will only give me access, as Reggie's solicitor. Although I suppose you could try invoking celebrity rank."

"No, you go ahead then. But I'll want a full report later."

"Done," said Nigel. He got up and moved toward the door.

Then he stopped and looked back. Laura hadn't budged. She was still keeping Reggie's chair warm.

"You're not going to just stay here, are you?" said Nigel. "This may take a while."

"I'm waiting to hear about Reggie's bail."

"Two million pounds? Not possible, is it?"

"It might be," said Laura. "If I've called in the right favor."

"What favor would—"

"Go along, Nigel," said Laura. "I'll just be here for a bit before I get some lunch."

Nigel knew the tone in her voice, and he knew better than to ask another question.

"Right, then," he said, and he exited the chambers, carefully closing the door behind him.

Laura remained seated after Nigel had gone. She had not quite told the truth to Nigel. There in fact wasn't any real need to wait to hear about Reggie's bail. Robert Buxton had said that he would get it done, and he certainly had the wherewithal to make it happen.

She was indeed thinking about Robert, and about Reggie, but she wasn't waiting to hear about one getting the bail for the other. She was just waiting to make up her mind, and all the events of the past two days weren't giving her the opportunity to do that.

She turned to looking out the window again, for quite some time, watching the rain and the traffic and the pedestrians on Baker Street, as she had been doing before Nigel had arrived, without really seeing any of them.

And then there was a knock on the chambers door. It opened, and there was Reggie's secretary.

"Oh, I'm sorry," said Lois. "I thought Nigel would be here. I have the address he wanted."

"The solicitor's address, you mean?" said Laura.

"Yes. Is Nigel gone already?"

"Yes," said Laura, "but no problem. I'll take care of it." And with that she took the written address from Lois's hand, eagerly, without even quite waiting for polite consent.

Lunch could wait. And so could deciding.

16

Nigel walked past the revolving sign that announced New Scotland Yard, and toward the steel and glass structure of the police station behind it.

As he entered the building, he began to feel odd that he would be representing himself as Reggie's solicitor. This had nothing to do with his license still being in suspension; no one would likely bother to check. But it did feel odd, because traditionally in the Heath family, Reggie had not been the one in need of anyone else's intervention. Reggie had been early to take on responsibilities as a child; Nigel had been late. For Reggie to be the one who needed Nigel to rescue him from dire straits seemed . . . well, odd to Nigel.

Of course, no one here had reason to know or care about that. From the front desk, Nigel successfully negotiated through two levels of authority and three different departments, and eventually got access to the evidence impound garage.

A young police sergeant escorted him to see the two

impounded Black Cabs. "Forensics has not quite finished with them," she said, "I can let you look. But you still can't touch."

They started with the cab that had been pulled from the Thames.

It was a Fairway; a make and model that had dominated the streets of London some ten years earlier, but which was now giving way to metro cabs and TXIs and IIs. Still, it was a classic—a shape that any Londoner, or for that matter any person who knew of the existence of London, would immediately recognize as a Black Cab.

Or they would once it got washed. At the moment it was still covered in dirty brown residue from the dried Thames water.

The forensics team had opened the driver's side window. The sergeant allowed Nigel to stick his head through for a look.

"Won't be much to see, I'm afraid," she said cheerily. "Do try not to sneeze."

And she was right. Any items of evidence had already been removed. And the same dry muddy haze that coated the exterior also coated the seats and floorboards and sidings of the interior, punctuated by the small areas where forensics had done its sampling.

"Let's have a look at the other, then," said Nigel.

The sergeant escorted Nigel past another dozen or so vehicles, either stolen or impounded for other reasons, until they got to the only other Black Cab in the garage.

This was the cab that had been taken from Walters's home upon Reggie's arrest.

And, presumably, it was also the cab that had been examined by the police earlier when they arrested Walters.

Nigel walked around it. This cab was nearly spotless. But to all appearances, aside from the dried Thames mud on one of them, both vehicles were exactly the same: same make, same model, same black paint (unadorned with the adverts that were just now beginning to appear on some cabs), and most important, the same license number.

Nigel walked back to the first cab again to confirm, and he wished the forensics team had lined them up side by side for that purpose, but there was no question. They were identical.

"Someone went to a lot of trouble," said Nigel.

"Just a bit," said the sergeant. "It's a common model."

"What about the engine numbers?"

"They're different," said the sergeant. "But that doesn't tell us much, because no one checks the engine number when a taxi license is issued."

"How often do you see vehicles with forged number plates?" asked Nigel.

"I've seen it before on private vehicles," said the sergeant. "You see it in insurance scams, and for passing off stolen cars."

"But on a Black Cab?"

"That's a first, I suppose," she said. "But it was bound to happen, wasn't it? Everyone trusts them. Sooner or later, someone takes advantage."

"Yes," said Nigel. "But if your only purpose is to pretend to be a Black Cab driver so that you can pick up trusting victims, why go to the trouble of matching the exact same number as another cab? Why do you need to make your fake cab identical to someone else's real one?"

She shrugged, unconcerned. "I can show the vehicles to you," she said. "But for the whys and wherefores, I'm afraid you're on your own."

Nigel thanked the sergeant and left New Scotland Yard. He took a taxi to Camden Town, to the maintenance center that had supposedly cleaned Walters's vehicle the day after the Chelsea murders.

The driver proceeded past the garage entrance where cabs

lined up for maintenance and cleaning, and stopped just outside the front office.

"Told you Caledonia Road would be blocked," said the driver, cheerily. "It's all up here," he added, pointing to the side of his own head.

"Yes, you were quite right," said Nigel, getting out. "I've been away for a while, is all."

Nigel got out of the cab and found an attendant, a man in his twenties, in the office.

Nigel asked him about the cab Walters had brought in.

The attendant laughed. "Do you know how many cabs we clean in a day?"

"I don't. Fifty?"

"Twice that."

"This is one the police may have asked you about as well."

"Ahh," said the attendant. "Right. The police were here, true enough. A few days ago."

"Then you remember the cab?"

"Just that we cleaned it."

"You did a bloody good job of it, too," said Nigel. "Forensics couldn't find so much as a hair."

The attendant nodded. "Think I could get a quote from the cops on that? It would make a fine advert."

"Ask for an Inspector Wembley," said Nigel. "I'm sure he'll oblige. Do you remember who brought the cab in?"

"The bloke who was leasing it brought it in," said the attendant, in a tone that meant it was a foolish question.

"Was he a regular?"

"Pretty much."

"Always the same time of the week?"

"Sometimes. Not always."

"Notice anything at all different or unusual about him on this particular occasion?"

"Same thing I told the police: I didn't notice anything about the cab, and whether that meant there was anything to notice or not about the driver on that day, I can't say. But you know who might?"

"Who?"

"You see the pub across Caledonia Road, just at the corner?"

"The Flounder and Dab?"

"Yes. The local cabbies go there. There's a bloke who's been a driver since the beginning of time. Bill Edwards. Knows everything, worth knowing or not, about every driver. If you're lucky, he might tell you some of it."

Nigel walked across Caledonia Road to the Flounder and Dab pub.

When he opened the door he heard a chorus of shouts and groans that meant either televised football or live darts.

He looked to his right and was pleased to see it was the latter; like Reggie, he hadn't cared much for football in a long time.

There was a dartboard at the far corner, with half a dozen patrons, all drivers by the look of them, and all probably with money on the match. There were murmurs now as the next contestant stepped up to the line.

Nigel went to the barman, requested a pint, and asked which of the darts enthusiasts was Edwards.

"None of 'em" said the barkeeper. "He's in the back room." Nigel looked in that direction—at a door at the opposite end from the darts—and the barkeeper nodded.

Nigel took his pint with him and entered the back room.

He heard no noise when he entered. Instead there was a hushed, suspenseful silence, enveloped by floating clouds of tobacco smoke and accompanied by the scents of chalk dust, leather, and felt.

Nigel knew immediately that he had entered a snooker room. And that was even better than darts.

In the center of the room was a full-size mahogany-and-slate snooker table, with deep, leather-mesh pockets, and green felt that had seen so much action over so many years that it was beginning to look just a little faded in the area of the racking dot, like the top of the heads of the older men in the room.

There were two men well past sixty; the other three were much younger. There was one young woman, who stood leaning into the embrace of one of the younger men, seated at a bar stool along the wall. Another of the younger men was involved in a contest at the snooker table with the oldest man; everyone else was watching.

No one was looking at Nigel as he closed the door quietly behind him, and no one was speaking. The only number ball left on the table was the seven, the final ball, and exactly the same color, and pretty much the same glossiness, as the Black Cabs. The younger man had a shot at it—but a very long shot—from the opposite end of the table.

The older man was close to eighty, or perhaps even a few years past. He had not quite a full head of hair, but he still had most of it; it was salt and pepper, mostly salt, but carefully slicked back. His trimmed mustache was like something out of a twenties Errol Flynn movie; he wore a long-sleeve shirt, crimson and black, in a narrow-stripe pattern that looked like it had been in style about a hundred years ago; his cuffed, slightly overlong gray trousers were held up by suspenders, not a belt.

He was leaning back against the wall, arms crossed patiently, eyes fixed on some point on the snooker table that apparently only he was aware of, as the younger man took a shot—a tentative, uncertain roller—that missed, with the black seven ball ending up flat against the green side-cushion.

"Didn't want it," said the older man, unfolding his arms and stepping over to the table. "You just didn't want it."

He lined up the shot with no apparent effort, leaned over the table slightly, and banked the seven firmly and cleanly into the opposite corner pocket.

The three younger men groaned, the girl laughed, and money was paid to the other older man, who sat on a bar stool and smiled.

Nigel smiled at it, too. And now with the game done, he knew he was allowed to speak.

"Bill Edwards?" he said, addressing the man who had just won the game.

The man nodded, said that Nigel looked like someone who could play, and offered that the table was open for the next challenger.

Nigel shook his head. "Perhaps when I was nineteen and foolish," said Nigel. "But not now. People say you know more about the licensed Black Cab drivers in London than all the databases at the Carriage Office."

"What people tell you that?" asked the older man, though he did not seem surprised at the assertion. He put a triangular wooden frame on the table and began to rack up the red snooker balls for the next victim.

"The bloke at the steam clean," said Nigel.

Edwards nodded. "He might be right."

"What can you tell me about Neil Walters?"

The man stopped, with the frame still on the table. Everyone else stopped what they were doing as well; one of the younger men stood up from his bar stool, snooker cue in hand, as if ready to turn it into a cudgel. All eyes were on Nigel.

"Why are you asking?" said the older man.

"I intend to clear Reggie Heath of his murder," said Nigel.

Now the room relaxed a bit, but just a bit. Apparently, among cab drivers, the jury was still out on Reggie Heath. Which made perfect sense, as Nigel considered it. They probably didn't know whether to regard Reggie as the inventive barrister who cleared their fellow cabbie's name, even if only temporarily—or as the duped and annoyed lawyer who killed his own cab-driver client.

The older man at the table, looking thoughtful, went back to racking the balls, as everyone else waited for him to speak. Now he lifted the wooden frame from the felt, with the balls in perfect formation.

"If Walters did what the police say he did," said Edwards, "then I hope your brother did drive a knife into him." He looked Nigel in the eye as he said this, to see if he had guessed right on the relationship. Nigel nodded slightly.

"And twisted it, too," said one of the younger men.

"Our reputation is our livelihood," Edwards continued, completing the rack by placing a red ball down perfectly in front of the six, "and anyone—even one of our own—who does anything to harm it will have me to deal with."

"Bloody well right," said the other younger man, tapping the base of his snooker cue on the ground for emphasis.

Edwards continued. "But I don't believe Walters had it in him to murder anyone. He's a big enough guy to have done it, all right. I'll give you that. But I've seen him deal with snock-ered toss-pots and fare-jumping yobs who flipped him off on the way out of his cab, thinking he couldn't catch them, and then when he did, he was as gentle as Gandhi."

Edwards moved on toward the other end of the snooker table as he said this, and Nigel wondered if that move was an evasion. He followed.

"So, it must have been the other driver who did it?" sug-gested Nigel.

"What other driver?"

"The driver of the other cab."

Edwards shook his head, and continued, unhurried, to place each numbered ball on its own spot on the green felt. "I don't believe there was another cab driver. Not a real one. Two Black Cabs driving about London at the same time with the same license numbers? Perhaps, perhaps for just a short time without me hearing about it. But two different drivers learning the streets of London and passing the Knowledge, the years it takes to do that, and then driving those two identical cabs without me knowing of them?" Edwards walked to the opposite end of the table now and put the seven ball down on its spot, with just a bit of emphasis. "Not bloody likely," he said.

"All right then," said Nigel. "If there aren't two Black Cab drivers, and Walters didn't do it, then what's your answer?"

Edwards started to chalk up his queue.

"Who said I had an answer?" he said calmly.

Now the door to the general pub area opened, and before Edwards could get a challenger for the next game, or Nigel ask his next question, one of the dart-playing cab drivers entered.

"They moved the time up, mates. It starts in an hour."

"Imagine that," said Edwards, calmly. "Who would have thought they'd change the schedule on us?" He and the other drivers in the room immediately put away their cues and picked up their macintoshes.

"You can ride along if you like," he said to Nigel.

Five minutes later, Nigel was riding in the back of one Black Cab in a procession of at least twenty Black Cabs, all of them heading toward the north end of Caledonia Road—so many shining Black Cabs all in a row that even for London it was a bit unusual, and pedestrians turned their heads to look.

"Where are we headed?" asked Nigel.

"To defend our livelihoods," said the driver. This cab driver was one of the younger men from the snooker room; there seemed to be something of a pecking order, and Nigel apparently wasn't of sufficient importance to ride in the cab with Edwards.

"From what?"

"Bloody satellites," said the driver.

Nigel thought about that. "Global positioning?" he asked.

"Right. Every year for the past three years they've tried to push this down our throats. Every year we throw them back across the pond. You'd think they'd get tired trying."

Ten minutes later they were at the London Transport Authority building in Penton. The meeting hall was quite ordinary: a large wooden emblem at the back wall behind the oak speaker's dais tried to be ornate, but the lime-green plaster walls and the two hundred folding metal chairs made it clear that this was a working-class meeting hall. Nigel felt quite at home.

All of the chairs were already occupied; and almost all of them by cab drivers, judging by the style of their macs. Nigel and his cab driver stood along the wall near the entrance.

Three people were seated in chairs on a platform directly behind the speaker's dais. One of them, farthest from the dais, was Edwards, apparently as the official representative for the cab drivers. The other two were not cab drivers: one was wearing a black blazer with an official gold insignia for the Carriage Office; the other man was wearing a corporate-gray suit, with the shade of pink shirt always worn by wearers of corporate-gray suits who want to demonstrate creativity.

A fourth person on the platform was seated unobtrusively in the dark of a full-length stage curtain at the far right corner of the platform. His face wasn't visible, but he sat with a posture that seemed familiar to Nigel somehow. But Nigel couldn't place it, and the man was probably just someone in charge of the hall facilities themselves.

The man from the Carriage Office stood, screeched the

microphone, and then introduced Mr. Trimball from Transatlantic Software.

Mr. Trimball was a lean, trim man, in his late forties probably, according to his bearing, but possibly older from his face, which was both more lined and more tanned that those of the other people in the room.

An unwelcoming murmur rippled through the audience of cab drivers as he stepped to the microphone. He looked out over the crowd, paused for the noise to subside just a bit, and then began to speak.

"The Black Cabs of London are the safest mode of transportation in the world," he began, quite loudly. From his accent it was immediately apparent that he was an American.

The murmuring stopped on those first words, as he must have hoped it would; there were even a couple of "hear, hears." He continued: "So it is said. So has it been said for one hundred years, and it has always been true. But recent events compel us to realize that it is true no longer."

Now the crowd emanated a tense silence.

"There was a time when you saw a Black Cab on the street and you knew what it was and the caliber of the person driving it, and if you were an elderly pensioner on holiday, or a stockbroker who had one or two too many after work, or even a honeymooning couple from America, you knew that if you took that Black Cab, your driver was licensed and bonded and had spent years achieving the Knowledge and the privilege of driving a Black Cab, and that you would be got safely home, without question, and with no wrong turns taken either.

"But no longer. Today, more Black Cabs are manufactured overseas than in the UK. We do not know where those cabs end up. Nor do we even know what has become of all the Black Cabs manufactured here at home. There is no legal prohibition against selling to anyone at all, whether at home or abroad.

Gangster drug lords in the US can own Black Cabs if they choose to, and some do, I've seen them. Anyone who chooses to do so can own one here as well. And as we have seen, a person of ill intent can forge a license placard and claim to be a licensed Black Cab driver on the streets of London when in fact he is nothing of the kind.

"Is the driver of a Black Cab still the best taxi driver in the world? Yes. But can we still say with a certainty that every apparent Black Cab serving the streets of London is indeed what it seems? Clearly, we cannot. And if we cannot vouch for the cabs, can we possibly vouch for the persons driving them?"

A heavy murmur rolled through the hall now.

"But there is a solution. What I propose to you here today will solve not only the rare problem of the bad-apple Black Cab driver, but also the problem of the false Black Cab, being driven by a false Black Cab driver. And—even better—it will make all of your jobs easier to boot."

Now, with a flourish, Trimball held up a small silver object, about the size of a cigarette case.

"Meet 'highway,'" he announced. "That's H-A-I-W-A-Y, otherwise known as "Here Am I, Where Are You?" A satellite navigation system so advanced that the US Department of Defense wouldn't even let us tell you about it until now. With HAI-WAY as a mandatory installation on every newly manufactured Black Cab and on every existing licensed Black Cab in the city, not only will you always know how to get where you're going without even thinking about it, but also, no person of criminal intent will ever again be able to create a fake Black Cab and use the impeccable reputation of the honest Black Cab drivers to help him commit his crimes."

Trimball paused just for a moment and smiled at the new round of murmurs.

"Why is that, you ask?" He looked back over his shoulder as

he said this, and on this cue, the man seated at the curtain stood and flipped a switch at the back of the platform. The lights in the audience went dark, and a projection screen descended into place at the back of the platform.

"It's because satellites are a two-way street," continued Trimball, over a slick audiovisual presentation featuring shining Black Cabs, a blue-and-green Earth, and animated, smiling satellites.

"Not only does the central processing system tell every Black Cab where to go and how to get there, but every Black Cab is at all times sending a signal right back to the central processing system, saying where it actually is at that moment. And more— every metropolitan police car in London will be equipped with a client device that will ping every Black Cab for its identity— automatically—and the police will immediately know if any cab is false. Because HAIWAY will tell them."

The presentation stopped now, and the lights came back up. Trimball looked out over his audience to gather their attention back in. He leaned forward on the podium.

"Think about it," he said, earnestly. "No one will ever dare drive a fake Black Cab again. And no one—not the *Daily Sun*, not the Crown Prosecution Service, no one—will ever again, falsely or otherwise, be able to accuse a Black Cab driver of committing a crime."

Now Trimball stopped and took a half step back from the podium to demonstrate that he was done, squaring his shoulders in anticipated triumph and looking out boldly over the crowd.

The man in the Carriage Office blazer immediately leaped to his feet. "Hear, hear!" he cried.

No one seconded it, but no one shouted it down either. There was a long silence in the hall. From his vantage point, standing near the doorway, Nigel could see the cab drivers, who had all seemed so certainly opposed on the way in, turning to each other in a confused state. By the look of things, they weren't necessarily all seeing the proposal the same way.

Nigel himself had not yet formed an opinion about it. In fact, for the past five minutes of the presentation, he hadn't been paying all that much attention to the content. He'd been trying to remember where he had seen Trimball before. The name wasn't familiar at all—but he knew he had seen the face.

"Huh," said the young driver standing next to Nigel. "Well, that's not exactly what I expected now, is it?"

"How is it different?" said Nigel.

"Why, the whole tracking and identification thing. I thought it was just going to be something that would make the Knowledge unnecessary, so that any wanker or unlicensed minicab driver could drop in and pick up a Black Cab license on his way to lunch. But always knowing the real thing from the fake . . . well, that's not a bad idea now, is it?"

"I'm not at all sure," said Nigel. He was watching Edwards, who had slowly stood after the presentation, said nothing to anyone that Nigel could see, and was now making his way toward the door. As the man drew closer, it seemed to Nigel that all of the starch had gone out of him.

17

Laura rode in a cab from Baker Street, down along the east edge of Hyde Park, toward the solicitor's home address in Mayfair.

In Mayfair, the cab turned onto a lovely street, lined with townhomes that by tradition had belonged to the likes of cabinet ministers and mercantile barons. All a bit stuffy for Laura's taste. But she had to admit that even with her recent success, if she herself wanted one of these stately white-stone Edwardians, she would hardly be able to afford it.

So . . . great legs and family money, thought Laura, as the cab came to a stop. The more she learned of Reggie's enigmatic solicitor, the less she liked her.

The home had a particularly nice front garden of pink and white roses. Great legs, family money, and good with a garden. Worse and worse.

Laura went up the short walkway and knocked. After a

short moment, a servant girl answered the door. She opened it only a few inches.

"I'm looking for Darla Rennie," said Laura. "Is this her residence?"

The servant girl hesitated. In a Russian accent, she said, "Yes. But she's not at home."

"Do you know when she is coming back?"

"No," said the girl, looking about rather helplessly, as though she wished someone else were there to answer for her. "I think . . . perhaps she will be gone a long time."

"It's very important that I get in touch with her," said Laura. "She is the solicitor for a friend of mine."

The servant girl thought about that for a moment, then said, "Is a solicitor a professor?"

"Not necessarily. But I suppose one could be, if one were teaching."

The servant girl thought about that, and then nodded. "I think she became one just recently."

Laura had no idea what that might mean. And she wasn't learning anything just standing on the doorstep.

"Do you suppose I might leave her a note?" Laura asked.

"Yes," said the girl. She had relaxed her grip on the door just a bit.

"You've been so helpful," said Laura, in her most soothing voice. "But I've nothing to write on out here. Might I come in just for a moment?"

The servant girl hesitated. Laura smiled kindly.

The door opened.

The servant girl escorted Laura quickly, as though to minimize the risk of letting a stranger in, through the front room, then the kitchen, and then out onto the back garden patio, where there was a nice wrought-iron table with a marble top.

"You can write here," said the girl. "It's where she always does. I'll get some paper."

The servant girl went away, and Laura sat down at the table.

Laura looked about. It was quite a pleasant place, really, a lovely garden, with a clear sweet scent from brilliant red roses. They were even more striking than the white and pink ones she had seen in front.

Near the patio door, on the cobblestone flooring, was a two-foot-high stack of newspapers, mostly tabloids. The one on top, Laura, could not help but notice, was the *Daily Sun.*

Now the servant girl returned.

"Your employer enjoys the *Daily Sun?*" said Laura, indicating the stack by the door.

The Russian girl nodded. "I read the headlines to her at breakfast."

"Really? Just the headlines, not the stories?"

"Sometimes she wants me to read the story, too."

"I see. You scan the headlines for her and then read whatever she says sounds interesting. Leaving her hands free to concentrate on more important things, like scones."

"Yes. Black Cabs and barristers."

"Excuse me?"

"Those are the only stories she has asked me to read."

Laura thought about that for a moment. "Perhaps you will show me a barrister story?"

But now a phone rang inside the house. The servant girl jumped up and went back inside to answer it. There was a brief conversation of some sort; Laura tried to hear what was said, but could not.

And then the servant girl came back outside.

"You must leave," she said nicely, but quite firmly.

"Was that your employer? Perhaps I could have a word with her?"

"No, that wasn't her."

"Oh," said Laura. "Who was it then?"

The servant girl gave Laura a startled look, and then clammed up tight.

"Of course," said Laura. "Rude of me to pry, and right for you to not reveal identities without permission. But perhaps just a hint as to the general category . . . Was it a friend calling? A relative?"

The girl said nothing; she looked back at Laura with deer-caught-in-headlamps eyes and lips pressed so tightly together Laura was almost afraid she'd hurt herself.

"Business acquaintance? Professional services? Gardener?"

Now there was a response.

"I do the roses myself!" said the servant girl, with some pride.

"Ahh," said Laura. That was just a bit comforting to know. Darla Rennie wasn't perfect.

"Under her direction," added the girl.

"Oh," said Laura, and then she wished she hadn't, because that slight note of disappointment seemed to give the girl her courage back.

"You must leave now," said the servant girl.

"Is someone returning? Perhaps I should just stay, and we'll all have a nice chat?"

The servant girl went do the front door, opened it, and looked at Laura with an attitude of desperate determination.

"Please. It will mean my job. You must leave!"

18

Nigel returned to chambers before Laura. It was early afternoon. That she had not returned first surprised him a little. It worried him a little, too, though he wasn't quite sure why.

Nigel pulled one of the smaller guest chairs up close to the desk, sat down, and stared at the edition of the *Daily Sun* that Laura had left unfolded there. It was still opened to the photo of the solicitor sliding her shining legs out of the Black Cab.

When he had seen the photo earlier, he had allowed himself to believe he might be imagining things. But that was before he had gone to the cab drivers meeting and seen Trimball, the man making the techno-pitch. Nigel remembered now where he had seen the man before. And given who Trimball was, Nigel no longer had much doubt who the solicitor with the lovely legs was. It just couldn't be a coincidence.

He would have to tell Laura and Reggie. But he wasn't looking forward to it.

Now the chambers door opened. Nigel looked up as Lois held the door open for Laura.

"It's . . . it is as I feared," said Nigel, without any preliminaries, or any remark about the large, apparently full, brown paper grocery bag Laura was carrying.

"What is?" said Laura. She put the bag down by the side of the chambers desk and nodded her thanks to Lois, who exited, closing the door behind her.

Laura sat down, again in Reggie's barrister chair. She looked at the photo Nigel was staring at. "Dare I ask?" she said.

Nigel hesitated, but then he got a reprieve—the door opened again.

"There you are," said Laura. "I was beginning to wonder."

It was Reggie.

Without being caught doing it at all, Laura quickly appraised Reggie's condition and concluded that other than some slight bags under the eyes, he looked none the worse for wear from his brief stay in jail.

He had clearly taken the time to put himself back together quite immaculately after getting out. He looked like a junior barrister at first appearance in court. Or just a bit older than that, but taller and with a nicer suit than most.

Reggie stood in the doorway, exchanged nods with Nigel, and then focused on Laura, sitting there in his chair. She was bright and inviting, she was looking right back at him, and for a moment Reggie forgot why he was angry with her.

Then he remembered, and he quite deliberately put on a sterner face.

"I thought I was clear about my bail."

"In what respect?" said Laura, innocently.

"That I did not want your friend Buxton—"

"Fiancé."

Laura regretted it the moment she said it. She wasn't even sure why she had said it. It wasn't even quite formally true yet.

Reggie heard it, comprehended it, and did his best to ignore it.

"Whatever. That I did not want him to have a hand in it."

"I mean probable fiancé, anyway, and, yes, I suppose you did indicate a preference for sulking in jail. But he's not the Godfather, Reggie, and you are not indebted to him for life. If you will refrain from absconding to one of those tropical places that have lots of Polynesian beauties but few extradition treaties, then he will get his money back, and that will be the end of it."

Reggie decided, wisely, not to mention that it was not himself feeling indebted that he was worried about.

But then he said something quite similar anyway.

"I'll remember that if you will," he said.

Laura gave Reggie a quizzical look on that remark, and then decided to drop the issue entirely. Instead, she said, "Your brother thinks there is something very important about your solicitor's legs."

Reggie thought that one over and chose the safest response possible. He just nodded slightly, mumbled "I see," and sat in the other client chair.

"The solicitor's legs in the photo," said Nigel, quite tentatively. "In the *Daily Sun* pic." He picked the paper up and showed it to Reggie. "I believe you've seen them? I mean, it? I mean the photo of them?"

"What of them?" said Reggie.

"Yes," said Laura, with just a bit of exasperation, looking from one brother to the other. "What of them?"

"I remember now where I've seen them before," said Nigel.

"The pic didn't even show her face," said Reggie. "You're saying you can recognize her just from her legs?"

"Yes," said Laura. "Apparently your brother has that faculty."

Nigel nodded, obviously taking some pride in it.

Reggie shrugged, indicating that it was no big deal. "I do as well," he said.

Laura looked at him.

"I do," said Reggie. "For example, do you know that behind your left knee—"

Laura waved that comment away. "You needn't try to impress me," she said. "I just want to know where Nigel met our so-called solicitor."

"At Bath a couple of months ago," said Nigel. "She was in my group at the Mental Health and Recovery Center. After I had my—you know—."

"Obligatory lawyer's stress leave?" offered Laura.

"Yes," said Nigel. "They funnel you into specialized groups that are specific to one's own particular . . ."

"Disorder?" said Reggie.

"Thanks for that; yes, one's own particular disorder. Or areas of challenge, as we liked to call them. My group was centered on careers, of course. Career-disappointment trauma is what the therapist called it. "Job Sobs" was the term the staff used. It was an exploration into the reasons why I—why all the members of the group—were such miserable failures in our chosen professions. Or as my group leader liked to put it, just couldn't seem to find our bliss."

"I've heard that phrase; it's all the rage in Hollywood just now," said Laura. "I think it's quite overrated."

"Point is, among all the heart surgeons who could not stand the sight of blood, and ballerinas with inner-ear problems, and timid rugby captains, there was one—and only one—failed Black Cab driver. She had great legs, a genius IQ—and was a sort of instant savant. Other people in the group would talk about their areas of expertise and she would respond as though she knew the subject matter better than they did. She talked about the coronary-bypass techniques with the cardiologist. She talked about data packets and throughput with the techno geek."

"And about briefs and motions with you?" asked Laura.

"Well, yes," said Nigel. "And I had the impression that whether it was from prior knowledge or some odd sort of mental osmosis, she could have gone out and performed a transplant, and filed a successful motion, and created a high-end software program all in the same day. But the point is, with all this brain-power, what she really wanted to do was drive a Black Cab. But it had turned out that she simply had no sense of direction what-soever, and as a result she had failed the Knowledge exam so miserably and repeatedly that she was advised to just give it up altogether."

"No one else ever failed at the Knowledge before?" said Reggie.

"Many, I'm sure, but no one else was in therapy for it at the time I was there."

"So," Laura asked, "just what was the form of therapy where you memorized her legs?"

"Well . . . there were group swim sessions . . . they did have a pool."

"You couldn't get *that* good a look in a pool," said Laura. She looked from one brother to the other again. "Could you?"

Nigel squirmed. "Well, no, there was more to it than that. Not as much as there might have been. I mean . . . well, I was actually just about to get to that—"

"Don't stop on our account," said Laura.

"We struck up a friendship. Not allowed, actually; they have rules. But we set up a rendezvous, the last night before I was scheduled to be discharged. She was to meet me at one hour past curfew that evening."

"And did she?"

"Meet me? Oh yes. She certainly did. She was a few minutes late, having got lost on the way apparently, but she did show up, and when she did, she seemed—if I may say so—quite eager about the whole thing, too."

"Oh," said Laura. "*She* was the eager one."

"Yes," insisted Nigel. "Surprisingly so. I mean, much more so than when we had made the initial appointment. It was as though she had spent the last several hours working herself into a state of high—" Nigel paused, searching for the right word.

"Yes?" said Laura. "High what?"

"Well . . . randiness, I suppose. Or at least anticipation. I could hardly believe my good fortune. But then—"

"Yes?" said Laura.

"Well, we were just getting started, and I had begun, as I said to take careful note of her legs . . . and such . . . progressively. When suddenly she began talking."

Laura shook her head slightly, in a way that indicated just how hopeless both the Heath brothers, and perhaps all men, were.

"I don't mean just that she was talking," said Nigel, alertly. "But so rapidly, and what she was saying."

"Nigel," said Laura. "If you are now going to claim that your touch made a woman speak in tongues, I'm leaving the room."

"She talked about her great-great-grandfather. On her mother's side. The American-Irish side of the family, it turns out. And how he met a mysterious death in Switzerland."

"Mysterious in what way?"

"She didn't say exactly, but she said it couldn't have happened the way everyone believed, because he was terribly afraid of heights and would never have been caught dead—so to speak—on a cliff, no matter how spectacular the view of the falls."

"Her great-great-grandfather died at a waterfall?"

"According to some reports, or so she said. But she was certain—vehemently so—that he was in fact killed, murdered, at a train station in Meiringen, and that she knew who did it, and that she would someday prove it."

"That she would someday prove who murdered her great-great-grandfather."

"Yes. And get her revenge. She was quite adamant about that. And it was at this point that I started to think twice about following through, despite how wonderful her—"

"Must we go there?" said Laura.

"Well, I didn't, finally, because she was truly railing on quite a bit. I kept waiting for her to jump up and say 'Fooled you!' and that it was all a sort of odd joke, and when she didn't, I decided to call it an evening."

"Wise move," said Laura. "So this woman with whom you did not engage in a midnight tryst—was her name Darla Rennie?"

"I don't know," said Nigel. "People didn't use their real names in the group. But I can tell you the name of the American-Irish great-great-grandfather on her mother's side. Or at least what she said it was."

"And that name is?" said Laura.

"Moriarty."

Laura and Reggie both stared at Nigel. He looked back, from one to the other.

"Well, it's what she said."

"Please," said Reggie. "Moriarty? A waterfall in Switzerland?"

"I've no idea about the waterfall thing," said Nigel. "But the name itself is not a stretch. Do you know how many Moriartys there were in 1890 in America alone, not even counting the UK?"

"No."

"Thousands. I looked it up. More than a hundred with first name of James. And Switzerland was a popular tourist destination for Americans who could afford it then, as it is now."

Reggie thought all that through for a short moment, and then he said, just a little irked, "You might have mentioned the patient's delusions when you warned me about the Moriarty threat letter."

"I would have done," said Nigel, "if you had mentioned that you were working with a solicitor who looked like this." Nigel held up the *Daily Sun* photo.

"Yes," said Laura. "Reggie was keeping rather quiet about her appearance. But what of her actual occupation? Was this woman in your group in fact a solicitor before she failed at cab driving?"

"She never said. Most of us were required to do so—that was the whole point, of course, of the group—but when it came her turn, Dr. Dillane, our therapist, said that she did not have to. The fellow rather played favorites, if you ask me."

"I've heard of a Dr. Dillane," said Laura. "'Prescriber to the Stars,' by reputation, at least in the circles that do that kind of thing. For those who just can't seem to find their bliss in the natural sort of way. But there was a bit of an overdose scandal."

"Probably someone else," said Nigel. "This Dr. Dillane seemed inclined toward less medication."

"And what happened after that night at Bath?" said Laura. "Did you see her again? Or did you just manage to run away and never ring her?"

"The next day, back at therapy, she seemed quite herself again," said Nigel. "Completely back to normal. Or at least back to usual. She said nothing of what had transpired the night before, and neither did I, but I happened to hear two of the nurses talking later that day, and . . . it seems that for the past two days before our rendezvous, she had stopped taking her meds. On doctor's orders apparently. I never saw her again after that. She was discharged, and so was I a day later. In fact, our entire Job Sobs therapy group was disbanded at that point, and I'm pretty sure the other members were discharged within days as well. Which brings me to the odd part."

"Good," said Laura. "I was hoping."

"I just came from a big meeting about this new high-tech navigation system that's supposed to revolutionize the job of driving a cab. The inventor was there on stage presenting it, a fellow named Trimball, and—" Nigel stopped again.

"Yes?"

"I could be wrong, but . . . I could swear he also was in my same therapy group at Bath."

"He was in Job Sobs? With you and Ms. Legs?" said Laura.

"Yes."

"Well, that's an interesting coincidence."

"Yes," said Nigel. "And I don't believe in coincidences."

"Neither do I," said Reggie. "But legs notwithstanding, I think we need a little more certainty that it was in fact Darla Rennie in your therapy group."

"Right," said Nigel. "And I know what we need to do to find out."

"Which is?" said Laura.

"Reggie needs to go to the Mental Health and Recovery Center at Bath," said Nigel.

"Excuse me?" said Reggie.

"One of us has to, and I don't intend to go back there any time soon. They're much too welcoming. I have a feeling they might think I still belong."

"Understood," said Reggie. "But it's a three-hour drive. Why don't you just give them a ring, keep your distance, and—"

"I did try that, actually, but I couldn't get through all the recorded options. And they are very tight-mouthed in the front office; you can't just ring them up and have a chat. I can't go myself in any event. I'm going to talk to this cab driver—sort of the senior statesman of cab drivers, as near as I can tell—who's hinting that he knows something about your client."

"Then the one to go see him is me," said Reggie.

"You aren't a popular figure where he takes his beer," said Nigel. "Most of them still believe what they read in the papers, which is that you murdered one of their own. Also, they seem to respect a good snooker game, and mine is better."

"Ha!"

"All right then," said Laura. She stood from behind the desk, and addressed them both like a couple of schoolboys. "There are only three of us, and we've only got so much time, so let's not sacrifice our chickens out of order. Nigel will go to the hearing and then interview this Yoda-of-Black-Cab-drivers person. Reggie will take a lovely drive into the country to see what the therapy center has to say about Darla Rennie. But first he and I have to take care of something else."

Nigel looked at Reggie, and then at Laura.

"So I can go," said Nigel, "but Reggie has to stay after?"

"Yes," said Laura.

"Right, then," said Nigel. He got up from his chair and went to the door, but on the way out, he leaned over to Reggie. "You're in it now. Whatever you do, don't mention Darla Rennie's legs again."

19

After Nigel exited, Reggie and Laura both remained seated in the chambers.

Reggie was watching her, and waiting, in quiet suspense. He liked how the pale glow of her face was framed and contrasted by the dark sienna color of the chair, and how the exertions of the previous conversation had caused the top edge of her blouse to dip slightly past the freckle line on one side, exposing just a bit more unfreckled skin than she intended—probably—at the moment.

That was just making the suspense harder to bear; he was certain that he was about to hear Laura declare something official about herself and Buxton. He didn't want to hear it, but there was nowhere to run.

But then, instead of taking a deep breath and starting out that she didn't know quite how to say this, she reached down behind the desk and picked up—with some effort, because the thing was stuffed—the large paper shopping bag.

She plunked it on the desk, and then, with a glance at Reggie that said he should have been helping her, she turned it over and emptied its contents—several dozen copies of the *Daily Sun,* the *Globe,* the *Mirror,* and assorted other daily tabloids—onto the broad mahogany desk

"What's all this?" said Reggie, standing, finally.

"I've learned that your solicitor seemed to be paying a great deal of attention to something in the tabloids," said Laura.

"Interesting," said Reggie. "When she first came to my office, she claimed not to follow them at all."

"I'm sure she made many claims."

Reggie offered no response to that. He leaned forward on the desk, looking at the newspapers.

"What specifically was she interested in?" he said.

"Black Cabs mostly, according to the servant girl."

"She might have been just following them to see what they said about the case we were handling."

"That would have been only about three days' worth. What she had stacked up in the garden went back much further than that."

"So the idea is to sort through the papers and see just what it was that interested her about the Black Cabs?"

"Yes."

"Where did you get all these, anyway?"

"From my aunt's laundry room."

"Your aunt stacks old tabloids in the laundry room?"

"Yes, why?"

"Just concerned. Next step after that is to keep fifty cats in the parlor, isn't it?"

"She has no cats."

"This is your aunt we're talking about, isn't it? Not just someone related to her?"

"My aunt, not me, and she happens to be a recycler. So let's just focus, shall we?"

"Fair enough."

"We'll stack the hits right here—anything about the Black Cabs, from the oldest to the most recent."

They began leafing through each newspaper in turn, scanning the articles and setting aside anything mentioning the Black Cabs.

After several minutes of sorting, Reggie began to move the *Daily Sun* editions—Buxton's paper—into a separate stack. Laura looked up at that, but said nothing.

Within half an hour, they had all the papers sorted.

The stack of *Daily Sun* papers that Reggie had assembled was as large as that of all the other tabloids combined.

Laura noticed.

"All right," said Laura. "I suppose you'll tell me what you think that means?"

Reggie did indeed have a theory, and he had already decided not to mention it. He had said something disparaging to Laura about Buxton once before, and the next thing Reggie knew, she was jetting off to a South Seas island to be in one of the man's movies. There had probably been no connection between his remark and her trip, but Reggie was not taking chances.

"Just sorting them, is all. Need to get them organized, do we not?"

"But there appear to be far more Black Cab crime stories in the *Daily Sun*," said Laura. "That's why you're stacking them separately, isn't it?"

"I'd say by two to one. Perhaps a bit odd, given the number of crimes available to be reported on is the same for all the papers."

"Well," said Laura, "perhaps we should compare what they actually say before we jump to any conclusions?"

"I agree," said Reggie.

"I'll read the *Daily Sun*," said Laura, "and you do the others. Here's the first; it goes back a few weeks: 'Black Cab Bully Bludgeons Broker.' It's on page two of the *Daily Sun*. What about the others?"

"Page five, or later," said Reggie.

"A few days ago there was 'Taxi Drivers a Terror to Tourists?'" said Laura. "Page four, a sort of summary of Black Cab crimes."

"None of the others have anything like it," said Reggie, a bit conclusively.

Laura looked up at him. Reggie realized he was beginning to lapse into the tone that he used when proving a case in court. He knew that wouldn't do.

"Let's look at the actual murder story," said Laura, eyeing him warily. She read it aloud. "'American Couple Killed: Cabbie Caught.' Page one, of course, but I'm sure the others put it there as well, didn't they?"

Reggie picked up the other papers to compare. "Yes," he said at first. Then he stopped and looked over at Laura.

"What is it?" said Laura.

"What's the date on the *Daily Sun* story?"

"The twenty-sixth."

Reggie put each of the other papers down on the table for Laura to see.

"All of the others are on the twenty-seventh," said Reggie. "A full day later, which is what you'd expect, given when the police report came in. But the *Daily Sun* story is barely six hours after the body was discovered."

Laura considered it. "Couldn't that just mean their news deadline is later in the day?"

"Not that much later. All of these papers are morning editions, with similar deadlines. For the *Daily Sun* to have picked this up before all the others, they had to have had a tip. They had to have been on the scene almost as soon as the police to get anything into that day's edition."

"A tip from the police?"

Reggie thought about it. "I doubt it. It's Wembley's investigation. He does what he is obliged to do for the press, but he doesn't cut them any favors, and he'd lop off the head of anyone on his staff who does otherwise. So the *Daily Sun* has a source the others do not, and I don't think it's the police."

Reggie stood. He could restrain himself no longer.

"I'm going to have a word with him."

"With who?"

"Your fiancé."

"Prospective, and you'll do no such thing."

"Laura, if he has inside knowledge of what has been happening with these Black Cab crimes, then someone's got to—"

Now Laura stood.

"Yes, someone does, and it will be me."

"No," said Reggie. "I'm the one who's facing jail, and I'm the one who's got the most to—"

"Yes? The most to just what, exactly? Reggie, you can't control yourself. If you go there, one of you will end up in a big geranium pot and the other will be off to jail. You aren't being rational about this."

"Of course I'm being rational about it."

"Really? Then how did you miss this?"

She slapped each of the *Daily Sun* editions down in front of him, pointing to the byline of each in turn. "There. There. And there."

Reggie stared. She had a point. Each story in the *Daily Sun* was by the same reporter. Emma Swoop. The same one who had done the story about Reggie's trip to Los Angeles, and the same one who had shown up so early at the crime scene at Lots Road.

Reggie realized he had done it again. He had been so annoyed with Laura's relationship with Buxton that he had made assumptions and was ignoring the more obvious connection.

Probably the reporter was the contact point. Perhaps it might be Buxton himself. It was impossible to know that—yet. What he did know was that he did not want this confrontation at this time with Laura.

"You're right," he said.

"Am I, then?" said Laura.

And then she stopped. She wasn't quite sure what to say next. Reggie had agreed much too quickly.

"Quite," said Reggie, picking up his mac. "I'll have a word with Ms. Swoop before I take my drive in the country."

And with that, he left the chambers.

Laura, still at the desk, watched the door close behind him.

That conversation hadn't gone at all as expected.

Perhaps there was something to this alpha-male thing after all. That was worrisome.

But worry wasn't productive. She sat back down. She started looking through the papers again, reading all the accounts of the Black Cab crimes, each in turn, from first to last.

Then she repeated the process, but this time comparing not the accounts of the crime itself, but the coverage of the hearings.

When she had finished doing that, she remained seated for several moments, staring at the stacks of the *Daily Sun*.

Then she got up, left the chambers, exited the Baker Street building, and caught a cab for Wapping.

20

Reggie entered a small pub on Fenchurch Street, looking for Emma Swoop.

He had called her as he left Baker Street Chambers, using the number from the TELL EMMA SWOOP hotline that had been appearing in adverts on pretty much every double-decker in London in recent months.

The number went to a calling service, of course, but he was put through immediately when he gave his name, and then Emma herself picked up the line, quite pleasantly. And eagerly—like a young and energetic spider with a fly tripping on its web.

This pub was her suggestion—a location far enough from both Wapping and Fleet Street that they could meet without necessarily every other reporter in the city knowing about it. She always protected her sources, she said, and for the moment Reggie had allowed her to believe that he was about to become one and that they would be talking about him and what he knew, rather than—so far as he was concerned—the other way around.

And besides, she said, she had skipped breakfast, was starving for it, and this pub served it late into the day.

Reggie found her in a back booth.

She smiled broadly and pushed aside an empty plate as Reggie approached. He caught the scent of bangers and stewed tomatoes.

"Very nice to see you again, Mr. Heath."

Reggie paused, still standing, and looked about. "No photographer this time, I trust?"

"Of course not."

He sat down opposite her in the booth.

"I have a letter I'd like to show you," said Reggie. "And then I have a question to ask."

"I have some questions as well," she said.

"No promises regarding that," said Reggie, "but in return for answering my question, I'll show you a letter."

"The letter first, then," she said.

Reggie took the tip letter—the one written to Sherlock Holmes—out of the pocket of his mac and put it on the table in front of Emma Swoop. Then he sat back to watch her reaction.

She began reading. Her eyes widened, and she read it again from the beginning.

Then she put her hand to her mouth, as if to stifle a laugh. She looked up at Reggie with amusement.

"You make my job much too easy. So now you're actually getting tip letters people write to Sherlock Holmes? And about your own cases?"

She took out a pen and began to scribble a note for herself.

"Not necessarily," said Reggie. "Perhaps just a tip letter from someone who knows that if she sends it to Sherlock Holmes, I will receive it."

Emma stopped scribbling.

"She?"

"A guess."

"Fine, I'll take your word for it. Anyone specific in mind?"

Reggie gave her the straight-on look he used for grilling a hostile witness.

"Did you write it?"

She laughed.

"Why on earth would you think I wrote it?"

"Three reasons. First is that you have an interest in stirring things up."

"Nonsense. People do gobs of stupid things all on their own—you included. I find it quite unnecessary to encourage anyone."

"Second reason is that you know my chambers address receives letters sent to Sherlock Holmes."

"Tons of people know that."

"Yes, because you told them all in the *Daily Sun*."

"Right, it's my job. So what? Point still is, tons of people know."

"Third reason is that your stories in the *Daily Sun* show more knowledge of the crime than anyone else's. And you made deadlines the other papers missed."

"Thank you. I do try."

"It almost seems you've had knowledge of the crimes before they occur."

She gave a derisive laugh at that.

"It might seem. But I haven't though, have I? I'd have a duty to report it if I had. But I only learn about them after. It's a big difference, knowing after and knowing before."

"But to know so soon after, you must have an informant."

She shrugged.

"Who is it?" said Reggie.

"I'm not saying I've got an informant, but if I have, I've no obligation to reveal him, her, or it."

Reggie shifted fully into his barrister mode.

"This has got nothing to do with your bloody rights as a member of the bloody press. This is not a corporate whistle-blower or a government informant exposing what needs to be to the light of day. This has to do with murder and you wanting to scoop the competition and make a reputation."

She bridled at that, and Reggie could see her searching for a defense.

"I take it you have a problem with ambitious women?"

"No," said Reggie, "I do not." But he decided to throttle it back a bit; he would get nothing if all he did was make her angry.

"I imagine you get fan mail," he said.

She hesitated.

"I do," she said after a moment.

"Fans who are so enthused about you that their life's ambition is to send you something that shows up in a story with your byline?"

"Occasionally. It's no secret; I'm sure you've seen my advert."

"Fan mail about your Black Cab series?"

She sat back in the booth and was silent for just a moment. Reggie knew he was guessing near the mark.

"All right," she said. "A little over two months ago I saw in the police blotter that a woman was drugged and fondled in the back of a Black Cab—by the driver. I thought it was a hot story, and I wrote it up right. A week after that story came out, I got a letter saying how wonderful it was and to keep up the good work, that the Black Cabs are overrated and an actual menace, and offering to help in any way possible. Which was a bit weird, but only a bit, compared to other stuff I get. And I thought that was all there was to that.

"But a few days after that fan letter I got an anonymous call, saying the police are on a robbery involving a Black Cab at Piccadilly. I got there straightaway, and sure enough, there has been a robbery, the police are there, and the victim is saying that the perpetrator was a Black Cab driver. I was the only reporter on the scene; I got good stuff that didn't get broadcast over the police radio, and so I had the best story and the *Daily Sun* gave it plenty of space the next day."

"Did you bother to wonder at all about the tip you received?"

"Not a bit. It could have been anyone at the scene: one of the local shopkeepers; bystanders in the street; someone passing by in a double-decker."

"But then it happened again after that, didn't it?"

"Yes."

"And then, again," said Reggie. "The murder on Lots Road in Chelsea. Another lucky tip from a bystander?"

"People read the paper. They know who to call when they see something happening. Nothing unusual about that."

"It was a different person that called each time, then?"

The reporter hesitated, shifting uneasily. If it was the same person, she won't want to admit it, thought Reggie. She probably hadn't even admitted it to herself yet. It was one thing to have a Deep Throat contact embedded in a political scandal. It was quite another if the contact was a participant in bloody street crimes.

"As I said, the calls were anonymous," Emma offered, sounding defensive.

"But was it the same voice each time?" said Reggie.

"What if it was? It could have been a bloody cop calling for all I knew. They leak things. They have their reasons."

"Not on Wembley's team," said Reggie. "So—was it the same voice each time?"

"I don't know. What bloody difference does it make?"

"The fan letter was the first step in encouraging you to give the Black Cab crimes a high level of coverage," said Reggie. "All the anonymous tips that followed were to make sure that you kept doing so, and they're all coming just a bit too early."

"What are you accusing me of? You seriously think both the fan letter and the anonymous tips were from someone involved in the crime?"

"Yes. Exactly that. And it's tit-for-tat: You receive the tips because your publisher gives the Black Cab crimes maximum coverage. I don't know why someone wants to do that, but I know it's what's happening."

"I don't know that at all," said Emma.

"All right, then. Here's the other piece of information I have for you. You can confirm it with Wembley later, if you like; I spoke to him a few hours ago when I got out."

Emma interrupted so eagerly that Reggie thought she must surely have a recorder running in her purse. "How did it feel being on the other side of the law—being in jail for the first time? This *was* your first time, right?"

"Nice try," said Reggie. "As I was saying, Wembley's forensics team has determined that the most recent Black Cab victim—the one that was thrown over the bridge—was not killed by brute force, as were the American couple. It was a gunshot, a single gunshot to the back of the head. Which makes my dead client not a good suspect at all. And although the clothes of the victim would indicate stockbroker or financial analyst or some other wealthy punter, his hands were as calloused as a dockworker's, and there is every indication that he was dressed in his expensive suit *after* he was killed."

"That's absurd," said Emma. "Why would anyone even try

to create a frame that would so surely be disproved by forensics?"

"Obviously no one would," said Reggie. "It's not a frame for a conviction, it's not a frame done for the consumption of the police or the legal system at all because, as you said, they would surely discover it, as they have done. So it's a frame for a very short-term goal, and since it's not a frame for the police, the only other possibility is that it's a frame for the press."

Emma looked back at Reggie for a long moment. Then—

"So you're saying I'm being played?" she said.

"I'm saying you can join the club."

She raised an eyebrow at that. Then she sighed and looked again at the letter Reggie had placed on the table.

"You showed me this on the record," she said. "That was the deal. So now I get to tell the world that you got suckered by a tip letter written to Sherlock Holmes?"

"Go ahead. At the moment, it's the least of my worries."

She laughed slightly, and then pushed the letter back at him. "The anonymous calls are from the same person each time—I think. It's hard to be sure; whoever it is speaks through something to muffle his—or her—voice. But sounds the same each time."

"You say the fan letter was two months ago?"

"Yes," she said.

Reggie considered that. It meant the fan letter had probably been sent just before Nigel's therapy group at Bath was disbanded.

"No return address on the letter, I presume?" said Reggie.

"Of course not. "

"A postmark?"

"Yes, I did check for that. The postmark was for Bath."

"Does that location mean anything to you?" asked Reggie.

"Well, it's rather a large area, isn't it?"

"True. Are you familiar with the Mental Health and Recovery Center at Bath?"

"No," she said with a laugh. "Are you looking for a recommendation?"

Reggie ignored that. "Do you know a man named Trimball?"

She paused just for a moment before answering. Then she said, "Heath . . . do you have any idea how many names of people and places I cycle through in a year? I can go back and check my files, but—"

"All right," said Reggie. "'Dr. Dillane'—does that name mean anything?"

"I think I've heard mention from some paparazzi acquaintances. Not sure of the context though. I can give you their names, if you're willing to go near them."

Reggie considered that. He nodded noncommittally. Then he pretended to check his watch. He paid the bill and got out of the booth to leave. "Thank you for your help."

She slid quickly out of the booth as well, clearly sensing a new story.

"You have a postmark and now you're off? It tells you that much?"

"No, not by itself."

"I'll go with you," she said, following along as Reggie went out to the street.

"Not likely. I'm not that foolish," said Reggie. "But if you need a ride, I can drop you before I leave the city."

"Never mind then," she said. "Thanks for showing me the letter. It might be worth a paragraph or two on page six."

"Sorry to disappoint," said Reggie.

Reggie walked around the corner toward his car. As he did, he glanced back over his shoulder and saw the reporter getting into a Black Cab.

Reggie drove out of the city on the M4, checking carefully at first to see that Emma Swoop had not waited to follow him in her cab.

Apparently she had not. But with cabs looking so much alike, it could be hard to tell.

21

At the Flounder and Dab pub, one of the younger drivers at the bar was telling a story to Bill Edwards as Nigel entered.

"She got into the back," said the younger driver, "took her fur coat off, leaned forward with all that bling and cleavage, and whispered through the window that she understood that Black Cab drivers have enlarged hippocampuses. Mine was, I can tell you, and I was ready to hop in the back with her to prove it, until I found out that hippocampuses aren't what I thought they were."

Edwards nodded, managed a perfunctory laugh, then got down from the bar stool and came over to Nigel.

"Someone did a study at Oxford," said Edwards, shaking his head. "And now I have to hear that same story every time I come into the pub. And if I thought he'd really hopped in the back with a fare, I'd boot his arse out of here. It's bad for business, especially when the driver has such a high opinion of himself. Take the booth in the back. I'll tell you a better story, but I don't want every driver in the place to hear it, and we've got just a few minutes before the crowd gathers."

A few moments later Edwards brought two pints. He put them both on the table, settled in opposite Nigel, and took a long draught before getting started.

"You hear all kinds of things," he said. "Half of 'em at least are made up, just variations on urban legends."

"No doubt."

"But a month or so back, I'm at the bar there, and I hear Walters telling a story, and I listen, because I never heard him tell one before. He wasn't causing much of a stir, because there really wasn't all that much to it, and everyone pretty much prefers a cleavage and hippocampus story when they can get one. But he told a story, and he told it again two weeks later, and I listened both times, because it was plain he wasn't telling it for the attention—he was telling it because it worried him."

"And now it's worrying you."

Edwards took a moment to look about the bar, and Nigel looked, too. Several more drivers had come in since Nigel entered, but no one had approached within earshot.

Still, when Edwards turned back toward Nigel, he spoke in a confidential voice.

"The bloody navigation system worries me. It will destroy the Black Cab profession as we know it. And these crimes are being used as a pretext to force it on us. If I can help you solve them, I will."

"So what was the story Walters told?"

"Before I tell you what he did," said Edwards, "you need to understand how it is when a driver first starts out. There's the tuition he owes from the Knowledge School. Payments on the scooter for driving about and learning the streets. Neither of them cheap for young lads just trying to get a leg up. And then there's the cab itself, which is hugely expensive. Walters just didn't have the cash."

"What about his inheritance?"

Edwards gave Nigel a quizzical look. "What inheritance?"

"Walters told my brother there was an inheritance," said Nigel. "He said his dad scrimped and saved it up, he got it when his dad died, and that's how he paid for the Knowledge School and got started."

Edwards shook his head. "Walters was an orphan. He lived in foster care until he was seventeen and then went out on his own. He was in debt to his eyeballs by the time he picked up his first punter."

"You're sure about this?" said Nigel.

Edwards nodded. "I heard it not just from him, but from blokes who knew him."

"Odd thing to lie to his lawyer about," said Nigel. "But go on, what did he do as a result of these financial straits?"

"Mostly, he did the right stuff. He signed up as a radio cab driver. You know how that works. A customer calls the radio dispatcher for a cab, the dispatcher sends the driver, and takes a commission for it. It's great for the customer, and better than nothing for the new driver who hasn't got established at the cab ranks yet. Walters wasn't too thrilled with it at first, because they weren't sending a lot his way. But then he comes in the Flouder and Dab one night and tells me about one particular fare.

"The dispatcher had called and said he had a customer who requested Walters specifically—requested him by his cab number, in fact, and you don't expect your average punter to be that observant. Walters had no idea who the bloke was, but that didn't matter; off he went, clear out to Hackney Downs, in the East End, which isn't normally your center of activity at that hour.

"He drives out there and picks up the fare. Then just being

sociable, he asks the gentleman where he had taken him before. The man said, 'Nowhere.' He said he had made the request just on the recommendation from a friend.

"As you might imagine, this made Walters even more curious, and so he asked the punter who the friend was. You know what the bloke said?"

"No idea."

"'Just shut up and drive,' is what he said."

"And did he?"

"Shut up and drive? Oh, he did. All the way down to Canary Wharf. Then around the perimeter of Isle of Dogs, and then back up to Hackney Downs again. Walters said he knew they had completed a roundabout, and most punters hate it when you take the long way anywhere, and so he asked the gentleman again where he wanted to go. Know what he said?"

"'Shut up and keep driving'?" offered Nigel.

Edwards almost looked offended at Nigel jumping the gun, but then he said, "Right you are."

"And—?"

"You mean, did he keep driving? Well, he almost didn't, I can tell you that. But right then the punter slides a fifty-pound note through the window to cover the mileage to that point, and then another one right after that, which wasn't even called for."

"So Walters kept driving?"

Edwards didn't answer immediately; he was looking past Nigel's shoulder now, into the broader area of the pub, and nodding to someone.

"We've got just a few more minutes," he said.

Nigel looked around, too, and he saw that the pub was now packed with cab drivers. And most of them weren't even drinking; they were milling about, talking loudly, waiting for something.

Edwards nodded again to someone else entering, and then he turned back to Nigel.

"He did keep driving, that same East End route again in the middle of the night, until finally the punter checks his watch, gets out at a corner, makes a phone call at a paybooth, and then tips Walters another fifty quid and says that will be all for the night.

"A week later, the same thing happens. A few days later, same thing again. But this time, the punter says he doesn't have time to ride along, and from that point on, he says he wants Walters to keep doing that same route at those hours on certain days—but all on his own.

"You mean, with an empty cab?"

"Yes. That's when Walters came in and told me his story for the first time. I puzzled over it with him, but we couldn't figure it out."

"Did Walters describe this vanishing punter?" asked Nigel.

"Walters said the fellow mumbled when he spoke and kept his face hidden in a hooded mac. Drivers learn when not to pry. Anyway, we couldn't see any harm being done. So I told him to keep driving."

Nigel nodded. "True, there's no law against getting paid to drive the cab empty. Nothing statutory, anyway. But why did Walters never tell my brother any of this? Surely he would have realized it was relevant to his alibi."

"Can't help you with that one. But there's something else. The day after your brother got Walters released at the magistrate's court, Walters came into the pub and bought rounds for everyone like he had bangers to spare. And I heard him on the phone saying he was going to pay off the loan on his cab the next day."

"And you can't see where he would get the money to do that?"

"Right. It would take just too much to do it all at once. And that's when I began to worry. And I realized that all these mystery rides were happening at about the same time as the Black Cab crimes across town. I made a list, and all the dates match up. I think it means something."

"It does," said Nigel. "It means one cab is being used to create an alibi, while another cab across town is doing dirty deeds. And if it was all just as you say, it probably also means Walters was guilty of nothing more than being a pawn in a much larger scheme." Nigel paused, then added, "At least up until the point he came into all that cash."

Edwards stood now.

"I've told you all I know," he said. "And we're about to get underway."

"What's the occasion?" said Nigel. Most of the cab drivers were now looking expectantly in Edwards's direction.

"The follow-up meeting for the navigation system is tonight. This time it will be before the full London Transport Authority. And just to make sure they understand that we understand that we have a stake in it, I intend that half the cab drivers in London will be there. So I've got a bit of organizing to do."

"Sounds like fun," said Nigel.

"It won't be if you're anywhere else in the city trying to catch a cab tonight," said Edwards. "And that's the point."

22

Reggie was an hour and a half out of London. It was very late in the afternoon now, but finally he reached the turnout from the M4. Within a few minutes, he was driving in a light rain on the narrow streets of Bath.

A mile or so past the town's Roman ruins, he found Old Bath Road. He turned west, driving another two or three miles on a country lane, until he reached the Mental Health and Recovery Center.

The structures of the center had at one time been a nobleman's estate. The main house, gripped on all sides by green ivy on old dark-red bricks, had been made into the main office for the center: to one side of that were the stables, which had become resident patient quarters; to the other side was a more modern addition, with placards identifying the therapy center and counseling rooms.

Reggie entered the brick structure and walked past the wood panels of the main hall to the reception office. It was fortunately still open, but it had to be near closing hour for the general public.

There was a reception desk, staffed by a middle-aged woman who was busy placing some items in a cardboard shipping box as Reggie entered.

Behind her were cabinets of patient records and a corridor that led to the offices of the psychiatric staff in the back. On the wall to one side of her desk were shelves of consumer brochures for the general public, and on the other side were shelves displaying professional publications.

It did indeed appear near to closing time; the office lobby was empty except for the receptionist. Reggie wouldn't even have to wait in line.

The woman looked up.

"How may I assist you?"

Her manner was professionally pleasant and artificial, in a bureaucratic sort of way. Reggie had a sense that she knew her job, and getting information from her would not be easy.

"I have an acquaintance who was recently a patient here," said Reggie, as offhandedly and routinely as he could. "Her name was Darla Rennie."

"I'm sorry," said the woman, "but I'm not allowed to give out any information about patients, or even to confirm if she was one."

"Yes, you're quite right," said Reggie. "Actually, I was just hoping, though, to get some information about a particular therapy group that she was in. Job Sobs, I believe it was called."

"Ahh," said the woman. "The career disappointment group."

"Yes," said Reggie. "Run by a Dr. Dillane, I believe. I understand about patient confidentiality. But perhaps I could speak with him in a general way about the group?"

"I'm afraid that won't be possible," said the woman. But

now she looked at Reggie appraisingly. "May I ask—is your enquiry in a professional capacity?"

For a moment, Reggie thought she was asking if he were offering his legal services. Then he realized she was referring to the doctor's professional capacity, not his own.

"No," said Reggie quickly. "Nothing like that. I would simply like to talk to him."

"Of course," said the receptionist. "And the woman you mentioned—she referred you to Dr. Dillane?"

"Actually, my brother Nigel gave me his name," said Reggie. "My brother was a patient here, too."

Now the woman nodded and smiled in an understanding way.

"Here's our preevaluation form. If you'd just like to fill this out, paying special attention to the question regarding any hereditary conditions that might—"

"That won't be necessary," said Reggie. "I'm not here for an evaluation. I'm just here because of a letter that came from Dr. Dillane's office."

"Oh. You are here because Dr. Dillane wrote you a letter?"

"Yes," said Reggie, hoping that answer, even if not true, would simplify things.

"Your name?"

"Reggie Heath."

She sat down behind her desk, opened a file on her computer, and did a quick search.

"I'm sorry," she said, "but I handled all of Dr. Dillane's correspondence, and I don't see anything outgoing to a Reggie Heath."

"Well, actually, the letter was sent to Sherlock Holmes," said Reggie, probably because he had not slept well in jail and was not thinking clearly.

There was a pause, while the woman assessed Reggie all over again.

"Sherlock Holmes?"

"That's not important," said Reggie. "What's important is that I speak with Dr. Dillane."

"He is no longer here," said the woman. "Sherlock Holmes, did you say?"

"Can you tell me where he has gone?" said Reggie.

"He was employed here until just recently; that's all I can say."

That meant, of course, that there was much more to it.

"Did he quit, then?" said Reggie. "Or was it a termination?"

"I simply can't say. But let me be sure I understand. You say Dr. Dillane wrote a letter to Sherlock Holmes?"

"Either he or someone in his therapy group did. That's why I need to talk to him."

"I see. And you are here in response to that letter?"

"Yes."

"I see," she said again, quite carefully. "Well, I'm sorry, Mr. . . . . Holmes, is it, then?"

"No, my name is Heath, as I said. Reggie Heath."

"Oh. My mistake. Well, I am indeed sorry that Dr. Dillane is no longer available. However, I'm sure we can find someone else to help with what seems to be bothering you." As she said this, she glanced back over her shoulder at a tweed-coated professional just now exiting at the other end of the office, and she looked as if she were about to run and fetch him.

"I don't think I've explained myself clearly," said Reggie quickly. "Nothing is bothering me."

"No need to feel embarrassed. All of us have something that is bothering us."

"I just need to talk to Dr. Dillane about someone who may

have been his patient. Do you have a number where I can reach the doctor?"

"I'm sorry, he never listed his personal number."

"Of course," said Reggie. "A forwarding address, then?"

"I'm sorry," said the woman. "I simply can't."

But as she said it, Reggie saw her glance fall just briefly to the shipping box that she had been packing. It was difficult to be certain from this angle—the shipping label on the box was facing the woman, not Reggie—but he was almost certain that the addressee's name was Dillane.

"Are these Dr. Dillane's items?" said Reggie. "That you're packing up for him now?"

The receptionist immediately pulled the box back from within Reggie's reach. Then she sat down behind the desk, planted her elbows there firmly, and clasped her hands together.

"Now please, Mr. Heath," she said, in her most officious manner, "you just tell me what is bothering you, and I promise, we'll find someone who can help."

"Very well," said Reggie. "What is bothering me is that the woman I love is about to marry another man, my legal career hangs by a thread, I spent most of the past twenty-four hours in jail, and I run a distinct risk of going back there again for a very long time. All of which—or at least most of which—I think I can begin to remedy, if I can just talk with Dr. Dillane."

Reggie paused. The receptionist was unmoved. Desperate measures were called for.

"Or," Reggie added, "some equally qualified psychiatric professional."

The woman smiled and stood. "Now we're getting some-where. You just wait right here," she said kindly, "and I'll find someone for you who's every bit as good as Dr. Dillane." She turned and moved off, in the direction of the tweed-coated man.

Reggie reached across the reception desk and turned the

shipping box just enough so that he could read the label. Yes, it was in fact for Dr. Dillane.

Reggie made a note of the address.

And then he turned and exited the building as quickly as he could without actually running.

23

Laura arrived at the *Daily Sun* publishing compound by cab. The security staff at the gate recognized her immediately and waved her on through.

As she took the private lift to Buxton's penthouse, she remembered that she had yet to give him an answer. He was being quite patient about it, actually, which was good.

But best to try to avoid that topic for the moment. Better to keep separate issues separate. She was making every effort to do that in her own mind, and until she made it up, she would have to do that in their conversation as well.

She found Buxton in his private office. He jumped up from the desk—he was quite nimble for a man of his size, and liked to prove it—and came toward her as soon as she opened the door.

He looked like a child on Christmas morning. She would have to be careful. He kissed her, and she returned it, but only as much as was necessary.

"This is not a social call," she said. She said it with a smile, as if half joking. She could ease into it that way.

"It isn't?" he was returning the half smile. That was good.

"No," she said. "I am here as a loyal *Daily Sun* reader with a complaint."

"We have a department for that."

"I don't deal with departments. I came straight to the top."

"Right, then," said Buxton. He went around behind his desk and sat down with his hands clasped together, in a pretense of receiving a very ordinary business appointment.

"What's the issue?"

Sometimes she liked him. That felt like a problem at the moment.

"It's these," she said. She plunked down half a dozen different editions of the *Daily Sun* on his desk. "There's a pattern in them, and it disturbs me."

"Now, I don't write the stories, Laura, you know that," said Buxton, shuffling through them to see what she was concerned about.

"You publish them."

"Five dailies on three continents. I can't read them all. What pattern is it that worries you?"

She rearranged the papers to show him where to start.

"This one was the the killing in Chelsea a few days ago. The two American tourists. Page one, and you managed to scoop all the other tabs."

"We do try," said Buxton.

"Yes," said Laura. "And the week before you had this one—a robbery in the financial district, not so glamorous as a murder, but newsworthy, I suppose, in that it was a driver of a Black Cab said to have done it."

"Yes," said Buxton. "Quite right."

"So much so that you threw in two pics where all the other papers had just one, and you devoted twice as much space to it."

"It was a good story, Laura."

"And here are three more, going back even further. In each of them, you've given them much higher play than any of the other press."

"Laura, I don't understand. Why are you being so hyper-sensitive about a few stories on the Black Cabs?"

"I'm not being hypersensitive at all," she responded, a bit defensively. "I just think it's odd. And—"

"This is about Heath, isn't it?"

"It's got nothing to do with Reggie."

"It's this one, isn't it?" said Buxton, holding up one of the front-page stories that blasted Reggie for getting the driver released. "I'll have a word with the editor about the 'Balmy Barrister' stuff, if you like. I don't kick a man when he is down. I mean, not repeatedly. At least not for personal reasons."

Laura considered that, then said, "I thought the 'Balmy Barrister' headline was rather clever, actually, possibly not even far from the truth. But Reggie can take care of himself, and it's certainly up to you whether you want to risk another shrub-bery. What concerns me is the sensational coverage—even for a tabloid—you've given all the Black Cab crimes. And in some of these, you not only gave them more play, but you seem to have scooped the competition, either on the timing, or on the lurid details, or both."

"Well, my journalists are very thorough, if they want to keep their jobs. Some evidence clerks can be bribed. That's Scotland Yard's lookout, if they can't keep their own staff on the straight and narrow."

"It's one thing to dig deep and be hard-hitting. It's another thing to go on a vendetta."

"Laura, what are you saying? That I have something personal against Black Cabs?"

"I'm saying that you are being used."

Buxton laughed. "That would be a first," he said.

"Someone is providing your reporter with inside information on each of the crimes, and the *Daily Sun* is in return giving the stories extraspectacular coverage."

Buxton wasn't laughing now. "Why would anyone do that?" he said.

"I don't know. To make everyone afraid to take a Black Cab? That seems to be what's happening."

"And what possible motivation would anyone have for doing that?"

"I don't know. But if that is the intent, aren't you concerned that with the way you're playing the stories, you are assisting them?"

Buxton sat back a bit on that remark. But then he recovered, leaned over, and patted Laura on the knee.

"I've been in this business many years, my dear. I know how it works, and I know what boundaries I can push. Your concern is noted, but I think you can safely leave the management of my newspapers to me. Now—while you were on your way up, I had a word with the chef at Club Gascon, and he's sending over an early dinner."

There are knee pats, and then there are knee pats. Laura was familiar with pats, squeezes, and caresses of all varieties. And this variety of pat, with the remarks that accompanied it, was the wrong one at the wrong time.

"Actually, I was thinking not so much dinner as a bit of shopping. I think Harrods is still open."

Buxton's look in response said that he knew full well how much Laura enjoyed the evening meal and how little regard she had for shopping as a pastime. He knew the tone of trouble when he heard it.

"Of course," he said. "I'm sure the filet mignon is reheat-able."

Laura almost sighed at that, because she knew it was not. But she held the sigh in and said nothing.

Instead, Buxton sighed.

"You can take my limo, if you like," he said. "But I'll call a Black Cab if you prefer."

"I'll take a cab," said Laura.

She turned and started for the door, but then she paused and looked back at him.

"Robert . . . when Reggie first came back from Los Angeles a few weeks ago, who was it that had the idea to do a story that told the world about his financial difficulties and those embar-rassing Sherlock Holmes letters. . . . Was it Emma Swoop all on her own? Or was it you who put her up to it?"

Buxton looked at Laura and then away for a moment, and then, after gathering all the courage he could, back at Laura again.

He said, "I can't recall."

Laura gave that response the look it deserved, and then she went out the door.

Moments later, riding in the back of a Black Cab that had appeared quite promptly at the Buxton Enterprises gate, Laura concentrated on the workings of her mobile phone and tried to ignore the center rearview mirror, which kept show-ing the driver's eyes shifting over to get a better look at her. These days it was getting difficult to tell sexual ogling from celebrity ogling—at least on first glance—and she was getting tired of it, regardless of whether it was one or the other, or a hybrid.

"Aren't all you Knowledge Boys supposed to be professional enough to keep your eyes on the road?" she said.

"Sorry, ma'am. Miss. Ms. Sorry."

She laughed at that, and finally got the phone to connect and ring Reggie's mobile. But there was no answer.

She closed the phone, and the cab driver, who had in fact not stopped watching her in the mirror, said, "Just surprised, is all. Would have thought you'd be taking a limo. Glad to have you though."

Laura smiled and nodded politely. Then she pressed the lever to turn off the driver-passenger intercom, and for the remainder of the trip she tried to ignore that the driver continued glimpsing her in the rearview mirror.

Twenty minutes later, she got out of the cab on Baker Street and took the lift up to Reggie's chambers.

"I just want to check something, it will only take a moment," she said to Lois, and then she went directly into Reggie's office. She closed the door behind her and took a moment to look about.

There were three combination locks in Reggie's office. There was a lock for the bottom right drawer of the desk. There was another lock for the center top drawer. And yet another one for the separate file cabinet. All of them, she knew, were among the office furniture that Reggie had owned when he first met her.

She went first to the lower right drawer of the desk, the one she and Nigel had been unable to open with her birth date earlier. But this time, instead of entering her birth date, as she and Nigel had done before, she entered the first six digits of her phone number—not her mobile, but the landline number she had given Reggie when they first met.

The drawer opened, sliding easily, with the silence of a well-made piece of furniture being treated properly.

She pushed it back closed again.

She went to the file cabinet and entered her digits again. It opened. She pushed it back closed.

And then she did the process on the center top drawer as well. The drawer slid open as if it had just been waiting for the opportunity.

Bloody hell. Every lockable item in Reggie's office was programmed with her phone number from when they first met. Why would a man do that?

Now she heard someone rapping on the door.

"Yes?"

The door opened and Lois stepped just inside. She was holding the Moriarty letters and some other slip of paper in her hand.

"The typewriter thing that Nigel asked about?" she said.

"Yes?" said Laura.

"I found it. I mean, I went to the museum, and I found a machine that has characters just like on the letters. It's a very rare model, more than a hundred years old. And I called every typewriter repair shop in the city—well, there are only three, actually—and I found someone who serviced such a machine this year. Should I call Nigel—?"

"Yes, call him," said Laura, taking the address note and the letters from her. "But tell him I've got it covered. And thank you very much."

Laura exited the chambers and went downstairs to the street. The air was beginning to condense a bit, but there was no need for an umbrella yet. She stepped to the Baker Street curb to get a cab.

A cab halfway down the block immediately started up and

came toward her, but another was already in motion in that direction, and it pulled in ahead.

"Thank you," said Laura, getting in. "The Standard Typewriter Repair on Portobello Road. Do you know it?"

"It's all up here, miss," said the driver.

"So they say," she replied.

24

A light rain was getting heavier now, as Reggie turned his Jag onto a narrow country lane, looking for Dr. Dillane's address.

He wanted to get there before the rain became a deluge. Small roads could become impassable in the Cotswolds, and the road back to the M4 looked capable of congealing in both directions. It could prevent him from getting back to London until very late in the evening.

And that would not do. The connection with the psychiatrist might turn out to be nothing at all, and Reggie did not have time to waste on leads that went nowhere.

He was already violating his bail conditions by being out of the city. And he did not want to give Laura any more reasons than she already had to spend the night at Buxton's compound. She might call Reggie at chambers, and he would not be there. Not an issue under normal circumstances. But these were not normal circumstances.

And something felt wrong. Whatever the reason, he was beginning to feel uneasy about being away.

He had driven through a little hamlet, out of the hamlet, and then past scattered farmhouses, and now the road was narrowing even further. More sheep. And more mud, beginning to run in rivulets along the side of the lightly paved road.

Reggie slowed. There was a turnoff to his right. There was no road sign, but his best reading of the map was that this might—or might not—be the direction to Dr. Dillane's house.

Even in the best weather, this turnoff would be nothing more than a farmer's dirt road. Reggie came to a stop for a better look, with rain beginning to come down in sheets now against the windshield.

He could see that the terrain was beginning to change. The flat, green, sheep-dotted fields were giving way to gentle slopes and valleys and in the far distance, to forested hills.

But between here and there, just a couple of miles out on the road, was a high, long hedgerow. There could well be a structure beyond it.

Reggie took the turn.

This road was even narrower than the lane he had been on, with a steep drainage ditch cut in the earth alongside it. The ditch was flanked by high grasses and an occasional copper beech; the road was unpaved, with infrequent sections of gravel to help things out, but not by much, and the rocky bumps and rain-worn creases tortured the Jag's undercarriage along the way.

Several minutes later, Reggie drove past the hedgerow and crested a hill; he was now above a long valley, and midway down the slope of this valley was a house.

Quite a large house actually, and impressive, situated where it was, with views down the extended valley and of the hills far and away. Even from a distance, Reggie could see that it wasn't one of the typical farmhouses in the area. It was a residence, built in recent years, and considerable money had been spent— the square-cut stone of the walls was either the yellow limestone indigenous to the area (and not easy to come by legally) or else a fabrication meant to mimic that stone.

Either way, thought Reggie, as he continued on the road toward the house, it's expensive. Even for a doctor.

The road was passing through fields now, not pastures; Reggie suspected he was entering a conservation area. There were no more sheep, just some black crows that startled up from a beech tree on the opposite side of the narrow road, as Reggie drove past.

Reggie hated crows. He instinctively glanced in his rearview mirror after he saw them. There were at least half a dozen, and several had hopped down to the ground, along the edge of the drainage ditch.

Probably they'd found a rabbit or the like. Bloody crows, and if anyone saw Reggie get out and just on general principle throw a rock at them in the nature conservation area, he'd probably get a bloody fine.

But it wasn't just the crows. There was something shiny and metallic visible in the rearview mirror.

Reggie put the Jag in reverse and backed up, swirling mud and water off the tires, until he was parallel with the crows and the object of their attention. But he still couldn't be sure. The crows were after something in the drainage ditch, and it was shielded by the high grass and reeds.

Reggie got out of the car into what was now a full-scale drencher; with rain running under his collar, he tromped several steps through the sucking mud to the opposite edge of the road. The crows scattered, but not far.

He looked down and saw it. A silver Audi A3 had gone off the road and was head-down in the ditch, crashed against the base of the beech tree from which the crows were staging their attack.

One crow kept its perch, on the rain gutter above the open driver's-side door, even as Reggie pushed toward it through the reeds.

Reggie found a pebble in the mud and threw it. The crow flapped and jumped away.

And then Reggie saw the driver—a white male, his head slumped, and his right arm dangling limply out the door.

He was not strapped in. No airbag had deployed, which was a little odd, but perhaps this vehicle didn't have one.

The man's head had hit the windshield hard enough to break the skin, and there was a nasty swelling on his forehead. Reggie knelt at the side of the car and checked for a pulse.

Nothing. The man was gone.

Reggie took out his mobile phone and pressed 999. He knew he himself would be identified by the call, and the police would discover that he was out of bounds if they bothered to look him up, but it couldn't be helped.

But bloody hell. The call didn't go through. No signal; in exactly the type of place where you might need it the most, no bloody signal.

At least not on Reggie's phone. But perhaps the driver had a better service.

Reggie leaned back into the car and began to look about. Several days' worth of *Daily Sun* editions were on the floor of the passenger side, getting soaked with the rain. It was interesting that the driver seemed to have more than a passing interest in that particular tabloid.

Still, Reggie's immediate need was for a mobile phone, and there was none—not on the floor or seats, not in the glove compartment, not in the driver's pockets. Which was a bit surprising, because the driver—mid-forties, expensive business-casual clothes—had the look of someone who should be carrying a mobile.

But the coat pockets weren't empty. Reggie found a small address book, a wallet with ID, and a passport with a stamp from three months earlier. The driver was Larry Trimball. An American and, according to his business card, the owner of a high-tech startup company.

Nigel's startup geek? Reggie looked in the address book. He flipped through pages filled with neat block characters, and on the next-to-last page, there it was—the address and number for the Bath Mental Health and Recovery Center.

Reggie put all of it back into the man's pocket. If the police arrived, it wouldn't do for Reggie to have the man's wallet in his possession.

He climbed back up to the muddy road and looked about.

If he went back out on the lane on which he had driven in, it would be a good half hour before he reached a farmhouse to make a call.

But the yellow stone house—the only house within sight in any direction—was less than a mile away.

Reggie got back in his Jag, started it, spun the wheels just slightly in the mud, and continued on toward the house.

In half a mile he turned off the muddy road and onto a long gravel drive.

He drove up to the front of the house and stopped. There were no parked vehicles. There were no exterior lights on. But there were address numbers carved into a placard above the door, and they matched the address Reggie had gotten—it was Dr. Dillane's house.

Reggie got out and went to the front door. He rapped the heavy metal knocker against solid mahogany and waited. Then he knocked again. No response.

It was twilight now, darkening rapidly. But Reggie peered

through the window, past folding wooden shutters, and saw a light source from some back room.

He walked on the wet, crunching gravel path of the drive from the front of the house, around the side, and to the back— where apparently a vehicle had been parked, leaving shallow depressions that were now filling with water.

The gravel ended at a terrace that was paved with flat sheets of more yellow limestone. There was no gate.

But apparently there was a security system. Glaring white flood lamps opened up on Reggie as he stepped onto the terrace, making him pause and blink.

He waited to hear an alarm. None sounded, but that didn't mean that some private security service somewhere wasn't being notified.

He had already tripped the alarm, but the nearest response had to be at least twenty minutes away. He would have to be alert to that; they would probably drive right past the vehicle and the body in the ditch to the house, and they would assume Reggie to be an intruder.

Which he was about to be. He wanted to talk to Dr. Dillane. Too bad Dr. Dillane wasn't there, but there was a dead body down the road, and there was no need to stick to the proprieties—he had the perfect excuse to break in and learn what he could.

He continued on to the wide back windows; they had shutters, too, like the front, but these shutters were open—this was the view side of the house, opening out toward the rolling hills of the conservation area.

Reggie looked in through the main window.

It was the dining room; he could see a long, heavy glass rectangular table and six chairs. But the interior light wasn't coming from the dining room. It was coming from an interior corridor.

It was time to make damn sure his presence was known, if anyone was here. He shouted. He rapped on the heavy picture window and made it shake.

No response.

Reggie stepped to the side of the picture window, to a sliding glass door.

When he had first stepped on to the terrace, he had thought the door was shut. But he saw now that it was not quite so. The door was unlatched, ajar by a quarter of an inch; rain was running down the edges and pooling at the metal runners.

Reggie pulled on the sliding door. It opened with a loud metallic screech.

He stepped inside. He was in the dining room. The dining table was in the center; to one side of it was the corridor. There was a mobile phone lying on the table—which would seem to indicate that someone was home.

Reggie shouted down the corridor once more for Dr. Dillane. No response. There was still that source of light from some room farther in—probably a cellar; through an open door at the end of the corridor, Reggie could see residual light reflecting on the highly polished wood floor. He continued in that direction.

He passed two side doors—a bedroom and a den—checking very quickly to be sure no one was inside.

There were bits of mud on the otherwise immaculate floor—what looked like same-day trackings of what Reggie had been tromping through outside.

Now he was at the open door at the end of the corridor. There was a descending stairwell, and light—a surprising amount of it—was coming from below.

Reggie stopped in the doorway, rapped on the doorjamb, and called yet again.

Still no response. He started down the stairs.

He saw immediately that this was no wine or storage cellar. It was a fully converted basement, brightly lit with fluorescents in the ceiling. There was a long work surface, of metal and white Formica, attached to one wall, and on that were personal computers, servers, and monitors. There was one padded office chair at the center of the workbench, filing and storage cabinets next to that, and a couple of smaller, more utilitarian stools for quick seating at the several PCs.

It was a small computer lab. Reggie immediately thought of the wild legends about garage startups making fortunes in Silicon Valley.

An odd sort of thing to find in an English psychiatrist's cellar, though. Even if the therapist was inclined to put his case histories and such online, he would hardly need an entire computer lab to do it. This facility had some other purpose.

And the American in the ditch had come a long way if it was just to render simple tech support.

On the floor at the near end of the Formica counter was a three-ring binder—a logbook, probably—which looked to have been dropped hastily; the binder and its pages were askew. Reggie set it on the counter, and opened it.

The first spread of pages were a calendar—two months, the current and most recent, were marked. Dates were circled in red and were annotated. Something was familiar about them, and Reggie looked closer.

They were hearing dates. And if Reggie was reading the notations correctly, the hearings were for Trimball's navigation system. They were spread out over several weeks, each of them progressively more final. One of them had been that morning— the hearing Nigel had attended. There was another circled for that evening, and the last date circled—tomorrow—was for the transport authority's final decision.

But something else about the dates was familiar.

Reggie took a pencil from the desk, and on the same calendar, he put a check mark for each of the dates on which a Black Cab crime had been reported.

At first they did not seem to match up exactly, which, for some reason, seemed to Reggie a good thing.

But then he looked again. There was, in fact, a pattern.

Except for the very first crime, the flurry of Black Cab robberies and other rudenesses at the start had all been in the same week—just prior to the first hearing for the navigational software.

And then, from that first hearing on, the crimes had gotten increasingly serious and more high profile, culminating in the murder of the American couple just one night before the second hearing.

The Black Cab crimes were not random. They were a scheme. They were deliberately timed and designed to create a perceived need for Trimball's software system.

But whose scheme was it? The software proposal was Trimball's. But the logbook and the computer lab were in Dr. Dillane's house.

Reggie began to flip rapidly through the pages of the logbook. The remainder of the calendar was blank, but in the log portion there were pages of handwritten notes with references to "C1," "C2," and "C3," and routes in London for each.

Cabs, Reggie realized. The references were to Black Cabs.

From the nature of the handwriting, it was obvious that two different people had been making journal entries. But neither of them was Trimball; Reggie had seen Trimball's address book, hand-printed in clean block letters. Both of the note makers in the book wrote in longhand; one was scrawled and almost illegible, like a doctor's signature. The other was old-fashioned and clear, and . . . and Reggie knew he had seen it before. It was the same elegant handwriting he had seen in Darla Rennie's briefing papers.

Reggie took a deep breath and sat down on one of the workbench stools. There was no doubt about it now—Darla and the woman Nigel encountered in Dr. Dillane's therapy group were the same person. That person believed herself to be Moriarty, and almost undoubtedly that person was the Moriarty wannabe who had written the threatening letter to Sherlock Holmes.

But what else had she done?

Reggie moved to the center terminal, found an attached mouse, and moved it to see if the monitor display would react.

The power was on, but he got no reaction from the mouse or the keyboard.

He swiveled the chair over to the other PCs and tried each in turn.

Nothing.

Of course not. It had been too much to hope for.

He got up to leave the cellar; perhaps he could learn more from something upstairs.

And then he heard a beep.

The central computer had come on.

And then, simultaneously, both the other PCs came on as well.

Timers. Reggie checked his watch and saw that it was exactly the top of the hour; the entire configuration must be on a timer switch.

And now all three displays lit up.

Reggie knew he could not have much time. The timer probably meant that someone was due to return, and in any case, he had already tripped the alarm.

He sat down at the center chair as the main display began to define itself. He waited for logos and icons to appear.

But they did not. All he had was a blinking log-on screen, and the system was demanding both a user name and a password.

He was no hacker, and any decent security set up would freeze him out after a few wrong attempts. If he was going to guess, he would have to guess right.

Certainly Dillane would have a user name on the system, but Reggie had no idea what Dillane's password would be. Trimball might have a user name on the system as well; after all, he had created it. That password might very well be noted somewhere in Trimball's wallet or address book, but Reggie had left both of those in Trimball's car.

But Darla also had made entries in the logbook. So she must have an account as well. For her, he could at least make a guess.

He typed in her initial and surname to log in. Good so far; the log-on screen was still blinking normally.

Now for the password guess. Reggie typed it in:

M-O-R-I-A-R-T-Y

The log-on immediately disappeared, the entire screen display disintegrated into thousands of pixels, and then—a moment later—it all reassembled again.

He was in. The display had opened directly into some kind of video link. Whatever was on camera was not well lit; Reggie stared, trying to discern what he was looking at. It was dark and shadowy, and the sides of the image were curved—he had to be looking through a small camera lens. There was slightly more light in the center, and there was some sort of movement taking place; but it was all blurry, like peering through dirty glass.

Reggie got up and tried the terminal display to his right, with a similar result.

But now he tried right-clicking the mouse, with the cursor on the image. When he did that, the angle of the image shifted.

And Reggie realized that he was controlling a bloody camera remotely.

He panned to the left and could make out essentially nothing—he was looking at a surface that was dark, solid, and textured, and something above it that was smooth and reflecting like glass, but he could tell nothing more.

He panned to the right and saw more black textured surface—but also a square patch of yellow. He right-clicked, left-clicked, double-clicked, tried the center wheel control—and finally he was able to adjust the focus and bring the yellow portion in more sharply.

It took a moment to register, but then he knew exactly what he was looking at: it was the interior of a Black Cab. The yellow square that had finally come into focus was the identification plate on the passenger door, and on that plate was the license number for the cab: WHAMU1

Reggie knew those numbers. They were ingrained in his memory from the court briefs. He was looking through a remote camera, tucked away somewhere inside a Black Cab—and, according to the numbers, it was his dead client's Black Cab.

Reggie stared point-blank at the screen.

Why in hell did Dillane have a remote camera set up in a Black Cab?

Reggie turned back to the monitor. He panned the camera up, down, left, right, and finally was able to get a view through the driver's side window. He could make out a plain gray concrete wall with black lettering on it, and now he knew exactly where the Black Cab was.

It was in the evidence garage at New Scotland Yard. He was looking through a remote lens so well disguised that the Scotland Yard team hadn't discovered it yet.

Reggie moved immediately to the next terminal, and repeated the same process. It was another camera in a Black Cab, and from the angle on the garage lettering, it was clearly a different Black Cab—but it had the same license number.

Both of the Black Cabs from Reggie's case were sitting in the Scotland Yard garage, just waiting for the surveillance devices to be discovered.

Well, give them time. They would get to it eventually.

Reggie went back to the central terminal, and knowing the controls a bit better now, quickly brought the display into focus.

It was a Black Cab. But this one was different. It had a different license number. And but this one wasn't in the Scotland Yard impound garage.

This one was in motion. It took a moment, but Reggie realized he was looking through the passenger window of a Black Cab as it moved through traffic.

Reggie stared at the screen, at fleeting, blurry images of London shops and street signs and pedestrians, and considered what this meant.

The Carriage Office would make its decision tomorrow. If the pattern Reggie saw in the logbook calendar held true, then there would be a new, and spectacularly high-profile Black Cab crime tonight—almost certainly another murder.

And there was only one cab in this scheme that remained available for it. Reggie knew now what he was looking at. He could almost make up the *Daily Sun* headline himself.

He was looking at a death cab driving through London.

From the current camera angle, through the passenger window, he could not see the driver of the cab. He would be able to see a passenger, at least partly, if one got in, but at the moment there was no passenger.

The cab turned left now. It passed more businesses and pedestrians. Through the limited angle of the window, Reggie saw a would-be fare trying to hail the cab. But the cab didn't stop. Apparently the driver had a specific destination in mind.

Another left turn. Then another.

Now the cab turned again, and Reggie began to recognize shops that he had already seen—a typewriter repair store and an Indian take-away deli next to it.

The cab was circling. And now, another man tried to hail the cab, but once again, the driver didn't stop.

It wasn't a particular destination the driver was looking for, Reggie concluded. It was a particular passenger.

Reggie manipulated the mouse and cursor, trying to get audio and another angle from the camera.

But now there was the sound of heavy tires on gravel.

Reggie jerked his eyes away from the monitor. This was a real sound, not a virtual one. It would be the security patrol.

He got up from the terminal and went quickly up the stairs.

His Jag was parked openly out front, so they surely knew someone was here.

The best plan was to be found doing what he had been intending to do anyway—calling 999 for the crash down the road.

He went down the corridor and quickly ducked into the home office he had seen earlier. He switched on the desk lamp and picked up the phone and dialed, while he waited to hear security knock on the front door.

But bloody hell. The phone did not connect—it was a landline, not a mobile, but there was no dial tone at all.

And, surprisingly, he still had not heard the security patrol rap on the door, not a sound from them at all after hearing their vehicle pull up. That was odd.

Reggie parted the window shutters slightly and looked out toward the drive. Yes, there was a vehicle, a late-model Land Rover. But it had no official insignia at all.

And now Reggie heard the annoying metal squeal of the sliding glass door.

Reggie realized now what was happening—the binder on the computer lab floor, the back door ajar, and Trimball's head injuries with no air bag deployed—he knew what it meant.

He turned and went into the corridor—but too late.

He found himself face-to-face with a man in a blue turtleneck and a tan sports coat.

This had to be Dr. Dillane. No one but therapists and car salesmen wore that combination anymore.

They were within a meter or so of each other, Dillane having apparently snuck around the back and come in through the sliding glass door.

There was a moment while each of them sized up the other.

They were equal in height. They were about the same age. Dillane had prematurely gray-white hair, but he looked fit. Still, Reggie would have liked his own chances better, if only Dillane had not been holding a semiautomatic Glock handgun.

"Ahh," said Dillane. "The XJS. The fancy barrister's chalk stripe." Now he gave a short, uneasy laugh. "I know which one you are. You're Reggie Heath."

Reggie just glared back at Dillane and said nothing in response.

"You're trespassing, Heath. Didn't your criminal clients teach you that's not a smart thing to do?"

"You're right," said Reggie. "I expect you should call the police."

"Yes," said Dillane. "And I will do so, shortly."

"I'm sure the security service is already on their way, in any case," said Reggie. "They've probably already found the accident you staged up the road."

Dillane raised an eyebrow. "And why would I have done that?"

Dillane wasn't even pretending he didn't know what Reggie was talking about. Given which of them was holding the gun, Reggie considered that a bad sign. And possibly Reggie should not have opened the discussion with an accusation. But there was no point in holding back now.

"Trimball discovered how you intend to use his brainchild," said Reggie. "He saw your lab book, he realized what you are doing, and he wasn't having any of it."

"And what is it that you think I'm doing?"

Dillane's voice was calm, patient, and smooth. Reggie found it annoying as hell.

"You make too much money, Dillane. You couldn't build this house on your NHS salary. You built it on your private celebrity practice. You made some money prescribing on demand to celebrities who need a fix. But you made even more with your inside knowledge of their lives, selling tips to the paparazzi about who is going to be doing whom, and where to catch them at it. But you overdid the prescribing; you created a celebrity overdose, and now all your famous and high-paying clientele have dropped you. You not only lose their fees, you lose all that bonus money you were getting by selling their private information to tabloid jackals."

Reggie paused. Dillane raised an eyebrow slightly, but he did not confirm or deny. Reggie continued.

"But no worries. You have a fallback plan. You conceived it when Darla Rennie and the American tech geek showed up in your therapy group. Larry Trimball with his new vehicle tracking system, and Darla with her hatred of the Black Cabs, and the ability to modify what Trimball had created so that it not only tracked vehicles but also spied on everyone who rode in them—it was perfect. You created the overall scheme, and you got Darla to implement it for you. Nothing short of a wiretap into every phone line in London could give you so much personal and inside knowledge as knowing what is said and done in the back of every Black Cab. You'd be back in the information-selling business, and bigger than ever.

"But Trimball was never in on that part of the scheme. He thought he was just marketing his navigation system. When he realized that all the Black Cab crimes occurring at the same time as his adoption hearings could not be coincidence, he came here to confront you. When he did, you killed him, and staged the accident."

Reggie stopped there and looked for Dillane's reaction.

Dillane glared back for a moment, and then spoke, with the calm in his voice rapidly vanishing.

"Well. What do I say now? Good job? You do indeed have a bit of it. But what if I do make a call to the paparazzi now and then? If these people want to be in the public eye, and I make a bit of money by helping them be even a little more in the public eye than they intended, who are they to complain? And if they want drugs, and I prescribe what they crave, and it isn't necessarily the best thing for them in some ways, whose choice is that?"

Dillane began to get animated now. He still had the gun pointed at Reggie, but he was moving about. Reggie shifted his position as well, as subtly as he could, until he was standing next to the mobile phone he had seen on the dining table.

"But this is just a start," Dillane continued. "Once the Black Cabs set the precedent, all the livery services will adopt this system. Stretch limo, Black Cab, minicab, it will make no difference—all of them will adopt the navigation system, unaware of the surveillance system embedded within it. I will know everything that is going on in the city. It will be a gold mine of information. But the politicians with their plots, and the stockbrokers with their tips, all the petty crimes and peccadilloes that everyone thinks they are discussing in private—all that will just be a bonus. The real bliss will be helping my new tabloid friends shoot down one or two of my former celebrity friends every month, and get paid for it in the process. If I can't make my money servicing them, then I'll make my money embarrassing them, and quite honestly, embarrassing them is more fun.

"But you are wrong about one thing," Dillane continued. "The security service is not actually on their way here." Dillane was settling down now, regaining his focus. "The alarm just goes directly to my own mobile phone. I'll call them myself in a bit. And what I'll tell them is that the crazed London barrister from the Black Cab cases cut my phone lines, broke into my home, and I had to shoot him."

"Why don't you just tell them now?" said Reggie. He picked up the phone off the table as he said it, and he quickly pressed 999. If Dillane was going to squeeze the trigger, might as well get it over with now.

And then the phone beeped in error, and the display showed these words: "Hi, Larry. What's the password?"

Bloody hell.

"Trimball's phone, isn't it?" said Dillane. "Bad luck, that. Not much use without the pass code."

"I suppose you're right," said Reggie. He resignedly closed the phone, transferred it to his left hand as if to place it on the counter and then, in a backhand flick, threw the ten-ounce device at Dillane's face.

The gun went off.

Reggie didn't wait to see if he had been hit. He leaped headlong at Dillane, grabbing for the gun with his left hand, and for Dillane's throat with his right.

Reggie shoved Dillane backward onto the dining table, slamming the gun hand against the heavy glass. Dillane let loose of the gun. But Reggie's own momentum, and a last-minute push from Dillane, propelled Reggie over the table.

Reggie scrambled across the floor, grabbed the Glock, and stood with it leveled at Dillane.

Dillane stood. He looked at the gun in Reggie's hand, looked at Reggie, and then nodded slightly, as if it were no big deal. Then he began offhandedly putting the collar of his shirt back in order. "Your brother did say you were always good in a scrum," said Dillane.

"I had him to practice on," said Reggie.

"Yes, I know. I should have kept it in mind, but he mentioned so many sibling things of that nature, I guess it just got lost in the whole bag of them. I know everything your brother told me about his life, you see, and as it happens, that includes a good deal about yours."

"I doubt that," said Reggie. "And keep your hands where I can see them."

"Of course. For example, I know why you became a lawyer— why you both became lawyers, in fact—which might include something you yourself didn't know; that like you, your brother went into law because of the injustice done to your father. Surprised?"

"No," lied Reggie. "I knew that."

Dillane smiled, in a doubtful and very annoying way.

"I know the guilt you carry," he continued, "thinking it was your fault things turned out the way they did at the football match, that if you had not gone, hadn't proudly insisted on wearing the cap, none of it would have ever happened at all. And so you became a lawyer, and you took on criminal clients, because you thought if you represented other defendants falsely accused you could balance things somehow. Erase the injustice of it. But you failed utterly in making things right. You merely got a guilty man released, making it possible for someone else to be killed. I can't imagine any failure that could be more complete. Failure is so wonderful when it comes as the result of what you thought would be your success and redemption."

"Balls," said Reggie, for lack of a better response.

"And I know your brother dated the woman in your life—Laura Rankin, isn't it—before you met her."

"That was years ago."

"Of course. I know that isn't news to you. But would you like to know just how far their relationship had gotten?"

"No."

"Now, that's just denial. I'm sure you'd like to know more. Why don't you sit down, we'll talk; perhaps I can tell you about it."

"I don't think so. Move over against the wall."

Dillane had been subtly shifting his position while he talked; Reggie now put one hand on Dillane's chest and pushed him back against the wall.

"You're on the verge of losing her, aren't you?" said Dillane. "Your brother predicted it, you know. He talked about it. He said he was afraid it would happen. And now it is, isn't it?"

"Tell me about the remaining Black Cab."

"I've no idea what you mean."

"Two cabs are locked up in New Scotland Yard. You've got one left. Tell me what it's doing. I know it's on the road in London. Where exactly is it going? What is it doing?"

"No," said Dillane, "I don't think I will tell you that. Shoot me if it will make you feel better. But I will tell you this much: You thought you would get Laura Rankin back? You won't. It's already too late, and you have failed, utterly. Once again. Lovely woman, though. And so is Ms. Rennie. Both of them are, actually. And both of them so useful."

Reggie had heard enough.

Though instinct told him this was exactly what Dillane wanted, he swung at Dillane's face with his free arm—and in the process, just for an instant, the weight of that motion caused Reggie's gun hand to shift to the left.

Reggie's punch connected, but Dillane was already in motion, it was only a glancing blow, and Reggie had not put his full force behind it. With the gun off target, Dillane threw a hard elbow directly at Reggie's face.

Dillane connected at a lucky angle, and Reggie fell back. For a short moment he could not see a damn thing. Dillane had caught him between the eyes, right at the bridge of the nose, and as his vision cleared, he saw the open front doorway. Dillane had fled.

Reggie got up and ran in pursuit, ignoring the pain in the whole center of his face and the blood that was beginning to pour down from his nose, and the fact that he had dropped the gun on the dining-room floor.

Reggie got to the doorway and saw Dillane's Land Rover roaring out of the drive.

It was full-on night now. Rain was coming down in torrents. The gravel drive was under water, the road that it led to had now turned completely to mud, and the surrounding pastures were rapidly becoming a shallow marsh.

Dillane was driving the Land Rover across the muddy road and out into those spongy fields.

Reggie drove the XJS directly after him, chasing the red taillights in the dark. The undercarriage of his XJS slammed hard in an expanding pothole as Reggie crossed the road, but he did make it across, and managed to maintain traction, at least at first, heading across the field.

The Land Rover was roaring along, sending out its own spray into the rain as nicely as in a television advert, and bouncing over little gullies.

And now Reggie struck two shallow washed-out gullies, one right after the other. The XJS took a bounce. The front axle came down in one washout, the rear axle in another, and the undercarriage of the Jag, with its shallow clearance, was actually now in contact with the ground, with the front wheels spinning and the engine screaming in vain.

Reggie got out, cursing like bloody hell, blood and rain streaming down his face. For just a moment, he watched Dillane's vehicle escaping over the fields.

And then he turned and began running for all he was worth back toward the house.

25

Laura exited the Indian takeaway on Portobello Road, carrying a paper sack with a container each of tandoori chicken and tandoori shrimp. She was famished. If it turned out that she finished it all off before she even got home, then so be it.

She tucked the sack into the crook of one arm and managed to get out her mobile phone. She was eager to call Reggie to let him know. The man in the typewriter shop had confirmed it now: the typed characters on the threat letters from the presumed Moriarty matched exactly the characters produced on a very old typewriter that the shop had repaired for one Darla Rennie, of Mayfair—Reggie's client's solicitor.

So Reggie had gone to court in the company of a woman who believed herself to be the descendant of Professor James Moriarty and who believed Reggie to be Sherlock Holmes, and who wanted to do something horrible to him—exactly what, apparently, was still to be determined—because of it.

Laura took out her mobile now and rang Reggie. No re-sponse; she got his mobile answering service. She left a message, but it was cut short—her battery had run down, which was an-noying. Now he wouldn't be able to return her call.

She walked toward the curb looking for a cab; she could see one approaching already from down the street. She'd had quite good luck today getting cabs, but she hoped the driver wouldn't be a talker. She didn't really want a long conversation. There was still too much to think about.

26

Soaked and muddy from his dash across the field, Reggie reached Dillane's house. He ran directly down the stairs to the cellar computer lab.

All the screens had gone dark. He sat at the central terminal and tapped a key; thank God, the displays appeared again.

Reggie stared at the main display, trying to get his adrenaline under control and to focus. In a moment he knew what he was looking at, and it was what he wanted—he was looking once again through the interior camera of the active Black Cab.

It was still on one of the same streets. Reggie recognized the shops. Apparently the cab had continued circling all this time.

But now it came to a stop. It held its position there in the street, in front of an Indian takeaway and a typewriter repair store.

And now the driver's arm reached over and tapped the meter on. Someone was approaching the passenger-side door.

The door opened. Reggie could not see a face, but he knew immediately it was a woman getting in.

Suddenly, and for the first time since he had sat down at the terminal, Reggie felt like a voyeur. But he could not look away. The woman was lovely: a nice length of red hair just visible over one shoulder, and long legs, with freckles behind the left knee that—

Reggie began frantically to work the controls, trying to get a view of her face, but he couldn't.

And then he right-clicked the correct corner of the display, and all at once he had audio.

He heard background noise from the street, and then the sound of the passenger door shutting. And then he heard the passenger speak.

"Elystan Street in Chelsea," she said to the driver.

The voice was clear as truth and unmistakable.

It was Laura.

The cab driver may have said something in response to her, or he may not have; Reggie couldn't tell, the audio configuration, like the video, was clearly focused on the passenger.

And now the cab was in motion.

Laura had settled back in the passenger seat, and though the camera angle still did not show her face at the moment, it did show part of her profile.

Reggie could tell by the tilt of her chin that she was perturbed at the moment. But she was not in active distress either; she was not physically afraid.

Of course not. She had no reason to be. She was in one of her trusted Black Cabs.

Reggie could see her taking something out of a white paper sack from the Indian takeaway. Then she held it up toward the partition window, as though the driver had said something to her.

"It's quite spicy," said Laura. "Would you like a bite?"

Apparently the driver did; Reggie saw Laura lean forward with the tandoori and then back again.

And then, after the driver said something, Laura responded, "Oh yes, I know what you mean. When I haven't eaten Indian food in a while, it is indeed as though I'm tasting it again for the first time."

The cab came to a stop at an intersection now. Laura was looking from one side to the other.

"Are you quite sure you know the way to Chelsea?" she said.

The driver didn't answer.

"Get out of the cab," said Reggie, under his breath.

The signal changed, and the cab was about to start moving again.

"It's very pleasant having a woman driver," Reggie heard Laura say now. "I've quite had it with trying to talk sense with any man of late, at least any that I know. But really, I think you have your direction wrong."

"Get out of the cab!" Reggie shouted at the terminal display.

But Laura heard nothing, remained in place, and the cab continued.

"Not to worry, miss," said the cab driver, and Reggie froze at the sound of the driver's voice. "I know exactly where we're going, and it's no good saying I don't."

"Get out of the cab!" screamed Reggie, recognizing the voice immediately. "Get out of the cab!"

But it was all one-way; he was receiving audio but could not send, and Laura was not responding.

And then, suddenly, Reggie caught a glimpse of the driver. The angle of the camera had changed, though Reggie was not touching any control, and now he could see the back of the driver's head—her jet-black hair not quite covering a shining silver headset—as she touched something next to her ear.

And then he heard Darla's voice again, so softly that Laura could not hear it, but Reggie through the audio feed could.

"What you value most, Mr. Holmes."

And now the video display went dead.

For several heartbeats, Reggie had absolutely no clue what to do.

There was no landline phone in the house. The XJS was keeping company with the sheep. He had seen no e-mail system on any of the terminals, and while there might be something a hacker could do, he was no hacker.

Then he remembered: Trimball's phone.

Reggie ran up the stairs and through the corridor. In the dining room, under the glass table, he found the mobile phone that he had thrown at Dillane.

Had Dillane's face cushioned the impact enough?

Reggie flipped the phone open. It flickered for a moment, and then the display lit fully. Wonderful.

And then, as Reggie knew it would, it demanded Trimball's password again.

With the phone in hand, Reggie ran out of the house and into the rain, across the crunching gravel drive, and then back down the muddy road toward Trimball's crashed Audi.

It was half a mile. It seemed longer. Reggie had no idea how long it took him, running in the nearly pitch dark; it felt like forever. The thick mud pulled at his feet; pits and potholes, invisible in the dark, twisted his knees.

With his lungs burning and gasping for more air, Reggie finally reached the Audi. He waved his arms wildly to scatter the fresh murder of crows that had gathered, and then he opened the door on the driver's side.

He reached in Trimball's pocket. The address book was still there.

Surely it would be on the very first page. It was Trimball's own pass code, he would not identify it, he would just write the numbers on the very first page.

Reggie looked at the top of the first page, peering in the light from the open car door, and yes, he saw five carefully hand-printed numerals. He flipped the phone open again, got the prompt, and entered the number.

"Welcome, Larry!" said the phone.

Thank God.

But the battery light was blinking. Reggie knew he had only seconds.

The hell with 999. He rang Nigel.

27

As Nigel sat with roughly six-score Black Cab drivers in the Carriage Office meeting hall on Penton Street, he was beginning to worry that he had made the wrong choice—he should not have insisted that it be Reggie who would go to the Bath Mental Health and Recovery Center. He probably should have gone himself.

And this was not simply because Nigel's excursion to the Black Cab meeting was turning out to be a bust—the meeting should have started twenty minutes ago, and the techno geek still had not shown up to make his final pitch.

And it wasn't because Reggie wouldn't be just as capable as Nigel of prying information out of the group therapist or whomever else he came in contact with. Reggie could certainly handle it; Reggie could handle anything. That had always been the case. Anyone (and that included Nigel himself) who had a brain and knew the Heath brothers would have the good

sense to send Reggie to do everything and let Nigel remain in
the pub quaffing ale and shooting snooker. Reggie would always get the job done.

No, Nigel's worry now was simply that he wasn't at all sure
that it was a good idea to have his older brother talking to the
therapist who had spent twenty days, four hours per day, listening to all of Nigel's own deepest darkest concerns.

Of course, it was all completely confidential. Surely there
was nothing to worry about.

Still, Reggie had a way of prying information out of people—

Now Nigel's worrisome train of thought was interrupted.
The man from the Carriage Office had stepped to the microphone, for the third time since they had arrived, probably to
announce yet another delay.

The Carriage Office apologizes, said the official. Mr. Trimball still had not arrived. The Carriage Office accepts full responsibility for the apparent glitch in scheduling, but for now,
the meeting is adjourned. Then he scampered off the platform
as quickly as he could.

There were annoyed murmurs from the audience of cab
drivers, many of whom were not going to be satisfied with just
leaving after the long wait.

"Bad move on their part," said Edwards, sitting next to
Nigel, "if they want to get this thing accepted."

"I agree," said Nigel. "You would think they'd want to . . .
Excuse me, one moment."

Nigel's mobile was ringing. There was a setting on the
bloody thing to mute it, but he still hadn't figured it out.

He flipped the phone open and took the call.

It was Reggie. He was talking rapidly, and in a stressed
pitch that was so unlike him that Nigel at first thought it must
be someone else.

"Laura's in the Black Cab. I'm hours away. Track Wembley down, tell him about Laura, get him to send out an alert, and give them this license number—"

"Reggie, what in hell are you—"

"Write down the bloody number before my connection goes out," said Reggie.

Nigel took down the number.

"But why do we need an alert about Laura being in a Black Cab?"

"Not *a* Black Cab, *the* Black Cab. I've identified the cabs being used in the crimes. There's one left. Something bad is going to happen tonight, to the passenger in that cab, and the passenger in that cab is Laura."

"Got it," said Nigel. And just in time, because in the middle of an adrenaline-rushed bloody-something statement, Reggie's connection went dead.

Nigel immediately punched in the numbers for Inspector Wembley. But all he got was an official New Scotland Yard recording. He shut that call off and punched in 999 instead.

"I want to report a . . . a . . . kidnapping."

"Who is it being kidnapped, sir?"

"Laura Rankin."

"Your name?"

"What bloody difference does—"

"Your name, sir?"

"Nigel Heath."

"And who is doing the kidnapping, sir?"

"I don't know. Someone in a Black Cab. The driver of a Black Cab."

There was a short pause.

"Did you witness this . . . Laura Rankin . . . being forced into the Black Cab."

"No."

"Did she communicate to you in some way that she is being kidnapped?"

"No, I . . . it's not like that; she may have gotten in voluntarily, the point is—"

"Sir, people get in Black Cabs every day, do they not?"

"Yes, but—"

"Typically they are simply going from one place to another. They are not being kidnapped. Do you understand that?"

"Of course I . . . now look here, just forget that I said anything about her being kidnapped, the point is—"

"Then you are not in fact reporting a kidnapping?"

"No, but she is in danger. You need to put out an all-points bulletin; I will give you the cab number; it's—"

"I'll transfer you to my supervisor, sir," said the operator, and now the line went silent.

"Bloody hell," said Nigel. "You'd think I'd get something right."

"Problem?" said Edwards, still sitting on the chair next to Nigel. Clearly he'd heard most of it.

"Bloody hell, yes," said Nigel, punching in Wembley's number again. Then, as he got another recording, he turned back to Edwards.

"How many drivers in this room?" asked Nigel.

"Something over a hundred," said Edwards.

"So there are a hundred Black Cabs, and Black Cab drivers, right here, at this moment?"

"At least," said Edwards. "And I can double that with a call to the dispatcher."

Nigel wrote down the cab number Reggie had given him over the phone.

"I take it you still want to find who is behind the Black Cab crimes?"

"There are a lot of lads here who'd give their right arm to

do that," said Edwards, "and at this moment, they're just itching for something useful to do."

"Find that cab, and that driver, and you'll have who you want," said Nigel. "But save the passenger inside."

"Just give us the cab number then, that's a good lad," said Edwards, "and Bob's your uncle."

28

Laura looked up from her tandoori and noticed where they were.

"Really, there's no question about it. You missed a turn," said Laura.

"Oh no, ma'am," said the driver. "I always know exactly where I'm going."

"I'm sure. But where I'm going is Chelsea. You can take the next right onto Park Lane, and it will be fine, or at least nearly so."

The driver made no response, but Laura wasn't concerned.

Until Park Lane came and went, and they were still traveling east.

"You missed the turn," said Laura firmly. "Take Regent Street. I'll direct you from there."

The driver made no response. Regent Street was approaching, and the driver was not getting in position to take it.

Either the driver had no sense of direction whatsoever, or

else she had her own destination in mind. Or it might even be both those things.

Laura thought about it. No reason to panic. She just needed to know what she was dealing with.

"Read the papers much?" she said quite casually.

"Every day, ma'am."

"That's quite something about that barrister over on Baker Street, isn't it?"

"You mean the one who got the cab driver acquitted and then murdered him?"

"Oh, I don't think it's quite settled that he did that second thing. And he had some help with the first."

There was silence for a long moment. As Laura waited for a response from the driver, another Black Cab came up quite close behind them. It flashed its headlamps.

Now Laura's driver said, "It's a ruse, you know."

"What is?"

"Oh, he's a barrister, all right. But he's not just that. And Heath is not even his real name at all."

"It isn't?"

"No."

"What is his name then?" said Laura.

"Sherlock Holmes."

"I see," said Laura, quite carefully, with no inflexion whatsoever.

Now she heard a soft thunk in the cab doors on either side of her. She knew what it was. The doors had just now been locked by the driver, and only the driver could unlock them. That could not be a good thing.

She was going to have to improvise.

"The man in the typewriter shop told me an interesting thing about a letter that I showed him. Would you like to know what it was?"

Silence for a moment from the driver. Then, "Tell me."

"He said that the typewriter that typed it was brought in for repair a while ago by a young woman named Darla Rennie. That would be you, wouldn't it?"

The driver did not respond for a long moment. Then she said: "You may call me Moriarty."

"That's fine," said Laura. "I've always believed in the right of anyone to choose their own formal name. We have so little control these days over what other people call us. But just so I understand—you prefer to be called Moriarty because—"

"My great-great-grandfather was James Moriarty."

"On your mother's side."

"Yes." Darla said that, paused, and then said, "He was killed by the man called Sherlock Holmes, and I shall have my revenge."

"It's a lovely name, Moriarty," ventured Laura. "Quite popular. In fact, not uncommon at all. And even adding the given name James to it is hardly unique."

Laura paused for a moment to see if Darla would get the point. But there was no response, so she continued.

"What I'm trying to say is—is there any possibility at all you might be mistaken? That perhaps your great-great—however many greats—grandfather was some other James Moriarty— perhaps one that actually existed? And it can be so difficult to extract revenge for the injustices done to one's family, even the real ones. Reggie could tell you that."

"His name is Sherlock Holmes," Darla stated again, quite emphatically. "He is a despicable person and I shall make him pay for what he has done."

"I'm so relieved to hear that you feel that way," said Laura. "I know him just as Reggie, of course, but I was afraid for a while that you rather fancied him."

Darla actually glanced back at Laura on the remark, but then quickly got her eyes on the road again.

"Certainly not," she said.

"Which would be very foolish on your part, because if you haven't noticed, Reggie is quite stodgy, even for a barrister. Everyone says so. And getting more so every day. What he'll be like at sixty I shudder to think, but I'm sure you would be quite bored with him."

Through the window partition, Laura could see Darla becoming quite upset. That was unfortunate; perhaps Laura had chosen the wrong tack. But it was too late for that now.

"His name is Sherlock Holmes, and I hold him in complete contempt."

"I'm so glad," said Laura. "There was quite a fire sale on Heath brothers there for a while, but I'm afraid they're all out now, right down to the store fixtures."

Now the Black Cab that had been behind them pulled up alongside, rolled down its window, and the driver started to shout something.

Darla took a sudden turn, cutting across a lane and narrowly missing a double-decker.

"His name is Sherlock Holmes," Darla stated again, quite emphatically. "He killed my great-great-grandfather. And I will have my revenge."

They were on the Strand now, approaching the Tower Bridge. A new Black Cab had taken a position alongside and just in front of them, eliminating one possible change in direction. And now another pulled in behind them.

"I've taken from him his reputation," said Darla. "I've taken from him his self-respect. And now I will take from him what he values most."

Laura was about to respond to that. But now a loud siren began to wail. It was coming from the Tower Bridge.

They had arrived at the bridge entrance from the Strand. All the other traffic had come to a stop; there were gaps between the lanes heading onto the bridge, but there was really nowhere to go—because the bridge was about to be lifted. A high-masted vessel was approaching on the river; the siren was already blaring, and red warning lights at the foot of the bridge began to flash.

"I hardly think you'll do that," said Laura. "What he values most is me."

Darla turned her head now and looked back directly at Laura.

"Exactly," she said.

And then she floored the accelerator. She drove right past the flashing lights and onto the bridge, heading toward the north tower, and weaving around the other vehicles that had already stopped.

Laura knew that within seconds the span of the bridge just beyond the north tower would begin to rise. Surely Darla knew it, too. The spans on either side of the bridge would rise and separate, and there would be nothing at the end of their road except a plummet directly into the Thames.

The metal gate in front of the tower was already in motion, and it was about to completely block the road in front of them.

Darla accelerated.

"You can't get across," Laura shouted. "It won't work!"

But the cab drove forward with everything it had.

The metal gate had now swung far enough to block half the roadway and was still moving. Beyond the gate, the two spans of the bridge had begun to rise.

Without slowing, Darla swerved the cab to try to go around the end of the gate.

There was almost enough room—but not quite. The front of the cab made it past, but the rear bumper of the cab, at full speed, clipped the end of the metal gate.

The cab spun forward, caroming up the rising span of the bridge, just as both halves of the span reached enough height to begin to separate in the middle.

Then the cab came to a stop.

For just a moment, everything inside was completely silent. Laura was dizzy from the two revolutions the cab had completed, and she was breathing rapidly, but it felt, strangely, as though they were now quite safe and secure.

And then she heard the metal undercarriage of the cab groan; in the same instant she looked out the window and realized, both from what she could see and what she felt happening beneath them, exactly where they were.

The cab was straddling the gap as the bridge span continued to open. The front wheels of the cab were on the parting edge of the southern span; the rear wheels were on the parting edge of the northern span, and in a contest between the hydraulic engines of the bridge lift and the undercarriage of the Black Cab, there was no question which would win.

The gap between the spans was straining to grow wider. The cab was about to be torn in two.

The front windshield cracked, and then burst.

But now the passenger-door locks sprang open with the stress; Laura pushed through the door, and without time to think, jumped out of the cab.

Her feet slid on the increasingly steep angle of the bridge span; she flung her arms out, grabbing for whatever she could.

She realized in a moment that she had not fallen. Her face was against the flat metal-joining edge of the road, at the end of one of the two parting spans. She had both arms over that edge from the elbows up, and it was just enough leverage to pull herself up.

She looked down. Below was the Thames.

She looked to her left. The Black Cab was not yet completely separated; the running board that ran the whole length of the cab was still in place, at least for the moment.

And clinging to the running board with both hands, with the rest of her body dangling straight down toward the Thames, was Darla Rennie.

The woman was desperately looking back and forth, from one span to the other, as the only thing she had to hold on to was being torn apart.

Only now, fully seeing her face for the first time, did Laura realize how young she was—younger than Laura—and, at this moment at least, how incredibly vulnerable.

Laura herself was now as secure as was possible, which was to say not terribly secure, essentially straddling the edge of one of the spans of the bridge as it continued to rise higher. But she pulled herself closer to the cab, and reached her right arm out toward Darla.

"Take my hand!"

Darla turned her face toward Laura. She was clearly terrified, but she hesitated.

"Take my hand!" Laura screamed as loudly as she could, her voice getting lost in the whirring from the bridge engines and the shriek of tearing metal from the cab. But she made her intent clear, and she stretched her arm out even further.

Now, finally, Darla let go of the cab with one hand and reached for Laura's.

And then there was one more terrible metal shriek, and the frame of the cab separated into two. The running board broke, the two halves of it slanted steeply downward—and the hand that Laura was reaching for slipped away.

Laura was vaguely aware of other sounds now, distant

shouts. That was probably a good thing; some assistance would indeed be useful. But she did not have the strength to turn and look. And the last thing she saw before losing consciousness herself was Darla Rennie plummeting into the Thames.

29

TWO DAYS LATER

Wembley was sitting in the barrister's chair in Reggie's chambers office. Nigel, seated in a client chair, was listening, and trying to remain patient.

Nigel had a plane to catch. The time difference and the expense had made his transatlantic calls to Mara too short and too infrequent. He was anxious to get back to Los Angeles.

So he hoped Wembley would not take long. Reggie had warned him that the man liked to talk, which presumably was why, at least in part, Reggie had ducked out already that morning, on the pretext of getting in a run—as if he hadn't had enough of that—before the day got too far under way.

"We caught up with the good doctor at Folkestone," Wembley was saying. "Where he was trying to board the Eurostar with a false passport. I love that about the Chunnel; it's the first place every fugitive runs to, and it makes my job that much easier."

"Did he confess?" asked Nigel.

"He wouldn't have if he could have avoided it, I can tell you that. But forensics has been all over his house and the crashed A3, and there's a Russian servant girl in Mayfair who filled in a bunch of pieces for us. We've already got so much on Dillane that he gave it up. We have him on murder of the American entrepreneur, accessory for the others, and more conspiracies to commit than I can keep track of. "

Wembley had his feet on Reggie's mahogany desk. Nigel considered telling him to remove them, but decided that if Reggie was going to leave this to Nigel, Reggie's desk could fend for itself.

"They rejected the proposal, you know," Wembley continued. "This one, anyway."

"Why? Just because of the spyware, or for other reasons?"

"Because it was put in without disclosure, of course. And also because the head of the company is deceased. That particular group won't be back. But that doesn't mean a rejection of the whole concept altogether. I'm sure it will be the way of things. A device that tells you how to get where you're going? Excellent idea, of course, and not just for cabs. I think they've got them already on some American cars. An added feature that notifies emergency authorities if you are in a wreck? Also a good idea. But recording everything said and done in the cab and sending it back to a database? That's a bit over the top. Even for my tastes."

"I believe the phrase for that is, 'too much information,'" said Nigel. "And I'm sure what Reggie really wants to know is, what is the status of the charges?"

"Against him, you mean?"

"Of course."

"Oh. Yes, naturally. Well, the Crown Prosecution Service is dropping those. Given the circumstances that have come to light, we're satisfied that Darla Rennie killed Walters. We found quite a bit of cash deposited in his account between the time of his arrest and the time he was killed. Apparently he got greedy."

"Yes," said Nigel. "He wasn't in on the original scheme, but after he was arrested, I expect he realized why it was that he'd been driving all around the East End every night for a fare who had no destination. I'm sure he wanted money to keep quiet about it—that, and a guarantee that he would get released, of course."

Wembley nodded. "And then they went looking for a barrister good enough to get the charges dropped. I sort of get why they wanted your brother for that. And I know he wouldn't have taken it on if he didn't believe his client was innocent of the murders."

"Which he was."

"Understood. But what I don't get is how they persuaded your brother to pick up a criminal case again at all. That had to take some doing. And some personal knowledge. How did they know which buttons to push?"

Nigel looked at Wembley, then away, and shifted uneasily in his chair. "I suppose it helped," said Nigel finally, "that Reggie had a brother blabbing away on family issues in the solicitor's therapy group."

"Oh," said Wembley. Then he nodded, almost sympathetically. "Very subjective stuff, that. Personally, I don't go in much for that touchy-feely sort of thing. I prefer forensics. Which is tying things up nicely in this case."

"You found her fingerprints, then?"

"Yes." Wembley seemed to want to not say any more about it, but Nigel wasn't satisfied.

"Where did you find them?"

Wembley cleared his throat. "On the detergent box."

"But surely not on the outside of the box itself?"

"No," said Wembley. "That of course had been wiped clean. As had everything else. We found the print—as you had suggested—on that annoying little tab that you have to either push in or pull out of the box in order to get the stuff to pour properly."

Nigel was so satisfied to hear Wembley acknowledge that the suggestion had been correct that he didn't even bother to point out that it was Laura who had first thought of it.

"And what of the other victim?" said Nigel. "The bloke that was unceremoniously pushed over the railing and into the river?"

"It took both Dillane and Darla Rennie to do that. She arranged the meeting and Dillane pulled the trigger; then they did their best to make him look like another Black Cab victim—when in fact he was their original Black Cab perp, doing all the robberies and killing that American couple. But once it all started to go down the crapper, they couldn't have him hanging about to get caught and testify about their plot. And according to Dillane—easy to say now, but it's what he says—the wanker was never supposed to kill anyone to begin with. The idea was just to make the Black Cabs appear unsafe, not to remove all their customers through sheer attrition."

Now there was a knock on the door, and Lois entered.

"Oh," she said. "Should I come back later?"

"Not at all," said Nigel. "We don't keep secrets from Inspector Wembley. I mean, not this afternoon, anyway."

"Well, I finally got a call back from the typewriter manufacturer. You know, the one used for the letter from . . . well, you know."

"And?" said Nigel.

"They found the original purchase record. It was bought in San Francisco in 1891 by an American."

"And?"

"That's all they had, sir. There's no record of it at all after that, until it was taken to Standard Typewriter here in London for repair—just last month—by Darla Rennie."

Lois stopped talking after that, but she clearly had something else to say.

Nigel looked at her suspiciously. "What is it that you're not telling us?"

Lois hesitated, finally she spit it out: "The name of the American who purchased it in 1891 was James Moriarty."

Nigel shrugged. "There were plenty of James Moriartys in England and Ireland and America then, as there are now."

"Yes," said Lois. "And that's why it's taken me so long; there were too many Moriartys who were not relevant, and I had to get into a bit of genealogy. But I do finally have it. Darla Rennie is indeed the great-great-granddaughter, on her mother's side, of the James Moriarty who purchased the typewriter. That James Moriarty was an American, who traveled to Switzerland in 1891, where he died in a railway accident. He left a considerable fortune to his heirs, which they apparently increased over the years, mostly during the American Prohibition, by importing British and Irish whiskey.

"Darla's parents—she has dual citizenship, British on her father's side, American on her mother's—both died in an automobile accident just less than a year ago. Darla inherited the estate, including, along with everything else, that typewriter, which her great-great-grandfather had owned before he died."

"Fair enough," said Wembley. "But it doesn't explain why she thought her great-great-grandfather was *the* Professor James Moriarty."

"Well, she was already schizophrenic," said Nigel. "Perhaps the death of her parents—and the discovery of something that her ancestor had owned—was enough to push her toward that particular delusion. That and the unfortunate coincidence of where and when he died. Perhaps she didn't even know about any of it until after her parents died; that would have only increased the impact of learning it. And then when Dillane took her off the meds for his own purposes, the delusion was reinforced."

"Well," said Wembley, getting up from Reggie's chair. "If we ever manage to fish her out of the Thames, perhaps we'll ask her."

"What?" said Nigel. "You haven't recovered the body?"

Wembley shook his head as he went to the door. "Given time and the tides, we might still. Or we might not. It's a big river, and anything is possible."

"You'll let us know?' said Nigel.

"If you like," said Wembley. "But if we do find her, I'm sure you'll read about it in the papers in any case."

Wembley exited.

Nigel checked his watch. "I have a plane to catch," he said to Lois. "Was there anything else?"

"Just these," said Lois. She showed Nigel a large mailer, stuffed with letters. Nigel looked inside.

It was filled with letters to Sherlock Holmes.

"I think Reggie was intending to mail them to you. But if you'll take them now, I suppose we could save on the postage?"

30

Laura got out of a Black Cab at the entrance to the pedestrian path at the north end of Regent's Park.

She was wearing long runner's pants that did not completely disguise her shape, but did cover all of her skin. Most of London had seen enough of that two days earlier. So although the weather would have permitted, she decided against runner's shorts.

She wasn't sure why she had blacked out momentarily just as the separating edge of the bridge span had reached its apex. What she did know—what she learned shortly after the fact—was that nearly all the cab drivers and half the bobbies in London had been waiting, arms linked, at the base of the span to catch her as she slid. And right behind them were any number of paparazzi.

She just wished she had not worn a skirt that day.

Today she set out on the Regent's Park path with the intent of running to the south end, where the park bordered on Baker

Street, and if things went according to plan, she would be re-
warded with lunch and a nice quiet row on the lake. She was
actually rather eager for it, and she started out at a quick pace.

Then, after a few moments, she slowed the pace just slightly.
No need to make things too difficult. Not if she wanted the
pleasant row on the lake.

At the west end of Regent's Park, Reggie was running north
on the circular path. He was nearly in full stride; he had started
at the south end some minutes earlier, and though his legs were
still quite sore, he could feel them beginning to loosen up. He
knew he could complete the entire circuit.

The soreness was, mostly, from his desperate run in the
Cotswolds two days earlier. After running at full tilt back to Dillane's house, and then to the crashed A3 to ring Nigel, he had
then run four miles back down the little country lane, through
the rain and mud, until he managed to get picked up by a lorry
carrying half a dozen sheep. That had gotten him to Bath, and
then a taxi took him from Bath to London—just in time to find
Laura in the hospital, getting checked out, surrounded by police
and reporters.

Now Reggie completed the curve at the north end of the park.
He was on the straightaway, heading south toward the Baker
Street gate, and in the far distance he saw a woman running,
her red hair swaying back and forth. It looked like a long way,
but he wasn't worried. He was only moments behind. He was
almost certain of it.